THE FALLING WOMAN

The
Falling
Woman

a novel

Richard Farrell

ALGONQUIN BOOKS OF CHAPEL HILL 2020

Published by
ALGONQUIN BOOKS OF CHAPEL HILL
Post Office Box 2225
Chapel Hill, North Carolina 27515-2225

a division of
WORKMAN PUBLISHING
225 Varick Street
New York, New York 10014

Printed in the United States of America.
Published simultaneously in Canada by Thomas Allen & Son Limited.
Design by Steve Godwin.

This is a work of fiction. While, as in all fiction, the literary perceptions and insights are based on experience, all names, characters, places, and incidents either are products of the author's imagination or are used fictitiously.

Library of Congress Cataloging-in-Publication Data

Names: Farrell, Richard, [date]– author.
Title: The falling woman : a novel / Richard Farrell.
Description: First edition. | Chapel Hill, North Carolina : Algonquin Books of Chapel Hill, 2020. | Summary: "The suspenseful story of a woman with terminal cancer who is the sole survivor of a plane crash, and the young NTSB agent who is sent to investigate"—Provided by publisher.
Identifiers: LCCN 2019048634 | ISBN 9781616208578 (hardcover) | ISBN 9781643750521 (e-book)
Subjects: GSAFD: Suspense fiction.
Classification: LCC PS3606.A7359 F36 2020 | DDC 813/.6—dc23
LC record available at https://lccn.loc.gov/201904863

10 9 8 7 6 5 4 3 2 1
First Edition

And now will drop in   SOON   now will drop

In like this   the greatest thing that ever came to Kansas   down from all
Heights   all levels of American breath

—JAMES L. DICKEY, from "Falling"

THE FALLING WOMAN

PROLOGUE

———

. . . *and then my seat gives way and black sky siphons me through a gaping hole in the fuselage, my body aspirating through the suddenly ruptured coach-class ceiling like a lottery ball in a pneumatic tube. Jagged teeth in the disintegrating cabin tear at the fingers on my left hand. Shattering aluminum nearly decapitates me. And suddenly, I'm outside. I'm outside. These are the words that flash as my body, still strapped to my seat, zooms past the tail. I'm outside. Lights flash by. I'm outside. I close my eyes. I tuck my chin to my chest. My body somersaults.*

And then I'm alone.

Falling through the night sky.

I fall toward humid cornfields, toward silos, barns, and bridges. I fall toward varsity quarterbacks dreaming of glory, toward farm girls with pet rabbits, toward meth heads riding the rails, toward retired veterans, librarians, lunch ladies, and lucid dreamers.

Down and down I go, accelerating earthward for nine seconds before I reach terminal velocity, a point at which the sensation of falling ceases. Freezing air riffles past. Sprays of rain and plinks of hail punch and jab, scratching my face. In my mind, I see my daughters, babies again, crawling along the kitchen floor, two perfect angels, reaching for me, and the pressure of their yearning, memories so deep and physical that, for a moment, I forget what's happening. But then the rush of air, and the rain and hail, become painful. The temperature warms as I drop. Humidity increases, the dewy sweetness of loamy farm smells rising up, my body spiraling, still strapped to that seat, twirling and twirling like a seedpod in a late summer breeze. I open my eyes. Lightning flashes in clouds. Then a split second later, I spot the flaming comet tail of the plane, my plane, disintegrating, its aerodynamic fragments still flying away from me, shedding pieces of itself. I think of Peter, Paul and Mary singing that song my mother loved—"Leaving on a Jet Plane"—until I pass through the densest parts of the storm and the plane disappears for good. And I'm still falling. Instinctually, I grab the side of my seat with my undamaged hand. I grip it with fury, with everything I have left. Streaming blood coats my face, stinging my eyes. My blood tastes like a cocktail of copper pennies and Communion wafers. Oh, if ever there were a time to still believe in God. My one remaining shoe rips off. Then my shirt flutters over my face and disappears into the night. A moment later, my bra peels away and then my underwear goes. I was always so modest growing up, always afraid to be seen. Bloodied and naked now, I begin to scream, only to stop in terror when I can't hear the sound of my own shrieking. How can I know that I'm outracing my voice? I fall and fall. And when it seems impossible to continue, when it seems that I'm trapped in a nightmare from which I will surely soon awaken, I begin to count. I count, slowly, in my head—one, two, three, four, five. I count all the way to fifty-seven. I'm still falling.

More than anything, I just want to reach the end, no matter what that means.

1

"COULD YOU STATE your name for the record?"

"My name is Charles Radford."

"And your involvement with the investigation of Pointer 795?"

"I was an investigator with the National Transportation Safety Board."

"In fact, sir, you were the lead investigator for the survival factors working group. Isn't that correct?"

How many times, he thinks, do I need to answer that question this week?

He reaches for the glass of water in front of him and glances down at his notes. Sixteen congressmen stare back at him from the stage. Behind them, pages, interns, and lackeys tussle with papers and phones. For the third day in a row, Radford has crossed the National Mall, checked his reports, sworn the oath, and sat stock-still in uncomfortable chairs waiting to testify. Three days of note scribbling, of listening to others, sidebars with attorneys, frantic calls home, and second-guessing. The entire Go Team—including Lucy Masterson, Shep Ellsworth, even Ulrich and the director herself, Carol Wilson—have gone before him. Now it is his turn. At his back, cameras record every move, every word.

"Need we remind you that almost twelve months ago, a commercial airliner exploded over south-central Kansas? Need we remind you that 123 people died, or at least that was the initial assumption from your agency? Need we remind you that this country has waited for a definitive answer? Terrorism, a bomb, a missile, a meteor, a short circuit in the plane's wiring, a lightning strike?"

"No," Radford says. "I'm well aware of what happened to Pointer 795. I've spent countless hours sifting through debris fields, maintenance records, and logbooks. I've waded into ponds to extract bodies. I've interviewed orphans and widows. I'd say I'm well acquainted."

"But you have no answers."

"I don't deal in answers," Radford says. "My job was to ask the right questions."

"For the record, sir, how many aircraft accidents have you investigated in your career?"

Radford shrugs. He knows the number but refuses to make this any easier.

"Would you classify the investigation of Pointer 795 as standard, as routine?"

"In the beginning," he says, "there was only havoc, devastation, and raw loss. Any solution seemed impossible. I needed to figure out which questions to ask."

"So, is that a yes, sir?"

"Events gathered in reverse," he says. "A chain of a thousand invisible mistakes had to be pumped back through time. Complex decisions teased apart, examined, challenged, abandoned, and reexamined. A forgotten switch closed. A valve not pressurized. A checklist item skipped. It's always about asking the right questions."

He knows he is rambling. Is he losing his grip on reality? He reaches again for the water and tries to organize his thoughts. So many others have sat here before him, men and women in positions of great power as well as the meek like him. Even this conference room, located in the bowels of the Rayburn House Office Building, imposes its will, with its bone-white ceiling, its sticky chairs and sweating pitchers of water. On the wall is a framed painting of the Great Seal of the United States. The American eagle—wings outstretched, talons clutching thirteen arrows in the left, an olive branch in the right—stares down at him along with the congressmen.

"Mr. Radford, what we're concerned about is where the investigation deviated from protocol. Why were you reassigned?"

"Sequences accrued," he says.

He knows they have no right to be doing this, no reason to challenge his expertise. He knows he has done nothing wrong. He simply followed the evidence. About the rest, about the way the rest unfolded, about that he has no regrets. The contradictions, the impossible contradictions of this investigation, these were not his fault.

"Sir, the investigation quickly went off track. Why did this happen?"

"The job demands you filter out assumptions," he says. "You gather the millions of scattered pieces and reassemble fragments into questions. If you ask the right questions, the rest will follow. To get from chaos to order, you have to trust cause and effect. This is how the work begins. Hours and days and weeks pass. Some pieces lost forever. The wreckage must be rebuilt, one rivet at a time."

He pauses and looks up at the eagle on the wall.

"Three babies were aboard that flight," he says. "Each body deserved a name, a next of kin to grieve it. That was my primary responsibility."

"Let's concentrate on the bodies. How many had you identified before you were reassigned?"

Why does he still hate uncertainty? Why is it still so hard to talk about? These congressmen don't understand his work.

"The short history of human aviation," he says, "is barely more than a century old. Flying used to be incredibly dangerous."

"Mr. Radford, we'd like to stay on track."

"You demand answers," he says. "You expect nothing to ever

go wrong. But your need for certainty is an illusion. You take it for granted because you fail to see the miracles anymore."

He's trying to explain why the sky is inside him. If they mined down into his soul, they would find wings. The sky runs through him, into places of himself he still hasn't mapped. A calling, perhaps, the way a priest is called, or like the passion of great lovers. Since the winter day when two brothers from Ohio closed their bicycle shop and fashioned together a rickety kite frame made from spruce wood and Roebling wire rope, thousands of others have been likewise called, and followed a path into the air. A coin flip and a steady Atlantic breeze changed history. What followed was more than just another invention. The airplane expanded human imagination, took us into places that we'd only dreamed about since we first stood erect and told stories. Radford has been more faithful to the sky than to anyone or anything he's ever loved. He has never doubted this love, not once, not since he was ten years old. But what has he been chasing all these years? For the first time in his life, he's not sure.

"Sir, refusal to answer this committee is serious violation of federal law."

"What a crock of shit."

"What was that, sir?"

"Do any of you," Radford says, "understand the first thing about flying?"

"You're walking a fine line here."

"I'm sorry," he says. "I didn't ask for any of this."

"Do you need a moment to gather yourself, Mr. Radford? We need a full accounting of the events."

Radford reaches yet again for his water, but the glass is empty.

"We need you to take us back to that day, sir. To the events that followed. A year has passed since Pointer 795 exploded. Why have millions of taxpayer dollars been spent on an investigation that has gone nowhere? Don't we deserve answers? Mr. Radford. Don't we deserve the truth?"

"You're asking the wrong questions," he says.

"What questions should we be asking?"

"My father was a stonemason," he says. "In many ways, that has been my work too. I reassemble fragments. I work brick by brick. Process is all that matters. I worry only about where the next brick will go. That's how you get to the end."

"What happened with Pointer 795? Why did the plane explode over Kansas? How did this investigation go so wrong?"

"I had obligations," he says. "I had a responsibility to follow the evidence, wherever it took me."

"And where did it take you, sir?"

"The hardest part is letting go of what you've been taught."

"Mr. Radford, what about the Falling Woman?"

2

(One year earlier)

CHARLIE RADFORD WAS working late again and ignored the vibrating phone in his pocket—which he knew was his wife, Wendy, texting him—so he could keep flying the simulator. He needed to get this report exactly right, even if every additional minute made his wife worry and fret. Radford flew the simulated plane around again, this time lowering a notch of flaps as he came abeam the end of the simulated runway. He cut the throttle, and the propeller slowed as he banked the port wing toward a narrow grass field, carved from a stand of Tennessee pine and hemlock.

Three months earlier, Cessna 417 *Yankee X-Ray*, a small plane flown by an inexperienced pilot, buzz-sawed the treetops on final approach into the actual William Northern Field. Now Radford was heading up the investigation of the accident, completely routine except for the fact that his immediate supervisor in this case was none other than Dickie Gray himself.

Before the *Yankee X-Ray* accident, Radford had only passing contact with Dickie Gray, a living legend at the agency, a man who roamed the halls in a faded blue windbreaker with a spiral note-pad always tucked in his shirt pocket. Gray had worked all the big ones: TWA 800, Delta 191, USAir 427, the bombing of Pan Am 103 over Lockerbie, Scotland. For more than three decades, Gray investigated and solved the most complex aviation accidents, long before Radford knew how to spell the word *airplane*.

A former fighter pilot, a Vietnam vet, a taciturn whiskey drinker, Dickie Gray was cut from the mold of classic aviators, men with thousand-yard stares and cragged faces. Radford had grown up idolizing men like Dickie Gray, who even looked a bit like Chuck Yeager. There were rumors that the old man had lost his edge, but Radford refused to believe them. Working under Gray's supervision was the single greatest stroke of good fortune he'd experienced since coming to the NTSB. A well-run investiga-tion would open doors for him. "There are no new ways to crash an airplane," Gray was fond of saying, advice so important that Radford thought of tattooing it on his arm.

In the simulator, Radford turned toward the airfield, half a mile ahead. The real William Northern Field, seven hundred miles southwest of D.C., consisted of three runways, one of them turf; it was little more than a patch of dirt and grass, where this pilot tried to land. The airfield once existed to train Army Air Corps pilots heading off to bomb Germany in World War II. On the screen, a half dozen simulated taildraggers and biplanes lined the makeshift taxiway in the lengthening shadow of a hangar. The simulator's graphics were incredible. Radford could hardly tell that he wasn't in the air. The runway appeared small and treacherous. Flying the approach brought back familiar feelings, thrills long forgotten. He missed being a pilot, missed that fraternity. Flying was all he ever wanted to do. The simulacrum of the small airfield reminded him of a bygone era, when flying was a simpler affair, when no one cared about medical clearances and training modules. In those days, a pilot still cut a dashing figure.

His phone buzzed again. Wendy was struggling of late. He wondered if perhaps pouring himself into the work was a way of avoiding the trouble at home. She worried so much. She catastrophized the simplest things, envisioned car wrecks when he was in traffic, imagined terror attacks when he wasn't at his desk. Just five more minutes, he thought. He needed to get every detail perfect.

Three hundred feet off the ground, he dropped the starboard wing and pressed the opposite rudder, initiating a slip, a maneuver that increased the plane's drag and accelerated it toward the grass runway. Not a complicated maneuver, as these things went, but flying into a short field with a ten-knot crosswind, the slip challenged Radford's limited skill set. With every botched approach, he felt a growing kinship with the pilot under investigation, a twenty-year-old flier with three hundred hours of flying time under his belt. At home, in a storage bin, was Radford's own faded logbook, which contained just less than two hundred hours.

As a boy, when he first became captivated by the elegance and beauty of flight—the sweep of a wing, the pristine lines and curves of a fuselage, the distant rumble of a turboprop—young Charlie

Radford would draw airplanes in his notebooks until the 747s he sketched at school bore some fine resemblance to the ones zooming through the sky. Squirreled away in his room like a monk, he built plastic models by the dozens and hung them from his ceiling with fishing line until his bedroom looked like a scaled-down version of the National Air and Space Museum. He internalized the mythology, the science, the history of aviation, as if the very notion of powered flight had been invented solely for him. The pilots who flew planes were his heroes.

His own flying career started out like gangbusters. Though his family could hardly afford vacations, his parents didn't flinch at paying for his flying lessons. He soloed at sixteen, obtained his pilot's license on his seventeenth birthday. He bagged groceries to pay for fuel and flew almost every weekend. But then disaster struck; almost as quickly as he soared through those early milestones, he came roaring back to earth. On summer break from college, he flew a check ride with an instructor. He'd taken a Cessna up to almost nine thousand feet when the world before him went black. He couldn't see. The instructor grabbed the control wheel, cursed at him, and flew back home. Two hours later, a doctor said his heart valve wasn't closing properly. Radford didn't care about his health; he just wanted to know what could be done to fix it so he could get back to flying.

"Son," the doctor said, "with this condition, you can't fly."

The blow felt tragic, a thunderbolt deadly enough to demolish his dreams. It was Wendy who saved him. At the time, they weren't even dating. They just played intramural softball together. She was the team's second baseman, and seemed to him off-limits, a nursing student with a serious boyfriend. They had talked quite a bit, so she knew about his passion for flying. Then, when an NTSB recruiter came on campus one spring day, she grabbed an application, brought it to his apartment, and waited for him to fill it out. Shortly after that, her boyfriend was out and she was dating Radford.

At the NTSB, he poured his love of flying into studying crashes, a grotesque reincarnation of his original desire, but if he couldn't fly, at least he was working in the aviation field. He had a nose for it too, a clarity of focus and detachment that let him thrive amidst the chaos of an accident. But behind his competence, behind the macho facade and bureaucratic bullshit that went into the work, was a boy who still dreamed of flying.

Quartering out of the southwest, the simulated wind pushed the simulated plane's nose off the simulated centerline. Radford applied more rudder to the slip. Bright green trees swayed and silvered in the breeze as ground rose up to meet the descending plane.

One more approach, and he'd feel confident signing off on the report. The hour was almost up. His phone buzzed again. The wings shuddered in an updraft of simulated air. He pressed the rudder harder, but the plane slowed toward stall speed. Don't let out the slip, he thought, refusing to ease up on the approach. The stall warning horn blared in the cockpit. Fifty feet above the ground, a football field away now. Radford killed the power. Ground rushed toward the lowered wing. Sunlight blared through the slowing propeller, creating a shimmering distraction, beautiful but vertiginous. Did the kid see this too just before the end?

Did his eyes and thoughts drift just long enough to lose sight of the mark? The plane leveled off, the nose straightened, twenty feet above the trees.

Radford fought the urge to push the throttle, resisting a deep instinct. The stall warning blared. The control wheel shook. Then the nose dropped and the simulated plane hit the branches. The propeller snapped, and clods of dirt, leaf, and bark raced past the computer screen.

3

THAT SPRING MORNING, Erin and Doug Geraghty sat in the oncology conference room at Johns Hopkins, waiting to see her doctor. She was thinking about Tory and trying not to dwell on the news she was soon to hear. Her older daughter (their inside joke; Tory arrived two minutes before her twin sister, Claire) had called the night before, asking to hire a tutor to help her get through the last month of college algebra. Doug had grabbed the phone and suggested she just have her sister help: "Christ, sweetie, Claire has had straight As in math since seventh grade." His suggestion sent Tory into a rage, which Erin had to placate. But for all the tears and shouting, Erin had welcomed the distraction. Anything to feel normal again, anything to get her mind off her illness. But like all distractions, it was short-lived. This morning, her scans were back.

It was all a bit much, the two of them waiting in this empty room meant to hold fifty people. No one had even offered them coffee or water. Doug paced along the perimeter of the horseshoe-shaped table while she tried to pull up Lehigh's academic tutoring web page on her phone. If the news was bad, as she expected it would be, she and Doug would drive the three hours up to Pennsylvania and take the girls out to their favorite Mexican restaurant for dinner. Erin made her husband promise, if that was the case, they wouldn't say a word. They would just spend the night with the girls and pretend like nothing was wrong.

"This room is absurd," she said, trying to sound light, sound confident. "Why couldn't we just meet in an exam room or in the cafeteria?"

Erin looked around the large room as if noticing it for the first time. On the walls, framed photographs of patients—she presumed these were the ones who made it—smiled down at her. Their cheerful optimism only mocked the twenty-pound ball of dread sitting in her stomach.

"I'm scared," she said to Doug.

He went to the window and pried open the blinds. She knew her husband was terrified too, but that he would never reveal it to her.

Had something eluded her in life? Had some vital piece of her existence been left out? She'd been telling herself she was ready for whatever was coming. For months she'd girded herself against the worst news. But it was all a lie. Every second they waited only added to her terror.

The tutoring-center web page appeared on her phone, but when she clicked on the "Schedule Services" tab, the page crashed.

"God damn it," she said. "They don't even have decent Wi-Fi here. How can we expect them to cure cancer?"

Doug didn't even laugh. She'd have felt better if he'd only laugh a little, but he kept pacing behind the table.

"Think positively," he said, which was all he ever said anymore, as if good thoughts and a positive attitude could overcome the cancer. He'd read all the books, studied journals. His belief in miracle cures rivaled any preacher's, though neither of them was religious at all.

After another ten minutes, the door opened and a young doctor entered the room. The man looked like he belonged in a freshman comp class with their daughters rather than holding the charts that would determine her future.

"I'm Dr. Orenstein, the oncology chief resident," he said. The young doctor glanced at Doug and then held out his hand to Erin. She had never seen him before but noticed that his skin was cold and clammy and that his breath smelled like stale coffee. A small stain on his lab coat's lapel needed to be daubed with bleach. She resisted the urge to ask him how old he was. She smiled.

"You must be tired from carrying all my charts," she said, trying to put him at ease.

Dr. Orenstein apologized for the delays and then asked her a few questions about side effects, which she answered mechanically. Since the last round of chemo, she'd been feeling better, almost normal again, she said. There'd been a low-grade infection in her right lung, but other than that, the postchemo time had been a welcome reprieve. She was tired of medical questions, sick to death of what she spoke of as "doctor talk." The doctor finished his inquiry and told them that the staff oncologist would be joining them shortly.

"Do you know the results?" she asked.

Dr. Orenstein said only that they would have to wait to go over her results with the attending physician.

"All those charts and data points and blood tests," Doug said, "but no one will give us a straight answer."

"There's a protocol," she said, interceding on behalf of the young doctor. She knew it did no good to be unpleasant to the overworked doctors and nurses. "The same way there were protocols for any transaction."

Doug frowned. "This isn't a commercial transaction."

Dr. Orenstein quickly glanced down at the charts.

How many times had she and Doug sat in similar conference rooms over the years? Buying a car. Selling a house. Listening to a career counselor talk about the girls' SAT scores. But this time, they wouldn't leave with an extended warranty on a shiny new SUV. This time, they wouldn't wonder about when they'd close escrow. This time, they wouldn't walk across the street for a drink. No, this conference room, however similar it looked to the others, carried finality. And she knew, even without Doug's angst, that the protocol meant the chief resident had to wait until the staff physician arrived.

The young doctor adjusted his gold-rimmed glasses on the bridge of his nose. Faint acne scars were visible on his forehead.

She wondered about him, about where he'd studied, why he'd chosen to go into cancer medicine. She tried to picture him as a child, before the serious work of life and death became his routine.

"Do you read much poetry, Dr. Orenstein?" she asked. "Lately, it's almost all I read."

The chief resident looked up but didn't answer her question.

"They say that the soul reaches for language at the end," she said. "The scariest things in life, those we can't describe. It's why children are so afraid at night. The demons and monsters in their dreams have no names."

The doctor remained mute. Doug continued to pace.

When had she become a person who spoke that way? She honestly didn't know. But lately, she'd stopped caring about what people thought, stopped filtering herself. There was a profound freedom to being on the brink of death, one of the unexpected fringe benefits.

Doug fiddled with the plastic wand attached to the window's blinds. When he twisted the wand clockwise, the room darkened, and when he twisted it the other way, the room brightened.

"Will you sit with me?" she said, firmly enough that Doug moved away from the window and sat next to her. "God, I could use a drink. I'd give anything for a glass of wine or a splash of whiskey." Finally, the doctor laughed, and even Doug managed a smile.

Her husband had taken the whole day off from work, expecting, no doubt, that the news, when it came, would ripple across the rest of their afternoon, if not the rest of their lives. But she didn't want to spend the day dwelling in sadness. Were she not so physically weak, were she not so uncertain of what was ahead, she'd have much preferred to do this alone.

"How much longer?" Doug asked. His voice was sharper this time. She squeezed his hand tightly. The young doctor glanced at his watch.

"Any minute now," Dr. Orenstein said.

How many patients had he already lost? She imagined his career running out in front of him. She pictured him at parties, smiling, laughing, and telling stories about his successes and failures. Her father had been a doctor. She understood how death became routine. Growing up, she hated the way her father's voice would change when he took a call in their living room. How he could be watching a ball game and cursing at an umpire one second and then delivering terrible news the next. *Your mother has gone into congestive heart failure*, he'd say, standing in the kitchen in his flannel pajamas. That false gravity, that rented solemnity, emotion cut off from genuine empathy. She loved the man but hated his work.

Doug fiddled with his phone. The doctor stared at the charts. She wished someone would tell a joke, anything to lighten the heaviness in the room. She tried to think of one, but nothing came to mind. Doug looked old, tired, like a shadow of the man she'd married.

Had they just grown old too fast? Or were they always this way? She tried to recall a time when she and Doug had fun together, a time when she saw passion from this man she'd spent half her life with. Nothing came to her. All along, there were hints, uncomfortable silences. Gaps hidden behind busy schedules and bedroom doors. A long time ago, long before she became sick, she started to feel stuck, trapped in a life that had taken on momentum of its own but that she felt detached from. More and more she wrestled with doubts. Was this it? Why were her passions constrained by protocols? It wasn't Doug's fault alone; that she knew. He'd been a saint through all this. But now, facing the end, she wondered about all that could have been.

The door finally opened and her oncologist appeared.

"I'm sorry I'm late," Dr. Shi said.

Dr. Evelyn Shi shook Doug's hand, gave Erin a small hug. The doctor was reed thin and short, with long straight hair that always reminded Erin, inexplicably, of a witch. The woman had no sense of style. Red ankle boots, nylons, and a skirt that seemed more suited for a picnic or a yard party. Her makeup was too thick, her glasses too cheap, her teeth too yellow, her voice far too chirpy. She looked like she worked at a nail salon, but she'd done her residency at Sloan Kettering, research at NIH. No doctor in the state came more highly recommended for treating non-functioning pancreatic neuroendocrine tumors. And Erin loved her. In a strange way, Erin wanted to get better so as not to disappoint her doctor.

Dr. Shi glanced at her notes. Was she just seeing them for the first time now?

Erin squeezed Doug's hand. She'd told herself again that she was ready, ready for whatever was coming. But she wasn't. Her calm demeanor, her brave face, it was all an act. Maybe it always had been. Maybe the whole goddamn thing was one great big act.

Dr. Shi studied the chart as if it were a sacred text, an Assyrian scroll dug from a cave after two thousand years. The oncologist's dark eyes scanned the pages from behind mocha-framed glasses. At last, she looked up.

"I'm cautiously optimistic," Dr. Shi said. The thinnest, palest smile broke across the doctor's lips. "The tumor has responded well to the chemo. Your scans look clean."

The words came as if from a great, long tunnel. Erin blinked. Waited for a "but." Instead, Dr. Shi offered another thin smile.

"We aren't out of the woods yet," she said. "But these results are encouraging."

What the hell was this woman, with her ruby-colored boots, actually saying? Inexplicably, a fiery rage swelled in Erin's chest. She felt the way a mouse must when tossed by a cat. She'd prepared for bad news, for the worst news. But this? It felt like hope had just tackled her to the ground.

"I don't understand," she said. "I'm in remission?"

"No," Dr. Shi said. "Remission is very different. This is a plateau. A truce. Full remission is extremely rare with your type of cancer. But we have bought you some time, which will allow us to try some other treatments."

As the news began to sink in, a blanket of meager optimism spread over the cold, grim reality of the past six months. Doug had questions, and began asking them in rapid-fire mode, without pausing for answers. Erin didn't even hear what he was saying.

"I know I'm not making much sense," he said.

"Dr. Orenstein will answer all of your questions," Dr. Shi said. "But you have to know, while the news today is good, this isn't over."

Goddamn oncologists. Were they ever happy? A dragon hid

behind every word, every test. She wondered what these two doctors were like in real life. But still, she would walk out of that room without receiving a final death notice. Something shifted, deep within, a tectonic plate of her soul.

"But the news," Doug said. "This is good news?"

"This is as good as it gets with pancreatic cancer," Dr. Shi said.

And Dr. Orenstein, the young chief resident, looked delighted. These doctors were like inquisitors, Erin thought, pleased that six months of their medical torture had paid off. She was converted. Dr. Shi closed the file and stood. Doug thanked her, and the doctor touched his shoulder, the feeblest expression of compassion. Erin said nothing, too stunned to speak.

"Congratulations," Dr. Orenstein said, turning to her like she'd just won a medal. The news filled the room like the milky light from a full moon. A governor's commutation, the execution stayed at the stroke of midnight. What came next?

Doug peppered Dr. Orenstein with questions. Would they start another cycle soon? Did she need more radiation? What were the five-year survival rates? The interrogation continued for a solid ten minutes, but Erin had stopped listening. She knew one thing with certainty now, a conviction forming in her gut even before she had the words to explain. It was time to sort out her life, figure out how to use what was left of it.

"No more," she said at last. "Let's go."

Doug and the young doctor both turned, as if they'd forgotten she was in the room.

"I have more questions," Doug said.

"Now," she said. "We are leaving now."

She had to get out of the room, out of the hospital. She needed to breathe real air. When they exited the hospital, a brilliant Maryland sun scorched her eyes. She'd forgotten and left her sunglasses in the car.

"What should we do?" Doug asked. She knew what he meant. He wanted to celebrate, to drive up to Pennsylvania and take the girls out to dinner.

"Take me home," she said. "Just take me home."

4

AFTER A WEEK of long nights to finish the report, once again Charlie Radford arrived home almost two hours late. Yeager greeted him at the door, the dog wagging his tail. A dinner plate sat on the counter, wrapped in plastic. Wendy was nowhere in sight, and their two-bedroom condo sounded eerily still. He grabbed a beer and microwaved his dinner.

She was angry, and he knew that he deserved his wife's ire, but at that moment, he needed her compassion more. Tomorrow, he'd present his work to Dickie Gray, and he was as nervous as a teenager taking the SATs. Only Wendy could settle his nerves. She was the person who could set his world back on its axis. He carried his plate and beer toward the stairs. Yeager followed at his heels.

Cardboard boxes lined the living room of their Alexandria

condo. As with most things, Wendy raced ahead of herself, packing up their belongings before they'd even put an offer on a house.
They'd lived in this condo for three years, and he thought of it
as their home. But Wendy didn't intend to spend her life in a
two-bedroom walk-up, despite its easy access to the restaurants
and bars of Old Town. She wanted a house, with a yard and a cul-
de-sac and an elm tree, a place for their future child to ride a bike,
sell lemonade, play hopscotch on the sidewalk, and jump through
sprinklers. And as much as he loved the idea, such a vision also
meant a longer commute, a yard to mow, a basement to clean, a
leaky roof, paint to deal with, wood chips, weeds, and dirty diapers. Moving meant an end to the life he'd come to enjoy. What's
more, he still hadn't agreed on having a kid. Once upstairs, he
could hear water running behind the closed bathroom door.

"I got caught up again," he said, knocking on the door. "I'm
sorry. I'm going nuts with these last details."

When she refused to respond, he knew things were bad. In
their growing repertoire of domestic thrusts and parries, closed
door/running water ranked just below lights out/asleep. Not a full-
scale nuclear attack, but the warheads were armed. He'd pushed
his luck with a string of late nights, and Wendy held grudges, not
forever but long enough to warrant some form of apology and
self-abnegation.

"Tomorrow, I'll have to sit across from Dickie Gray," he said.
He lowered himself to the floor and sat with his plate on his lap.
"The man's forgotten more about accident investigations than I'll
ever learn." He hoped exposing such vulnerability might soften his

wife's hurt feelings. The water kept running. The door remained closed. "The man's a legend. I'm not kidding. He's the real deal."

He heard her feet shuffle across the bathroom floor. Was she softening? Was she moving toward forgiveness?

Wendy Luard Radford always carried herself with a nonchalant charm. She never tried to impress, never needed to show off her beauty. After they started dating, and Wendy confessed about the abuse she'd endured at the hands of her ex—a semipro kickboxer, part-time DJ, and full-time scumbag—Charlie could barely contain his own rage. He wanted to find the man, rip his head off, literally kill him, consequences be damned. Even now, years later, he still struggled with that possibility and wondered if he would ever be able to let it go. The thought of that man touching Wendy's body still made him sick. But Charlie knew that if he ever thought he was saving Wendy, if he thought she needed his protection, he was sorely mistaken. The ex-boyfriend was her one lapse in judgment, the single regret that she'd admit to.

The woman he married turned out to be tough, durable, and strong. Most days, she needed him far less than he needed her. He loved her, plain and simple, a classic old-fashioned love. He never wanted to be with anyone else. Never felt tempted. He marveled at the combination of her resilience and decency. At times, he felt foolish, loving a woman as much as he loved Wendy. He never talked about it with the guys, never participated in the male banter of coveting other women or reducing them to sex objects. He loved her so much he was almost embarrassed by his feelings. And with each passing year, she became more mysterious, not less.

He knocked on the door again. For all her strength and charm, Wendy could also tumble into despair without warning. More and more, a darkness overtook her, like a spring storm blown across the prairie. During those times, Charlie could only stand back and watch. He'd find her sitting in the dark, an empty wine bottle on the floor. Other times, she wouldn't get out of bed. Once she fell asleep with an open bottle of sleeping pills next to the bed. She swore that she wasn't suicidal, swore that she had simply drifted off to sleep after taking one pill, but he became more attentive after that, worried about her more. And when she fell into melancholia, no amount of attention, kindness, or love could draw her out. And the source of Wendy's despair was within his power to solve. Wendy wanted to have a child.

Not having kids was something they'd agreed on together. He'd been honest with her from the very start. At the time, she seemed to feel the same. A life together without complications. Only their love to sustain them. Simple. Clean. But she was seeing her OB tomorrow, and reluctantly, Charlie agreed to go with her.

At last, she opened the door. Soft light backlit her.

"Why do you put yourself through this?" she said.

Wendy's long red hair fell across her freckled shoulders, which he loved almost as much as he loved her. She'd been a swimmer in high school, and her muscles remained ropy, rounded, perfect. His heart still raced when he touched her skin. She stepped out of the bathroom and sat next to him. He stroked her arm. Thin, golden hair glistened in the light.

"I'm so nervous for tomorrow," he said.

"Should you put so much stock in a first meeting with this guy?" she asked.

"He's the best at the agency," he said. "This doesn't always have to end poorly."

"I worry you're setting yourself up for more heartache," she said.

"I need this, Wend," he said. "His approval matters to me."

"Can we talk about the other thing?" she said.

He didn't want to switch gears, but she leaned into him and her hair fell across his chest.

"My feelings haven't changed," he said. "I love you more than life itself, but I'm not cut out to be a father. You know that. You know why."

"Nothing is worse than this, Charlie," she said. "It's like I have this hole inside me."

He reached out and held her hand. Her skin felt cool and soft.

"I want to be a mother. I want to have a child with you. I'm not going to give up." She kissed him lightly on the lips. "Now tell me about the magnificent Dickie Gray."

5

BENEATH THE SPUN-ALUMINUM finial ball, her grandfather's American flag fluttered in the breeze. The flag's field of red and white stripes unfurled, folded, unfurled again, its canton of forty-eight white stars on blue cloth snapping as another gust lifted its edge. Chipped paint and rust freckled the lower pole. At the flagpole's base, sprigs of marsh parsley and skunk weed threatened to choke the just-emerging shoots of tulip bulbs that Erin had planted last fall.

Out of the slate-gray sky, two eastern crows arrived. She loved birds, though she hated crows, with their iridescent coats and arrogant squawks, bullying the lesser birds away from her feeders. The first crow hopped along a brick pathway that cut through the fallow gardens, followed by the second. Where the brick path widened to the patio, dried leaves swirled in intermittent wind. The leaves scattered up to the porch. One of the crows squawked, and they both startled and flew.

Their house was a turn-of-the-century Colonial Revival with weathered shingles and burgundy shutters. A side door faced the Chesapeake like a sailor on starboard watch. Standing at an upstairs window, she stared toward the water, trying to avoid her reflection in the glass. Thin and gaunt after the session with the doctor, she knew she was still sick but not yet dead. The news was still settling over their lives.

Behind her on the bed, a suitcase sat open. She'd packed and unpacked three times already that morning.

"I don't want you to go," Doug said.

Instead, Doug wanted her to begin a third cycle of gemcitabine. They'd been arguing about it for a week, ever since the oncology report came back. But the prospect of six more weeks of stomach pain and debilitating headaches—no. Enough was enough. She'd agreed to two cycles to buy time. She'd done that.

"I'll be fine," she said, turning from the window. "It's only a few days."

Once again, Doug listed the various risk factors associated with her planned trip: delays in treatment, disruptions in routine, fatigue, anemia, infection, relapse. A litany she knew by heart.

"What happens if you throw a clot?" he said. "From where you'll be, it's more than two hours to the nearest hospital."

She returned to the window and imagined oceanfront cabins, sugar pines, books, and a string of silent days on the Marin Headlands, away from all this disease, treatment, and madness. Away from Doug.

"The crows never go hungry," she said.

Doug didn't respond.

Her husband was a practical man, kind and sincere too but contemptuous of her whimsy. As he'd done since they first married, he ignored her musings. They were an ill-suited match, except they'd been together a quarter century, raised a family, built a beautiful house in Annapolis, sent the girls to a private university in Pennsylvania. Cancer never fit into their plans. Though the latest reports were encouraging enough—the tumor had not grown, radiation and chemo had checked the spread, no metastases, no evidence of trouble in her diseased body's hinterlands—the news did not signal a victory but, as her doctor had said, a much-needed truce.

Erin refolded her jeans when Lexie entered. The stout English bulldog snorted and paced back and forth near their bed. Lexie was her dog, loyal to her. She wondered what would become of the dog after she was gone. More and more, these questions stole into her thoughts: What would become of the dog? Who would care for the gardens? Who would take out the recycling? She worried about the most mundane details, as if her death would simply interrupt the routines.

Lexie hated suitcases. Like Doug, the dog was a creature most comfortable with habit. The sight of packed luggage triggered a primordial fear, manifest in frenetic hip shakes. Erin scratched Lexie's chin until the dog settled.

"A retreat for cancer survivors?" Doug said. "It sounds nothing like you."

"I need a break," she said. "I'm pretty sure I've earned it."

He shook his head. "You've always been so," he said, checking himself, "so damn impulsive."

He avoided anger the way another man might avoid a downed high voltage line. In a moment, he'd back away and apologize for cursing. Sometimes she wished he'd just stand and fight.

"Don't worry about how it affects the rest of us," he said.

Or he'd cut the power and pout. She hated this more.

"You need a break too," she said. "You've been taking care of me all winter."

She'd made him lists. Doctors to call. Appointments to cancel. Insurance claims to complete. He needed lists. Doug measured self-worth through task completion. His use of lists had become one of the great strains in their married life. After the girls went to college and she became sick, Erin began to feel like little more than another item on his endless lists. But ever the masterful accommodator, she learned to adapt to his behavior, even came to appreciate the security and comfort in the contours of his rigidity. Outside, the crows returned to her gardens. She crossed the room, wrapped her arms around her husband, and kissed his cheek.

"This disease has taught me patience, compliance, even a measure of grace over the last six months," she said. "But self-pity has no place."

Her words wounded, but perhaps some wounds were unavoidable. She released the embrace, zipped her suitcase, stared out at the crows, and thought of Adam.

Adam Moskowitz worked upstairs from her at Hawkins, Lemenanger & Walton. Erin was in contracts, with its monotonous days that compensated for accuracy, not style. The litigators orbited a different planet. She knew Adam only by reputation. He'd been lead counsel on a class-action suit against a major

Japanese automaker. Airbags kept exploding. Instead of saving people, the airbags were killing children. In his closing statement, he quoted Shakespeare: "Out of this nettle, danger, we pluck this flower, safety."

For weeks after, everyone at HLW was talking about him.

One morning, a year before she was sick, Adam joined her in the lobby elevator. He was on his phone, on the way to the tenth floor. Tall, with broad shoulders, a pleasant, easy smile, he looked like an athlete, deeply confident, like he could do anything, with penetrating blue eyes that softened when he smiled.

"I know you," he said.

"I doubt that," she said, trying to suppress the shameful surge of schoolgirl energy rushing through her chest. She'd never cheated on Doug, never really even been tempted until Adam came bursting through her defenses.

More than a year passed before anything happened. Sometimes they'd eat lunch together or send occasional emails that grew more personal over time. He told her he was leaving his wife; she complained about Doug's habits, the absence of passion. Eventually, they wound up together in Atlanta for a meeting. By then, the outcome was inevitable. For three days, they stayed on the same floor at the Hyatt without so much as a hug, until she lingered after the HLW partners' dinner and they shared a bottle of Lodi zinfandel. He walked her to her room, touched her wrist, and they kissed.

6

THAT MORNING, RADFORD was so nervous about his meeting with Dickie Gray that when he entered L'Enfant Plaza, he forgot to clip his ID badge onto his shirt pocket. A frustrated security guard directed employees around him while he fumbled in his briefcase. By the time he reached the elevators, his starched shirt was already soaked through with sweat. Photographs of vintage airplanes adorned the walls. Constellations, Comets, old DC-3s. The NTSB also investigated highway accidents, train and subway wrecks, maritime disasters, but if the agency were the athletic department of a high school, the aviation investigators were its football team. And if Radford were to push that logic, he was the JV water boy while Dickie Gray was the varsity quarterback.

Radford hoped *Yankee X-Ray* could finally get him on the field.

But he needed his report to be perfect. If he screwed up in front of Gray, he might not just get cut from the team but possibly be expelled from the agency itself. In the past year, there'd been a hiring freeze, with more cutbacks rumored.

He spent the morning proofreading his work. Four times he talked himself into making changes to the report, and five times he reprinted the whole damn thing, all fifty-one pages. After lunch, he wrote up an addendum to the final draft and slipped it into the back of the folder. As he printed the final copies, he thought of a dozen more questions he needed to ask.

He called Wendy before heading up to up to Gray's office.

"God, Wend, I'm so nervous. What if he doesn't accept my report?"

"You'll be fine," she said half-heartedly. "Don't forget my appointment this afternoon." She was still upset over yesterday's unresolved argument, but he'd called to get a last-second pep talk, not to continue their talk about having a child.

"Don't be mad," he said. "Please don't be mad at me now."

"Nothing ever changes," she said. "Good luck, Charlie. You'll do great."

On the sixth floor, a receptionist directed Radford to wait in Dickie Gray's office. "Mr. Gray will be back soon." Radford welcomed the reprieve and silently rehearsed his opening statement.

Gray's small office possessed a commanding view of the Washington Channel, but the room was a disaster. Boxes were stacked on the floor in haphazard fashion, boxes containing years' worth of evidence, reports, and technical data. But it was as if Gray never had filed a single document in his career. Toward the rear of the office were more files, while folders, pens, and empty root beer cans littered his desk. The trash can overflowed with paper. The office suggested disorder but not quite chaos. The backlog of true diligence, Radford thought.

There'd been rumors about Gray, that he was only hanging on, collecting a check and pushing paperclips. Radford refused to believe that the mess was a symptom of a man who didn't know when to quit. Newspaper headlines and photographs, mostly aerial black-and-whites of accident sites, hung in Gray's office. Radford recognized a few of the photos. A shattered L-1011 in Dallas. The grisly pieces of the Concorde at de Gaulle. A famous image of the Pan Am logo on the plane's tail in ruins at Lockerbie. Standing there, in the midst of the man's work, Radford suddenly felt very small, a movie extra called in to talk with an aging star. He'd spent two months laboring over every detail of *Yankee X-Ray*, worrying about the weather, the tire pressure, the goddamn fuel quantities, but Dickie Gray had done the real thing. For a second, Radford considered signing the report, leaving it on Gray's desk, and slinking out of his office.

"You crack the case?" Gray said, coming up behind him. Radford stood and awkwardly stuck out his hand, which the older man shook quickly. Gray crossed through his office, navigating around the labyrinth of boxes to sit at his desk.

Dickie Gray was tall, with a beer gut ballooning over his belt. He resembled a truck driver with a Tennessee drawl more than an ex-fighter pilot with two air medals. In clear violation of agency protocol, Gray wore jeans, work boots, and a plaid shirt. His close-trimmed white hair thinned at the back, and his skin was deeply tanned, a generational fuck-you to sunscreen companies everywhere. He'd spent most of his time in the field, in contrast to the majority of sun-starved bureaucrats imprisoned in this building. Radford knew nothing about Gray's personal life, but everything about the man's appearance screamed lifelong bachelor, a man married to his work. There were no arguments over children, no distractions. If there were a Mrs. Dickie Gray, Radford imagined her on the shortlist for sainthood. His gray-blue eyes were steely and intense, though wrinkles now encircled them, softening his face. Gray scanned his messy office, spotted his target, and reached across his desk. He grabbed a manila folder and handed it to Radford.

"Your overtime forms," Gray said. "All signed and approved."

Radford suspected a secret order to all the seeming chaos, an esoteric system that made no sense to an outsider. He bet that the old man could find any file in the room in six seconds.

"Let's get a drink," Gray said. "For obvious reasons, I no longer hold meetings in here."

Without waiting for Radford to agree, Gray stood, grabbed his faded blue windbreaker off a hook, and turned off the office light. Radford checked his watch. He didn't have time for a beer, but he certainly couldn't pass up the opportunity. Wendy would have to understand, even if he arrived a few minutes late to the doctor's appointment.

Outside the headquarters building, a bright spring afternoon greeted the two men. The cherry blossoms were peaking late, and tourists swept over the city with their cameras. They crossed the Mall, passing art museums, the cavernous buildings of the

Smithsonian, before turning left up Pennsylvania Avenue past Lafayette Park. Gardeners in green jumpsuits mowed the White House lawn in the fading light.

As Dickie Gray walked, he favored his left leg, but he still moved quickly, purposefully, despite the limp. At the crosswalks, he fiddled with change in his pockets. Radford sensed that the man's mind was elsewhere. A busload of tourists passed, the fumes from the coach mixing with the smell of mown grass. There were a thousand questions Radford wanted to ask, a lifetime of experience and wisdom he wanted to absorb, but he took his cues from the elder man's silence. Radford had grown up around silent men. He understood their cues and codes.

They passed a dozen perfectly acceptable bars and restaurants before they stopped at Sam's. The facade was white brick; inside was an Irish pub with dim lighting. The Clancy Brothers played from overhead speakers. Radford liked the place immediately. It was worth the twenty-minute walk.

The bartender waved at Gray, who ordered whiskey and a beer, along with a Reuben sandwich. Radford asked for a Belgian IPA and held off on food. No reason to compound the trouble brewing across the river. He told himself he'd have a quick drink, go over the results from *Yankee X-Ray*, and get to the appointment. Wendy would have to understand.

"How long have you been at the agency?" Gray asked.

Radford told Gray that he'd been an investigator for four years, omitting his first three years—when he'd worked at the agency as an analyst—as if they'd never happened.

"You need more experience in the field," he said. "It takes time to get good at this work. Investigating a crash is one part archae-ology, one part guesswork, and one part origami. You don't learn this job overnight."

Radford nodded. He wanted to be an expert, to command the same respect he felt toward Gray. But how did he get there without more experience? There were fewer major accidents these days, fewer opportunities for him to prove himself.

"Things are changing," Gray said, sipping his whiskey. "Everything today is by the book. Investigators are losing the feel for this job. I'm happy I'm on my way out."

Radford didn't want to use the slice of lemon or the glass that came with his beer. Somehow it seemed effete, something that Gray would notice. He fingered the juicy flesh and then pushed the lemon aside.

"You know what you need to succeed in this job?" Gray said. "You need to ask the right questions. If you ask the right questions, you won't need to worry about the answers. Now tell me about *Yankee X-Ray*."

Radford detailed the information about weather, runway con-ditions, and the pilot's logbook. "Tox screen came back clean," he said. "On the pilot and the injured passenger."

"So, what are the questions you need to ask?" Gray said.

"Was this kid in over his head?" Radford said.

"You ran some simulated approaches?" Gray asked. "You have what, about four hundred hours?"

Radford had less than half that flight time, but he didn't correct his boss. He was ashamed of his scant experience. Gray probably had logged twenty times that number in the sky.

"Take me through the approach."

Radford took his boss, step by step, through the landing approach. He described the winds, the tree line, and the displaced threshold at the downwind end of the runway. He resisted the urge to tell the old man how much he admired him, and how much he wanted Gray's approval. The sandwich arrived, and Gray ordered another drink, but this time Radford demurred. He needed to be across the river thirty minutes ago. Wendy was already texting him.

Gray listened to Radford's summary of the investigation, nodded, and asked direct and pointed questions. By the time Radford had finished, Gray had spotted more holes in the report than were in the Swiss cheese on the Reuben. He felt sick to his stomach and began to apologize for mishandling the report.

"I want to do good work," he said, certain he'd failed his first real test.

"I'll say it again—ask the right questions. You're never smarter than the evidence. Always let the evidence provide answers."

His phone vibrated once more. He worried that Wendy might divorce him after this. Gray flipped through the written report and ripped out the addendum.

"Keep this," he said. "Remind yourself from time to time. Always learn something. This work will demand more than it will return. It will require you to see things no one should have to see, pay attention to details no one cares about. The work will keep you away from people who love you, and will leave you to fend for yourself."

The phone kept buzzing. Gray's words already coming true.

Radford wanted to know if he'd passed. Would Gray sign off on the report? Would he get any hint of validation? He knew better than to ask.

Gray said, "We've gone almost a decade without a major. I'm going to retire on that streak. Ten years without a major. Ten years without any fatalities on the commercial side. But no one is going to build a statue of me. Find a balance, son. Don't make this job your life."

Then he took out a pen, signed the report, and handed it back to Radford.

FORTY-FIVE MINUTES LATER, Radford arrived at the doctor's office. Wendy waited in the building's lobby. He was over an hour late. He expected her to cry, to shout and fall into despondency right there on the spot. Instead, she calmly asked about his meeting with Dickie Gray.

"The man's incredible," he said. He knew better than to go into details, but he told her about the bar and their conversation. She listened and smiled while he finished.

"Well," she said, "Jesus, Charlie. Don't make me ask. Did he sign the report?"

Radford smiled and pulled her close. He felt her warm body press against his, and was happy.

"What happened upstairs?" he said.

"I went alone, Charlie. What choice did I have?"

7

THE CONCOURSE AT Dulles International Airport brimmed with the Friday-evening energy of businessmen and lobbyists rushing home for the weekend. Spring storms over the Midwest created delays across the system. Lines queued at the gates, at customer service kiosks. Irate passengers demanded drink coupons, hotel vouchers, upgrades to first class. Crowds gathered around chain restaurants, jockeying for tables and overpriced hamburgers. Outside, the delays clogged taxiways, the air heavy with jet fuel and Piedmont humidity.

Erin dragged her suitcase through the bustling departure lounge at Dulles, wondering if it was too late to reconsider. Doug was right. She was in no condition to travel. She should've stayed home, resting, watching television, or getting her hands dirty in the zinnias. Her lower back burned. Both her knees had swollen to the size of grapefruits. With every step, her feet felt pierced by nails. She worried that she might collapse before reaching the gate. There was a time when she ran two marathons a year. Qualified for Boston. Won her age group more than once. Not anymore. This level of physical debilitation was staggering. She couldn't walk a hundred yards without pain.

At last, an airline agent waved her forward. The woman smiled, a familiar mix of pity and disgust. Erin knew that no amount of makeup could mask the consequences of sixteen weeks of poison. Her once lustrous hair grew in clumps and patches beneath her head scarf, like meadow grass in winter. After a few keystrokes and much consternation, her bags were checked and boarding passes printed.

"Do you need assistance to get down to the gate?" the agent asked.

Erin didn't answer, just grabbed her ticket and left.

It was all so normal. Long, hot security lines. Crowds of people staring into phones. As she approached the checkpoint, her bowels slackened. A cold sweat spread down her back.

On the long list of cancer's many miseries, incontinence ranked near the top. She'd made it six months without fouling herself in public, a streak verging on the mythic among pancreatic cancer patients. Most of her peers could make no such a claim. At all times though, she tracked a mental map to the nearest restroom, every step tethered to her turbulent bowels. She planned escape routes, backup plans if she encountered a full house. Already, she was worrying about the departure, those interminable minutes while the seat belt sign glowed. Mercifully, the security line moved quickly.

She hadn't planned to call Adam, but the relief she felt when she reached the gate buoyed her spirits. The next thing she knew, his voice was on the phone.

"Jesus, it's good to hear from you," Adam said.

What was it about that man's voice? His sincerity felt like warm rain on her skin, like a burst of light shot through darkness. She told him about the trip—one week among other cancer survivors, a term she hated, with its implicit finality. Surviving, perhaps, but not a survivor. Survivor implied a category that simply didn't exist.

"How are you?" he asked. "What are they telling you?"

She lied about her prognosis, about the headaches and nausea. She exaggerated her chances for a full recovery. She didn't want his pity. She wanted his desire, which she knew was gone.

"I wish you'd told me," he said. "I could've come out to see you."

Adam's voice, the implication of his offer, unsettled her. Something stirred in her hips, in the place she thought had gone dormant.

"I need this trip," she said, doubting her own sincerity. "I need to be alone."

She wanted to crawl into Adam's arms, to feel his shoulder against her cheek, to rub her hand across his stomach. But what she couldn't tolerate, what she wouldn't risk, was his rejection. She pictured the shape of his back, the way his lips once felt on her thighs. For a bright moment, she imagined slipping away from the retreat center, finding him at a café in Nob Hill, going upstairs to a hotel room. So much time had passed since she'd felt passion.

Adam used to visit her in the hospital until it became too much. He'd sneak away from the office—bring her books, little bars of Belgian chocolate. She was in and out of hospitals so much at the beginning. Once, he actually passed Doug in the hallway. After that, she told him, no more. But she never regretted one second of their time together. How foolish not to take grand chances in life, she thought. How seldom they arose. How quickly it could all be snuffed out.

"Listen," he said. "I could get away. I can fly out for the weekend. I'm not trying to push it, but I miss you."

Then she caught her reflection in a window. Her once-high cheekbones had sunk, as if someone had carved out her skull like a pumpkin. Her long honey-colored hair was now a sparse desert of patchy fuzz. Her battered body was only a shell of her former self. He'd take one look at me . . . , she thought, letting the notion go unfinished.

"Not now," she said. "Soon, though. I promise," lying to him only to spare herself the truth.

Soon. What did the word mean anymore? *Soon* used to mean the vague but certain future—a month, next fall, before the kids graduated high school. *Soon* used to mean not now, noncommittal time borne out of abundance. So much time to waste, so many limitless tomorrows. She used to measure life by bountiful *soons*: soon-hours, soon-days, soon-decades. Now *soon* led only toward darkness. Termination.

"I'm serious," Adam said. "Say the word, and I'll be there. I'll book my ticket right now."

"They have birds here, in the airport," she said. "They're amazing."

"*Birds?*"

THIRTY MILES AWAY, Charlie and Wendy walked along the Potomac River, on the Virginia side, down South Union Street just a few blocks from their condo. Charlie loved the brick buildings of Old Town, where restaurants and shops retained a village feel in the midst of the crushing power of urban commerce and government. He loved cobblestone sidewalks in snow, dew-slick bike trails on an early morning jog. They spent many weekends walking these streets. Sacred time reading books in Waterfront Park, leisurely breakfasts, and catching movies at the cinema and drafthouse. They had fallen in love here, built a marriage here. Did she really want to abandon all that? He couldn't shake the feeling that her desire for a child would pass. He didn't want to be a father, maybe because his own father hadn't exactly blazed a trail for him. Wendy, on the other hand, had come from good stock, a good home, Currier & Ives to his Clampetts.

She spoke little as they walked. A thick layer of clouds settled over the buildings. The air smelled of rain. For the first time, he worried about the integrity of their marriage. Would they still be together in ten years? He would never leave her, but he worried he wasn't enough, worried he'd disappoint her as a husband, as a man. It was an odd, unsettling thought. The way everything felt so tentative. He wanted to forget about work, about children, about everything but Wendy. She'd worn the long blue dress he loved. A dark sweater covered her shoulders. To him, she was always beautiful; it didn't matter what she wore. He wanted to kiss her, to take her home and make love to her.

He tried to imagine a future without her. Tried to picture her on a date with another man, in the bedroom. The thought made him feel nauseous.

She took his hand as they passed Kempers, his favorite restaurant on Prince Street, and kept walking south, to where the neighborhoods became less gentrified. A raw smell of the tidal basin fouled the air. They walked four blocks in silence. He wanted to tease apart the nuances of her mood. She seemed happy tonight, despite the trouble they'd been having. He wished he could bottle up this feeling, to save it for when her darkness returned. Finally, she turned a corner and stopped at an Italian place. Flecked paint on the sign out front against brick walls gave the old building a rustic feel. Thick red curtains on the windows. She led him inside, ordered a glass of wine, and he ordered a beer. The waiter brought a basket of warm bread.

He talked more about the meeting with Gray. She offered him a taste of her wine. Her voice was calm, soothing and familiar, and the wine softened her eyes, brought a hint of color to her cheeks. He remembered their first date, a fumbling affair after the night she'd brought the application to his apartment. He fell in love fast, so that when he saw her again a week later, and knew that she still had a boyfriend, his emotions and desire were horribly conflicted. They'd gone out to dinner four blocks from where they were now, a restaurant that had long since closed. That night, he couldn't eat, could barely say three coherent words. But she smiled at him and touched his arm across the table. After dinner, they walked through an old Civil War era cemetery on the way back to her apartment. She told him she loved going to that spot. They sat on a step and she rested her head on his shoulder. Later, curled up together on his couch, in a trembling voice, she'd confessed about the abuse, about the awful things her boyfriend had done to her.

Why couldn't things stay simple and pure?

"We need to talk about it," Wendy said now, breaking his reverie.

"I know," he said.

8

THE PLANE ARRIVED and taxied to the gate. The pilots' faces appeared in the windscreen, like those of innocent children playing a grown-up game. From the plane's bulbous nose, gold and blue stripes traced down the length of the craft. Tiny American flags adorned the upturned wingtips. Lights flickered on the plane's tail.

"Birds?" Adam asked. Erin held the phone close to her ear, hoping to feel something more tangible than sound.

The hallway behind the departure gate was decorated with porcelain cranes, modeled after origami paper cranes. An artist had affixed scores of these bone-white creations to walls and ceiling tiles, some birds in flight, others perched against the various signs in the cavernous concourse, fluttering over gift shops, soaring above the food court atrium. She'd read about the installation—a thousand cranes, all carved by local Japanese artists—to be hung inside the airport. Adam listened as she described the birds. Unlike Doug, he never changed the subject, never made her feel ridiculous for rambling.

"Like the book you used to read me," she said.

"Kawabata," he said. "Some of our best days. How are your kids?"

She told him about the twins, their first year of college almost behind them. Claire made the dean's list, while Tory was eking out a C minus in algebra. He responded by talking about the tribulations of raising three prepubescent boys, all of them athletes and fiercely competitive. During their time together, they never talked about their kids. They understood what they were risking. She never shared a photo of the twins with him. Their children were off-limits, terra incognita during their brief but passionate affair. It felt strange, almost healthy to talk so openly about them now. The guilt she carried centered entirely on notions of family, of what family meant, and what it meant to risk that security. She knew that through their affair they weren't gambling with their own lives but with the lives and destinies of all those people who depended upon them.

He offered again to go to California, but the last thing she needed was more pity. She'd wallowed in pity for six months—her own, her family's, and that of her friends. Anything but that. She told him what she needed most was solitude.

"I'm tired," she said. "I just want to disappear. I can't expect you to understand what that's like."

"I'm trying," he said.

"I have to go," she said.

There were other words she wasn't saying. Perhaps there always are.

"Wait," he said.

What did he want? What did she? She wanted him to confirm that she was once desired, once loved deeply. But only silence followed his imperative. After her initial diagnosis, she was ashamed to tell Adam. She hated the thought of him viewing her as sick, dying. He found out at work. She knew her sudden break of their relationship must have rocked him, but he bounced back quickly. Nothing rattled him for long, which was one of the reasons she was so attracted to him. Equanimity of the highest order. As with a knight, adversity only glanced off his armor. On the other hand, she seemed to suffer punishments out of proportion for her sins. How many times had they actually slept together? Did that level of infidelity deserve a death sentence? By the time she began the first cycle of chemo, she'd almost convinced herself the affair had been a mistake. A wonderful, exquisite mistake, but a mistake nonetheless. With disease dominating her life, it was an easy lie to believe. Mired in despair, she reached out for anything to cling to, and for a while, especially those early weeks, she'd clung to Doug. She remembered why she'd loved Doug in the first place.

Doug. Attentive, so positive, so certain in the efficacy of aggressive treatments, Doug chased down every medical option with a tireless, almost ruthless aplomb. He never complained, never expressed doubt or sadness. In a certain sense, her cancer brought out the best in Doug, a revelation she at first found startling, but one that, over time, grew troubling. But he'd been right.

The treatments had worked to an extent. Six months of hell had passed and she was still here. Doug had been right. But at what cost? Misery as routine? The anguish becoming ordinary? Her days chained to IV drips, needle sticks, and radiation blasts; nausea, vomiting, diarrhea, nosebleeds, skin bleeds, yeast infections on her tongue. And in the fading background, a memory of passion that had run its course, a sliver of pulsing life fading away.

"I miss you," Adam said at last.

"I KNOW YOU haven't changed your mind," Wendy said at the restaurant. "But I have. I want this, Charlie, as much as you want a career. I want to have kids. Why can't you see how important this is?"

Wendy talked with her hands, waving them higher as she spoke. He took another sip of her wine and tried to surrender to her excitement. More than anything, he wanted to share her joy over nursery colors, video monitors, strollers, and diaper bags. He wanted to believe in family too. But the more she talked about it, the more he felt his own dreams slipping away, and the more he felt the shadows of his past creeping in.

"I'm going to see a house in Vienna tomorrow," she said. "I want you to come with me. I need you to believe in this."

"Nothing has changed for me," he said. "At the very least, I need time to process all this, to think about it."

"This isn't a math problem," she said. "You have to feel it. You can't solve it—you can't collect data and reach a conclusion." She paused and took a bite of her food. Charlie had lost his appetite.

"Show me the house," he said.

Between shifts at the hospital, where Wendy worked as a critical care nurse, she'd been house shopping, in a progressively widening arc away from D.C. While she talked about the local schools, Charlie calculated the traffic. While she extolled the virtues of the eat-in kitchen bar, he pondered how much a nanny would cost. Water bills, home warranties, gas money, property taxes, wear and tear on the car, hours and hours in traffic. He loved seeing Wendy happy. He loved seeing her dream. But he suddenly felt a wave of sympathy for his father. No wonder his old man worked extra jobs on the weekends. No wonder he drank so much, was always tired and cranky.

"I'm scared," he said, interrupting his wife's analysis of plantation shutters versus drapes.

"What?" she asked.

"I don't know the first thing about being a father. I don't know how to raise a kid."

He thought about Dickie Gray. How would Charlie ever get to the top with all these distractions? Or would he, like his father, short-circuit his family by working too much? Either way, he lost. Why was he worrying about fatherhood before changing his first diaper?

"You'll be a wonderful father," she said.

"My old man was a prick," he said. "My mother was in church most of the time. They loved me, Wendy. I know they did their best. But I don't think either one of them smiled more than three times in eighteen years."

She ordered another glass of wine. A wonderful blush spread

high across her cheekbones. Had he ever loved her more than he did at that moment?

"I want to be someone you're proud of," he said.

"I am proud of you," she said, reaching for his hand. "I want to start a family with you. I want to be the mother of your children."

"I'm a goddamn bureaucrat," he said. "I might as well work in an office."

"You love your job," she said. "You're good at it."

He told her he didn't understand why she needed to make this decision now. They were still young. Maybe in a year or two. Maybe once he had more security in his job. Maybe she didn't understand what he was saying.

"Charlie, there are no road maps in life," she said.

"I need clear paths," he said. "I always have. If I can't see where I'm going, I shut down. I stop moving."

"No, you don't," she said. "My god, look at the work you do. More than anyone I know, you make sense out of chaos."

"I wish that was true," he said.

"Charlie, all you have to do is love a child. Everything else is a bonus."

"I love you," he said.

"If you love me, then you'll understand how important this is."

Outside, the rain had started. The wind picked up. Charlie watched a young couple on the sidewalk duck under the restaurant's awning. They curled into each other, laughed and then dashed back into the rain.

9

——

THE COOL SPRING evening began to give way to darkness, and the general boarding began, for Pointer Airlines flight 795, with non-stop service from Washington Dulles to San Francisco. Passengers queued and gathered their belongings. Text messages radiated out from the departure gate.

Seated across from where Erin stood, a young mother combed the tangles from her daughter's hair while the girl tapped on a cell phone. An elderly couple shared a coffee and a bagel. A soldier dozed against the wall. Others packed up, flipped through fashion magazines, played video games, talked on phones, stared out windows. All those private desires, those common sorrows. And above their heads, a flock of porcelain cranes. What beauty. What abundance! They thought only about where they were going, whom they would see, and, of course, the people they were leaving behind. It was only a cross-country flight, something that happened hundreds of times daily. They simply took it for granted, this flight ahead of them, such blind faith in the next hour, the next day, the next year.

Out of nowhere, Erin Geraghty filled with pure joy. She wanted to hug all the people around her, to break out a notebook and write poems about them and the wreath of birds circling overhead. Who were those people? What secrets did they possess? Who was grieving? Who was in love? Didn't they realize how tentative all of it was?

She thought about how selfish she'd been. For almost a year, she wore selfishness like a shell. As her world collapsed into misery and disease, that shell hardened. Even toward her family, she became cruel and tyrannical. She shoved everyone away. Doug. The girls. Her parents. Doctors and nurses resented her. *A most difficult patient.* The entire world was fighting for her, but she just wanted to be left alone.

Inexplicably, standing in line at the departure gate, the shell began to crack and splinter. She filled with something she would describe only as gratitude. Gratitude not only for being alive, but gratitude for the disease itself, for cancer, for the journey through hell that delivered her to the other side.

She sent Doug a text: "See you in a week. Thank you for letting me have this time. I love you."

He deserved so much more than that text and a wan message of love, but at that moment, a few words and escape were all she could muster. For months, Doug cared for her without complaint. He took time off work, drove her to every appointment, bathed her, wiped her ass when she couldn't. He deserved a medal, and she'd have happily pinned one on his chest, if only he'd shown some honest emotion, betrayed some depth of feeling, some sadness, some joy, even anger. His attention and anxiety were, at times, harder than the cancer itself. His care came from duty and obligation, not choice. Doug stopped choosing her years ago. They were married; they had children, obligations. Adam chose her. Cancer chose her. And both those choices only exaggerated her husband's deficits.

A young woman stood beside her. The woman had long curly hair, natural blonde. Pristine skin. Perky breasts. Slender legs. Three silver rings on her right hand. None on the left. This woman filled Erin with a boundless curiosity.

"Where you heading?" Erin asked.

The woman glanced over and shrugged.

"Away," she said.

Then the young woman popped on headphones and turned aside. Erin felt a flash of embarrassment, as if she were still a child excluded from the group. But the feeling passed quickly, a cloud moving across the sun. The beautiful woman had no idea. Even her rudeness didn't matter. This was simply how she carried things that day. There was no right way, no wrong way. Only the carrying.

Then she laughed. Right there at the departure gate, Erin laughed out loud, like a madwoman. For the first time in almost a year, she felt happy. Light. Like she could float. The young mother seated across from her looked up.

"Say goodbye to the birds, sweetie," the woman said to her daughter.

"I don't want to go, Mommy," the girl said.

Erin followed the line moving forward, still caught in a private reverie. What was it, she wondered, that ecstasy? She would wonder about that moment many times after. She would swear it was real, like a drug, blocking the pain in her legs, shielding her from the constant worry in her gut. She would wonder if perhaps that sudden joy was some sort of withdrawal, a sign of the toxins at last draining from her body. But even as she exalted in it, she sensed its shadow too. Her cancer had only gone dormant. Once it returned, the disease would devour her for good.

The mother hugged her little girl. The soldier hoisted his bag. The elderly couple packed up their belongings and ambled to the jetway. Even the rude woman with the golden curls glowed. And above them all, the flock of porcelain cranes. She never wanted to forget this moment. She wanted this feeling to rise above the others, above all the darkness that had surrounded her. Her whole body trembled.

The line moved slowly. A man stepped backward and plowed into her. She stumbled, almost fell over. The man turned, apologized.

"These damn bags," he said.

She smiled.

"It's such a beautiful night," she said. "Where are you heading?"

The man nodded. "My sister's getting married," he said with a slight accent. South African? German? He was strikingly handsome, like a movie star from another era.

"That's wonderful," she said.

He handed his boarding pass to the gate agent and moved away. Erin smiled as she handed over her pass.

"Have a good flight," the gate agent said.

Halfway down the Jetway, Erin approached the man again. He turned.

"Hurry up and wait," she said.

He really was Hollywood handsome, much like Adam. The man wore suit pants, a sapphire shirt, no tie. Salt-and-pepper stubble shadowed his cheeks and chin. She wondered what the man did for work, imagined him as a father, a son, a lover. The line stretched to the fuselage door. The smell of fuel wafted in from outside.

"Where are you heading?" he asked.

"I've been sick. I'm going to a cancer survivors' retreat. It sounds ridiculous to say it out loud."

"My sister," he said. "The one who's getting married? Had brain cancer two years ago. It doesn't sound ridiculous at all."

Everyone getting on the plane possessed an incredible story. Only the shells had to be cracked, Erin thought. She fought an urge to hug him as the line inched forward. The man said that his sister went through hell but seemed okay now. He spoke without the guarded optimism of most well-wishers. He seemed to understand the bleakness, the need for truth instead of pandering.

"She bought her own casket," he said. "She really did."

How many hours had she spent on funeral home websites? Too many to calculate.

"You just never know," he said.

They were almost at the jet's door. She wanted to ask him to sit near her. How wonderful it would've been to continue that conversation. But she didn't. She was trying to let go of control. She said goodbye to the man and stepped aboard the plane.

ALONG THE POTOMAC, on the Virginia side, a light rain glazed the cobblestones. Charlie Radford paid their dinner bill, pulled out his wife's chair. They walked home over slick sidewalks, laughing as they entered their condo, closing the door, turning on lights, and stepping around boxes. He took Wendy's hand and led her upstairs, kissing her neck at the top of the stairs, slipping off her sweater, unbuttoning her dress as her breath warmed his chest.

Thirty miles west, Pointer 795 taxied to the active runway at Dulles. Final checks were performed. A full moon rose off the plane's starboard wing, casting yellow reflections on water in a catch basin along the runway. Seat belts were fastened low and tight about the waist. A baby screamed. The plane rumbled down the runway, climbed into the clouds, and began a long, slow turn to the northwest. Climbing through twenty thousand feet, it crossed the Blue Ridge Mountains, a range formed more than four hundred million years ago, its isoprene falling back to the earth as the cool evening raised pockets of fog deep in the hollows. The passengers settled in for the long flight ahead as the plane picked up the airway that directed it west over the Appalachian Plateau, toward the Rust Belt, toward the once-grand cities of the Midwest—Pittsburgh, Cincinnati, and Dayton, where, just over a hundred years ago, two brothers, Orville and Wilbur Wright, once operated a bicycle shop but secretly dreamed of powered flight.

By the time Charlie Radford fell asleep beside his wife, Pointer 795 had crossed the Mississippi River south of Saint Louis, before turning in a southwesterly direction, lightning flashing in distant clouds.

10

MARTIN RADFORD NEVER played ball with his sons, never took them to an Orioles game in the city, never vacationed with his family on the Eastern Shore. A stonemason by trade, Martin worked long, grueling days building garden walls, resurfacing buildings, and repairing fireplaces. He'd come home sore, tired, bloody nicks in his hands, silica dust in his hair. The family's happiness and misery were chained to the boom-bust cycle of the Tidewater economy, always dependent on the metric-ton price of granite and the vagaries of home construction. The only good memory Radford had of his father was the air show at Patuxent River.

Charlie was eleven that summer, heading off to the sixth grade. Already something of an airplane nerd, he had begged his parents to take him to the show for weeks, but they'd ignored him.

Charlie's mother hadn't driven out of Aberdeen in five years, and Saturdays were sacred time for Pops—reading the paper, pushing the mower around the yard, the first highball before noon. But the night before the air show, his father came into his room and told him to get to bed.

"I want to get on the road early," his father said.

"Where are you going?" Charlie asked.

"Just make sure you're up."

Rolling south out of Baltimore, they picked up Route 2 before the sun rose. His father turned on sports radio but didn't speak much. It was one of the few times Charlie had ever been alone with the man. They stopped for breakfast at a McDonald's, and Charlie asked for a taste of his father's coffee. Martin laughed when his son could barely choke down a single sip.

Charlie was excited, and the anticipation he felt over this adventure was unlike any he'd ever experienced. The world he inhabited and the world he dreamed about were suddenly merging. Though he hadn't confirmed it, Charlie knew his dad was taking him to the air show.

Martin lit a cigarette and cracked the window. His father's companionship felt strange to Charlie, uncomfortable at first, but the tension eased as they drove south and the Calvert Peninsula thinned. On their left, through gaps in the trees, the bay came into view. Between puffs of his glowing Pall Mall, Martin pointed out various birds, some in flight, some on the shore. Herons, egrets, wading bitterns, and black cormorants. His father talked so eloquently about migration patterns, alluvial plains, and the salt line.

Charlie wondered where such knowledge came from. What other secrets lay hidden behind the man's usual, deep silence?

Martin lit another cigarette. "Okay, tell me—what makes this damned air show so important that I had to give up a whole Saturday for it?"

Only then did Charlie begin to talk about the Blue Angels.

"They fly six jets, Pop. They fly so close together that it looks like one giant plane." He'd seen a video at school and it set the hook. And Charlie had bitten. "I want to do that, Dad," he said. "When I grow up, I want to be a navy pilot."

Martin held the wheel steady with his left hand and grasped the cigarette with his right.

"That's a lofty goal," he said. "It's important to dream, but it's important to be realistic too."

As they approached the Governor Thomas Johnson Bridge, Martin cursed.

"God damn it," he said. Ahead, a steady stream of brake lights halted their progress.

Charlie wanted to apologize for the traffic souring his father's mood. As much as he wanted to see the air show, he would've happily traded any zooming jet for a chance to stay longer in the moment with his dad.

"Reach in the cooler and grab me a beer," Martin said, his voice blistering with familiar wrath.

He'd never contradicted his father and wasn't about to start, but he was sure that his father shouldn't be drinking beer while behind the wheel. Ice water chilled his hand as he fished out a can of Carling Black Label and wiped it dry with his shirt. The traffic had come to a dead stop.

Martin drank three beers before they pulled through the gate at the naval air station. Men in uniforms directed a long procession of cars into orderly rows. By the time they found parking, the beer had steadied his father's mood. Charlie relaxed and fiddled with loose change in the ashtray when the roar of an approaching jet rattled the windows. It was a sound unlike anything he'd ever heard before.

"Lookee there," Martin said, climbing out of the car and shielding his eyes from the sun.

A great roaring beast was sucking air from the sky itself. A moment later, Charlie spotted it, a black dot, low, coming fast out of the east. Two thick, oily exhaust trails streaked the sky. A split second later, the air exploded around him. The lumbering jet screamed low over their heads, so low that Charlie could almost see the pilot's helmet. The ground shook as the jet climbed, banked left, leveled off, and then banked sharply right. Martin was still tracking the jet as it disappeared into the sky, dark trails diffusing in the air.

"You know what that one was?" Martin asked his son.

Charlie nodded. "Yes, sir," he said. "That's an F-4 Phantom."

His father lifted him up onto the car. Charlie worried that he'd dent the roof, but as soon as he turned, he spotted the Blue Angels on the tarmac. Six blue Hornets with insignia-yellow numbers painted on their tails. They were magnificent even while at rest, parked in a precise row, each plane's fuselage polished to a mirror's sheen. He studied the jets, noting the position of the wings, the way the sun glistened on the canopies, the blue wooden chocks nestled beneath the planes' tires.

For the rest of the morning, they walked among static displays of aircraft. Charlie waited patiently in long lines for his turn to gaze into each plane's cockpit. All those dials, switches, and instruments, a world still completely foreign to him. He knew every plane, from the vintage World War II Spitfire to the Harrier jump jet, from cargo planes to an AWACS. Every half hour, another plane would take off and go through a routine of maneuvers over their heads: rolls, loops, ballistic climbs. Charlie watched them all carefully, noting which planes flew faster, which turned sharper, which could climb higher and which could land shorter. More jets flew, mock dogfights, parachutists with smoke streaming from their ankles, the smell of jet fuel and hot dogs, and the roar of the next thundering jet starting up. He was mesmerized, and the Blue Angels still hadn't flown.

By lunch, they walked back to the car and Charlie dragged his father's cooler into the shade of a hangar. He wanted to go back and see more planes, but Martin flopped down in the shade and shoved a beer into a paper bag. He told Charlie to grab a Coke from the cooler. Two six packs of beer floated in icy water, along with a single can of soda.

Behind the hangar, away from where all the air show jets were parked, a pair of navy Corsairs taxied past. The attack jets' cockpits were open at an odd angle. Charlie stared at the pilots with a mix of admiration and awe. One pilot's gloved hand rested casually on the side of his jet. The jet's gray fuselage was festooned with shark teeth near the cavernous intake at the plane's nose. At low power, the engines sounded like a shriek, more keening whistle than thunder. As they taxied past, the pilot spotted Charlie and lifted his gloved hand in a greeting. The boy was so stunned he didn't even wave back.

Martin reached into the icy water, snagged another beer, and sat down on the cooler.

"What do you say, sport?" he asked. "You wanna call it a day?"

Charlie's stomach heaved. For a split second, he thought he might vomit. The Blue Angels weren't scheduled to fly for another two hours, and his father was already trying to leave.

"Can we stay a bit longer?" he asked.

"I don't want to risk getting stuck in traffic again," Martin said. "Let's not be like all these other assholes."

Charlie tried to appear nonchalant, but inside, he wanted to explode. He had never loved his father more than he had that day, but he'd never hated him more than he did at that moment. He thought about running away, disappearing into the crowd.

"I haven't seen the C-5 yet," Charlie said, indicating the massive gray cargo jet parked on the south side of the base. The plane's nose had been retracted so that people could walk through like it was a tunnel.

"You go, sport," Martin said. "But be back here in twenty minutes. I'll start packing up."

Charlie wondered if he really could disappear, get away from his father. He thought of heading off toward the first-aid tent, perhaps feigning an illness. But then he thought about the long drive home, about what would happen back in Aberdeen. His father's rage would linger, spreading across their family like a storm. But he'd come here specifically with the dream of seeing the Blue Angels. He glanced out at the flight line. The six blue-and-yellow jets, lined up wingtip to wingtip, would soon perform, but he'd be on his way home. Quietly, reverently, with the serious purpose that only a ten-year-old boy can muster, he committed himself to do whatever it took in life to fly with those men.

RADFORD THOUGHT ABOUT the long-ago air show at Patuxent River as the NTSB jet descended before dawn at Wichita's Dwight D. Eisenhower National Airport. He remembered staring out the back window of his father's car, watching white smoke from the Blue Angels' jets mark the bright Maryland sky. He wondered if Martin would be proud of him now, if he'd done enough to be worthy of the old man's approval now that he was investigating his first major plane accident.

Radford rebuckled his seat belt. Near the front of the plane was the man who'd be leading the investigation into the crash of Pointer 795, Gordon Ulrich, "Gordo" as he preferred to be called.

In every way, Gordon Ulrich was the polar opposite of Dickie Gray. Short, stocky, nervous, and talkative, Ulrich never shied away from reminding his investigators that he'd graduated from MIT. A nonpilot, Ulrich had made rank at the agency with an unrelenting reliance on statistical analysis. Where Dickie Gray talked about intuition and experience, Ulrich relied on data and numbers. Career advancement over culture. At the agency, he was reviled, but respected too for his brilliance.

"Our first priority is to secure the accident site," Ulrich said as the jet taxied toward a hangar.

It was 5:00 a.m., and Radford hadn't slept at all. With him on the plane that morning was the rest of the NTSB Go Team, an advance cadre of investigators rushing to figure out why a 737 apparently had exploded. Most were only now waking up. Ulrich spoke over the noise of jet engines spooling down.

"Document everything," he said. "It didn't happen if it isn't documented."

He thought of Gray's advice. *Ask the right questions.* In no small way, Radford was getting his shot because of Gray. Only on Gray's positive recommendation would he be leading the survival factors working group, a huge step forward in his career if he didn't screw it up. He'd be collecting evidence, finding bodies, identifying the remains of 123 passengers and crew, which, from the initial indications, would be scattered over miles of Kansas prairie farmland.

But inexplicably, Gray had been left off the Go Team. Radford had no idea why. That decision seemed like a fatal misjudgment, leaving behind the most experienced investigator at the agency. Whatever analytical talent Ulrich possessed, whatever brilliant minds he'd studied with, Ulrich lacked the very thing Gray possessed in spades: wisdom. Radford had plenty of questions about why Gray had been left off this investigation, but right now, more important questions needed to be asked. The answers waited, scattered in the smoldering wreckage on a Kansas prairie. Ulrich stood up and cleared his throat.

"All right ladies and gentlemen," he said. "Last night a plane exploded, and over a hundred people are dead. This is what we train for. This is why we get up in the morning."

11

An hour later, dawn broke over Kansas. Radford sat in the cramped back seat of a state police helicopter, scanning the ground below, where the smoldering wreckage revealed no discernible pattern. A piece of wing blocked the passing lane on Highway 400. A landing gear strut had wedged into a fallow cornfield. Aluminum panels littered rooftops. In Lake Afton, seat cushions, luggage, and a human torso bobbed atop the water's surface, while wires and the port engine casing washed up onshore. Every thirty seconds, police scanners crackled with reports of more wreckage and body parts. Near Murdock, jet fuel had sloshed onto a clapboard farmhouse, where fire crews sprayed the adjacent outbuildings with foam. Elsewhere, hot spots burned like signal fires across the open prairie.

In his lap, Radford held a chart. He was marking the debris fields with a red pen, but the chart was already stained with so many red dots that it seemed useless to continue.

He had never seen anything like this spectacle of ruin. The destruction was not just staggering; it was unimaginable.

A quarter mile off the port skid, a pile of debris smoldered along the edge of a road. They circled the wreckage several times. The young Kiowa pilot said nothing as he held the helicopter in a tight orbit. To the west, a piece of the downed plane's tail assembly lay shattered in mud. Radford could identify the Pointer Airlines blue-and-gold paint on the rudder.

"Not many pieces of wreckage larger than hay bales," Ulrich said over the intercom. Radford only nodded.

"How do you get used to this?" the Kiowa pilot finally asked.

Radford didn't know. He didn't even want to speculate. He'd trained for this, studied, worked grueling hours, read books and journals and accident reports. But below him was the real thing, the ultimate test. None of the accidents he'd seen before were this extensive. Nothing he'd studied in training videos or read in old case files prepared him for such carnage: broken pieces of airplane littering golden winter wheat fields, bodies floating in catchment ponds.

He asked himself, Am I ready?

"What we knew so far," Ulrich said, "is that last night Pointer 795 came apart in midair and showered its contents over a massive swath of south-central Kansas."

The helicopter hit a thermal, forcing the contents of Radford's stomach upward.

They crossed a highway overpass and approached a larger

section of fuselage. A black crater in the earth marked a large impact point. Seats and body parts were visible on the ground. Radford added more red dots to his chart. Such devastation was hard to put into any context. Reconstructing this accident would be like building a house of cards in a hurricane.

"These early hours are the toughest," Ulrich said. Radford wondered if his boss was trying to sound confident. Was he trying to convince himself he was up to the challenge too? Radford wished Ulrich would just shut up. "It looks like pure chaos. But we'll make sense of this."

"How?" the helicopter pilot asked.

"It's all about the data," Ulrich said. "We pick up the pieces and organize the sequences."

Radford bit down on the side of his cheek. "What's the old joke?" he said, trying to comfort himself as much as the young helicopter pilot. "How do you eat an elephant?"

"Right now, I need to find a spot to establish the operations center," Ulrich said, cutting Radford off before he could deliver the punch line.

The truth was, Radford had no idea how this accident would ever make sense.

"We'll need highway access," Ulrich said, "and space for a temporary morgue."

"You might as well have set up back in Wichita," Radford said. He estimated the accident zone covered forty square miles.

The young pilot tapped the windscreen and pointed toward what appeared to be a rest stop. The helicopter banked left toward the road, where no cars moved.

"The entire highway's shut down," the pilot said.

"We haven't ruled out terrorism," Ulrich said.

Radford wondered if a bomb could've caused this. The screening measures throughout U.S. airports were rigid, and the likelihood of slipping a large enough explosive on a plane was far exaggerated in the popular consciousness. But if not a bomb, then what? They would need to demonstrate that some other factor was responsible, and given the positive safety record of airliners, he had no earthly clue what that might be. Planes just didn't blow up in midair, not anymore.

On the horizon, swirling black smoke trails rose, pushed along by steady southwesterly winds. The scene looked like something out of a B-grade apocalyptic movie. The pilot cycled the collective, slowing them into tight orbit, two hundred feet over the truck-stop parking lot.

Cars and trucks had been abandoned along exit ramps and breakdown lanes. How many were dead on the ground? How the hell did this happen? Radford's thoughts filled with questions. He thought of Dickie Gray back in D.C. Gray should be here.

Radford cringed when his boss twisted his body around to make eye contact with him in the back seat. "This look like a good spot?" Ulrich asked. What the hell could he say?

Radford shook his head. Nothing about the scene was good.

How would this carnage affect him? Would he carry pieces of this day for the rest of his life? He thought of Wendy back in Virginia. He'd wanted this chance to prove himself as an investigator, to prove himself to his wife as much as to anyone else. He'd said the words to her: "I want to be someone you're proud of." But now that he was here, he felt like an impostor, a fraud.

Ulrich signaled with his thumb: take us up.

A thousand miles in either direction, at the departure and arrival airports, hundreds of families began gathering. News of the disaster arrived overnight. Lives forever altered. Children waking up as orphans, wives as widows. Devastation echoed like thunder across the plains. An airliner crash was a spectacle. Every media outlet, every TV channel, every newspaper in the world would soon carry pictures, stories, rumors, and tales of what was just now coming into view. And Radford was here now, at the center of it. "Almost a decade without a major," Gray had said at the Irish pub. A streak he'd hoped to take with him into retirement. Gray's lifework. And the poor bastard couldn't even be here to help figure out what had happened.

Radford folded the chart as the helicopter zoomed west, tracking over power lines toward more wreckage in the distance.

12

THEY WORKED PAST nightfall on Saturday, and by breakfast on Sunday, they'd mapped the major debris fields, established a perimeter, set up a temporary morgue at the old Cheney High School field house. The critical first forty-eight hours were almost up. The more debris they gathered, the more bodies they found in those first two days, the higher the likelihood they'd have secured the most vital evidence. *You're never smarter than the evidence*, Gray had told Radford. The first rule. But with each hour that passed, the scrutiny and pressure continued to build.

The hordes of media—print, TV, streaming—relentless and uninformed, had arrived. They took over every motel room in southern Kansas and began spilling over into trucker motels in northern Oklahoma. Relatives were now arriving too, along with onlookers, curious farmers and truck drivers, high school kids and old men. Public spectacle mixed with private misery. Radford worried about the temptation to grab a piece of history. Hard to pass up a souvenir from a crashed plane. Hard not to pocket a scrap of aluminum, a rivet, a ball of wire. He knew that even body parts had been snatched before. He tried to block out the distractions and follow Dickie Gray's second axiom: *Ask the right questions.*

As head of the survival factors working group, Radford's primary focus would be the bodies. With an in-flight breakup, many of the bodies were in pieces, though some were largely intact, still seated, with hands neatly folded in laps. What could explain how, earlier that morning, Radford had pulled a severed leg from a car's windshield? How could the extreme violence of the accident so easily mingle the absurd and macabre at the same time? He concentrated on the work, not the grim reality of what he was seeing. So far, the biggest distraction was not the wreckage on the ground but the borderline incompetence of his boss.

If Dickie Gray was a walking classroom, then Gordon Ulrich was a nervous vice-principal facing budget cuts. Despite his reputation as the agency whiz kid, Gordo appeared overwhelmed by the scope and complexity of the work. His primary concern seemed to be getting a clean shave before each press conference. He badgered his investigators, blaming them for the slow pace of the operation, for the lack of answers. He kept interrupting the all-important fieldwork by calling unnecessary meetings, filling their phones with useless texts, and micromanaging even his most experienced investigators to the point of mutiny. And this was only their second day in Kanas.

What Radford couldn't fully appreciate was the intense pressure Ulrich faced from D.C. How his bosses had to respond to questions from congressmen and senators, all of whom wanted answers now. Ulrich was simply the extension of the political will. Every move would be scrutinized, every facet of the operation watched and judged. This was the reason Dickie Gray had been left off the team. Twenty years ago, investigators could be mavericks and cowboys, but now appearances mattered as much as evidence. Now public perception drove the decisions made on the ground. These were all things Radford didn't yet understand but would discover in time.

So far, the only thing Radford knew with certainty was that an explosive decompression had ripped Pointer 795's fuselage apart in flight. But as for a source, any number of things could've initiated the explosion. A bomb, a fuel-tank explosion, an engine coming apart and spraying its metal shards into fuel. Radford knew the answers would come eventually but Ulrich wanted results now.

Later that morning, Radford and Ulrich went to investigate a report that the plane's nose cone had been located. They stood near their rental car at mile marker 118 on Highway 400. Locating the pilots' bodies was the most critical phase of Radford's recovery operation. It should've been done yesterday, but thunderstorms and nightfall restricted their work. A bright, clear sky was overhead now, but the path into the field looked miserable. Dark, relentless clods of mud for as far as the eye could see.

"We need to hire more crane contractors," Radford said.

"I'll worry about the big picture," Ulrich said. "You focus on your bodies."

Radford hoped the pilots' bodies were waiting out in the field. Ulrich leaned against the car and slipped on blue-mesh shoe covers.

They set out, swatting away bugs, alert for rat snakes and knee-shredding gullies. Five minutes in, and Ulrich already lagged behind, sighing and huffing with each labored step. The going was slow, but Ulrich's whining made it tortured. Two hundred yards ahead, the plane's nose cone finally came into view. Mud sucked at his boots as Radford crossed a furrow. For weeks, spring thunderstorms had dumped heavy rains, filling the reservoirs and catchments, soaking the emerging crops, and making the ground soft, doughy, and almost impassable. Flies and gnats swarmed. Rows of shin-high soy plants swayed in a light breeze, creating a dizzying effect.

Every five minutes, Radford's pager went off: notification of a piece of wing here, a section of the tail there, bodies and fuel and wires and more bodies. He formed questions while they slogged ahead. What did the pattern of injuries show? How did that pattern explain the nature of the explosion? Where were the passengers seated? Trust the process, Radford thought.

Ulrich groaned. He'd worn the wrong clothes for fieldwork. The blue-mesh covers long gone, his dress shoes were mud covered. Bug bites glowed on his neck. A day into the investigation, the man already looked beaten and broken.

"I want theories," he said, talking as much to the soy stalks and insects as to Radford. "I don't want explanations and hunches."

Radford began to understand the complexity of what lay ahead. This plane had shattered into a million pieces at thirty thousand feet, and now those pieces were buried in dirt on hillsides and at the bottom of ditches. Short of clear-cutting every wheat field in Sedgwick County, he didn't know how the hell they'd gather everything together.

"Fuck," Ulrich said, swatting at his neck.

Fifty feet away now, the crumpled nose cone lay sideways. It was an eerie sight. Enough of that section of the plane remained intact and recognizable that it looked almost new, but transformed as this grotesque fragment, like a decapitated head in a basket, minus the guillotine. The field reeked of manure and jet fuel. If they didn't get the bodies out soon, the smells would only get worse. As he approached, Radford noted the absence of burn marks on the nose cone's aluminum skin. It lay on its side, like a child's Lego carelessly left on the floor. He thought of Wendy, of home. He tried to forget that among the dead out here were eleven children.

"This is ridiculous," Ulrich said. "Why couldn't they have choppered us in here?"

"It looked more accessible from the ground," Radford said.

"I'm going to need clean clothes," Ulrich said. "God damn it, I've got a press conference in two hours."

Ulrich lived for the media. His whole demeanor, even his voice, changed when he was talking to a reporter. And for the foreseeable future, he would be the public face of the Pointer 795 investigation, handling the press, coordinating the daily progress meetings, teleconferencing with D.C. Maybe that was a good thing. Maybe keeping Ulrich high and dry would make the day-to-day work more bearable. Just in front of the nose cone, a large drainage ditch blocked their way. The ditch contained foul, brown-green water. A swarm of mosquitoes skimmed the murky surface.

"No way," Ulrich said. "I'm not wading through that."

Radford spotted a section of wood fencing nearby. He placed two boards over the ditch to form a makeshift bridge. As he crossed, Ulrich's phone rang, providing an excuse for his boss to remain on the other side of the ditch while Radford approached the wreckage.

"It's Kansas," Ulrich said, almost shouting into his phone. "Not the goddamn Indian Ocean. Find me those black boxes!"

Radford was suddenly aware that Lucy Masterson, another member of the Go Team, was approaching on his left. Her pants and shoes were spotless. In her left hand, Lucy carried three plastic evidence bags with small fragments of metal inside. She glanced at Ulrich and rolled her eyes.

"You geniuses forget how to read a map?" she said. "There's an access road from the north. Five minutes of preparation saves an hour of effort."

"Ulrich is the biggest horse's ass in the entire stable," Charlie said.

"Yeah," Lucy said. "But it's *his* rodeo."

Lucy Masterson had started at the NTSB a few months before Radford. She was one of the few female aviation investigators. In Iraq, she'd flown navy helicopters, and from what Radford had been told, she didn't rattle under fire. Compact, almost masculine in her attire, Lucy was an attractive woman if you looked past her bulldog attitude and personality. She kept her hair short, wore little makeup. Except for pearl earrings and an occasionally warm smile, you might not even notice her gender. Radford liked her, even though they were essentially competing for the next promotion. She was also unencumbered: no partner, no children, nothing to worry about apart from the work.

"The son of a bitch is right though," Lucy whispered. "No reason we shouldn't have found the boxes by now."

The black boxes were in fact orange in color and two in number: the flight data recorder and the cockpit voice recorder. The first would contain a record of all Pointer 795's systems the moment before it came apart: engine thrust, fuel levels, avionics, electrical systems. The cockpit voice recorder saved communications between the pilots during the flight. Both would yield critical clues once they were found, a task Radford would have preferred to gathering bodies. Together, he and Lucy walked the last few paces toward the nose cone. Twice she bent and gathered pieces of metal from the mud, slipping them into evidence bags and marking the locations on her electronic map.

Behind them, a man Radford didn't recognize crossed the makeshift bridge with Ulrich. From the sidearm holster and the suit coat, Radford figured him to be FBI.

"We're not going to get into a pissing contest over this," the man said. "Until you can definitively rule out a bomb, this is a crime scene and we have the lead."

"You really think a bomb did this?" Radford said. He didn't suspect a bomb. The explosive patterns were wrong, and the likelihood of sneaking a bomb on a plane was low. But he immediately knew he already had violated Gray's first principle: *You're never smarter than the evidence.* He should've kept his mouth shut.

There was so much to learn, so many nuances of the work that he didn't yet understand. The FBI agent turned and looked at Radford with a dismissive glance.

Were it not for the gaping hole where the cockpit door should be, the plane's nose cone was remarkably intact. Puckers in the aluminum skin revealed impact forces, but whatever decapitated the plane in flight made the cut cleanly and decisively. Several panels below the windscreens had blown clear. Radford grabbed his flashlight and took off his windbreaker.

"I'm going in," he said.

"Be careful," Lucy said. "I'm not crazy about its structural integrity."

Wedging through a narrow opening into the cockpit, Radford stopped cold. The destruction was staggering. The cramped space, no larger than a closet, smelled coppery, earthy, almost sweet in an eerie way. Several interior panels had ripped away from the ribbing. Insulation and wires dangled like viscera. He poked his head farther inside, where four of the six cockpit windscreens were blown out. Sharp smells—fuel, metal, the faintest odor of bodily waste—greeted Radford as he shone his light on the cathode-ray instrument panel. All the screens were shattered. Fluid oozed from the throttle column, which had snapped off from its attachment braces and hung at an odd angle. He carefully pushed aside a fallen metal hatch. Behind it, more wires and cracked metal pointed toward the copilot's lifeless body, still strapped in his seat.

Jack Delacroix, Radford thought. In the briefing he'd read that morning, the notes said Delacroix was a father, a husband, a former high school teacher who'd finally landed his dream job at Pointer Air six years ago. Delacroix's left arm had been ripped from the shoulder socket. His femur protruded through his blue uniform pants. Petechial hemorrhaging in the man's cheeks and nose indicated that he didn't have time to don his oxygen mask. His skin was ghostly blue, *cyanotic*, that was the medical term, Radford remembered. But despite the obvious blunt trauma, there were no burns, no char. In the port station, where the captain's body should've been, an empty seat raised more questions that would need answers. Radford flicked off his light and shimmied back through the small opening.

Ulrich was on his phone. "Find me those black boxes," Ulrich said. "Stop pussyfooting around."

"Copilot, strapped to his seat inside," Radford said to Lucy, who offered her hand to help him down. "Longitudinal sheering. Most of the starboard station is gone."

"Captain?" Lucy asked.

Radford shrugged. Finding the copilot's body was important. It was like finding a corner piece of a jigsaw puzzle. But where was the captain's body? Why wasn't he in his seat? What did that mean? For all the questions Radford asked, he worried more about the hundred other ones he hadn't thought to ask.

Lucy crawled into the cockpit with a tech. They needed to photograph the copilot's body before it could be taken out. Radford thought about the man's wife, about his kids. No, all the classes, all the study, none of it had prepared him for this.

Coming down the access road, Shep Ellsworth, another member of the Go Team, suddenly appeared. He stood near a crumpled fuselage panel ripped from the nose. A structural engineer and former marine fighter pilot, Shep Ellsworth now sported a beard and a ponytail. Shep had joined the agency right after 9/11. He was notorious for being a cold, cruel human being. But he was also brilliant, an investigator cut from the same cloth as Dickie Gray. He might well have been the smartest investigator at the agency, but he possessed an outright antagonism toward authority as well as toward his colleagues. The beard, the ponytail, the forearm tattoos, Ellsworth bucked the bureaucratic image. Radford hated to acknowledge it, but he admired the man's confidence. Radford had to prove himself in the field, and working in Ellsworth's shadow wouldn't make that any easier.

"They finally let you out of the dugout?" Ellsworth said. His breath smelled like coffee, cigarettes. "And the dyke too?"

He reminded Radford of a younger version of his father, the same inappropriate, cutting humor, the same cruelty toward the world, an utter disdain for anyone who didn't see things the same way he did.

Begrudgingly, as if such a task were beneath him, Shep Ellsworth outlined the most likely time line for Ulrich. The FBI agent listened too.

"Pointer departed IAD at 0010 Zulu," he said. "Vectored west. An hour or so later, they begin a series of course changes to avoid heavy weather."

Radford imagined the crowded sky, all those jets jockeying for smooth rides while they zipped through an ever-narrowing gap in the storm front. Ellsworth's tone remained detached, nonchalant, as if he were reading a grocery list, and not standing in a world of wreckage.

"What's that all mean?" the FBI agent asked.

"They were trying to slip through a line of massive thunderstorms," Radford said.

"Could that be the cause?" the agent asked.

"It's possible," Radford said.

"Listen to Encyclopedia Brown," Ellsworth said. "And here's his sidekick, Penny Parker."

"Bite me, Shep," Lucy said, emerging from the nose cone. A stain of blood or hydraulic fluid smudged her cheek.

"Lines up with the major debris," Ulrich said. "Within ten to maybe fifteen miles. If we assume the plane held together for a while after the initial event."

"No Mayday?" Radford asked.

Ellsworth glared at him but didn't answer.

"We need those black boxes," Ulrich said.

"We'll get 'em," Lucy said.

The key was to filter out emotion. You had to look past the raw carnage. You had to see the victims as bodies, as evidence. To look beyond the death and destruction. To picture order. To see the end, even in the havoc of the beginning. The key was to start asking the right questions. Radford wiped the smear from Lucy Masterson's cheek with a handkerchief. He admired and appreciated her tenacious approach, but you had to expend your energy evenly. A major investigation might take two years to conclude. They were only into the second day.

From the access road, a frenetic-looking Willie Hernandez jogged toward them, violating another of aviation's most sacred principles: *never panic*. Hernandez was the most junior member of the Go Team. The dumb son of a bitch already looked sick, like a frightened kid after a nightmare. He arrived at the nose cone sweating and out of breath.

Hernandez turned toward Radford, almost as if he'd forgotten where he was or why he'd come. For a moment, Radford worried the man might be cracking. The bodies, the wreckage, the sheer chaos, he knew it could overwhelm a person. Hernandez was a big muscular guy. Sometimes the giants cracked first.

"They found someone," Hernandez managed to say.

"What?" Lucy asked.

"What the Christ are you babbling about?" Ellsworth said.

"They found a passenger," he said. "She's alive."

13

Radford clears his throat. An aide delivers another pitcher of cold water, and he immediately fills the empty glass. He takes a sip, glancing down at his detailed notes.

"The report was that they'd found a passenger alive," he says.

"What did you do upon hearing this news?"

"I commandeered a state cop and his car, and raced toward the barn in Goddard where she was said to have been found."

"At that moment, Mr. Radford, what did you think you'd encounter when you reached the barn?"

"The details were sparse at best," he says. "In those early hours, very little provided context. You grope about in the dark for a long time. That's why we don't speculate. That's why we gather evidence."

"Answer the question, sir. What did you expect to find? What did you think you were walking into?"

"A woman was found alive in a barn," he says. "Along with debris. I didn't know why the assumption was that she'd fallen from the plane. That story made no sense. I assumed the woman was injured on the ground, in the barn."

He doesn't tell them that his second thought was that someone played a hoax. He avoids using the word *hoax* in front of the Congressional Subcommittee for Aviation Affairs. He hopes to keep the word *hoax* out of the public record, since the resolution of this story itself remains in doubt. He wants to provide no headlines for the evening news. He won't say the word, not to these men and women, even if that was the exact word that ran through his mind all the way to the barn.

"So, you approached the barn with skepticism?"

"I tried to approach the barn the way I approached any other piece of wreckage. Whatever I found would be part of the story, and whoever was alive had a story to tell. My job was to ask the right questions."

On a screen behind the congressmen, a photo appears, an aerial shot of the farm, the now-famous red-clapboard barn center left, a few dozen acres of feed corn, more rows of soy, a modest-sized ranch house, two huge bur oak trees. Other photos are projected onto the screen: open barn doors, a John Deere tractor parked inside, bailers, shelves stuffed with tools and chemicals. Radford remembers walking past a traffic jam of emergency vehicles to get to the barn. He remembers the fireman, the cops, the sheer chaos of that moment, and everyone looking to him for an explanation. They all answered an emergency call, but apparently the woman was no longer there when any of them arrived.

Then another photo flashes: Shep Ellsworth and his bushy ponytail, tattooed forearms, standing next to Radford, both men in blue NTSB windbreakers, staring up at the barn's roof. Just over their shoulders, the dark sky and threatening storms. This photo appeared on the front page of the *New York Times*. In the distance, Radford can almost see again the lightning flashes.

"Mr. Radford, what happened next?"

"I went into the barn," he says. "More than twenty uniformed men and women were inside. Cops, firemen, paramedics." Even now, over a year later, Radford remembers the town names on the back of the firemen's coats: Murdock, Cheney, Goddard, Kingman.

The final photo now appears behind the congressmen. This one Radford took with his phone's camera. A huge, jagged hole between two rafters in the ceiling. Splinters of wood and light. Clouds moving past the open timbers.

"Was the woman still there?"

"No," Radford says. "They'd already taken her to a hospital."

"How badly was she hurt?"

"Apparently, a number of abrasions," he says. "No significant trauma. As I said, they took her to the hospital."

There is a long pause before the next question is asked, this one from an Alabama congressman. Until now, this man has been quiet. Radford recognizes the man from television. He is old, black, with a ring of bone-white hair. The man's jowls are wide, and he is hard to understand at first, the thick Alabama drawl, an old man's croaky voice. Radford thinks the congressman marched with King. He even may have been in Memphis.

"Mr. Radford, thank you for being here today. Let's get to the point. Did you believe the story about the Falling Woman?"

Radford stares up at the man. It is the first good question of the hearing, the right question. He doesn't mean to insert a dramatic pause, but one follows the congressman's question, while Radford registers its implications.

"Belief is not part of an investigation," Radford says. "Never try to be smarter than the evidence. This is how we work."

"Mr. Radford," the Alabama congressman says, "who is Alan Magee?"

A murmur rises in the room. Radford admires this congressman's thoroughness. He would like to thank the man for doing his homework.

"Staff Sergeant Alan Magee," Radford says.

"Can you tell us about Sergeant Magee?"

"Magee was a tail gunner on an American B-17 in World War II," Radford says. "In 1943, while on a bombing mission over occupied France, Magee's plane took flak and caught fire."

Radford remembers reading about the story. The details seemed fake, an urban legend propagated on the internet. At first, he could find no hard evidence to verify its claims, but he also couldn't debunk the story's truth. Finally, after hours of digging through old news clippings online, he found the original article from *Stars and Stripes*.

"What happened to Sergeant Magee?"

"He bailed out of his plane from twenty-two thousand feet. Without a parachute."

The congressman nods. Others pass notes to their interns.

"Magee," Radford says, "fell through the glass roof of a train station in Saint Nazaire, France. He survived. When the German soldiers found him, he'd suffered little more than a few broken bones."

Radford hears the cameras and reporters coming to life. What did Magee's story represent to them? A precedent? Evidence that such a fall could occur?

"And who is Juliane Koepcke?"

Radford smiles.

"Miss Koepcke fell from a plane in Peru. The plane was struck by lightning above ten thousand feet. She was a teenager at the time. I think it was 1971."

"She lived too?"

"She fell into a tree, climbed down, and then stumbled around in the rain forest for eleven days before they found her," Radford says. "She only broke her collarbone. She published a book about it."

A murmur spreads in the hearing room. The Alabama congressman then asks about Vesna Vulović, Nicholas Alkemade, and Ivan Chisov, men and women who survived falls from airplanes coming apart in midair. The congressman is smart, Radford thinks; he wants to buy the man a beer. Instead, he shares details about each case, cases he's come to know well.

"So, I'll ask again," the congressman says. "Did you believe her story?"

"I didn't want to believe it," Radford says. "But the more I looked, and the more of these stories I found, the more I considered it plausible."

"And you decided to do what with this information?"

"I decided to keep an open mind. That's what the job demands. I let the possibility exist."

"What possibility is that, sir?"

"The possibility of the impossible."

14

"THIS FUCKING PLANE went full piñata at thirty thousand feet," Shep Ellsworth said, sitting next to Radford in the state police cruiser. It was Sunday afternoon, and they were heading to the hospital where, the police said, the woman from the barn had been taken. "Why are you wasting my time?"

Radford didn't reply. He'd never been in the back seat of a police car before. What was it his father used to say? *Every good Irishman should spend a night in jail.* The old man attributed that bit of working-class wisdom to Jack Kennedy, but Radford never verified the source nor lived up to the adage. Yet another reason he'd disappointed his father.

They passed two debris fields along the highway. Still-smoldering wreckage, yellow tape, police cars idling, red flags planted in the earth to indicate body parts. An hour earlier, the lieutenant governor arrived at the command tent to insist they reopen Highway 400, though few cars were visible on the straight, flat road.

"I need this distraction," Ellsworth said, "like I need to be kicked in the balls by a horse."

"You aren't buying it?" Radford asked.

"Jesus," Ellsworth said. "I know you're new at this, but for Christ's sake, use your brain."

Ellsworth's presence was toxic. Radford already hated the man. He was no better than a high school bully, constantly looking to put people down, and his outright cynicism made things worse. His attitude ruined what little flickers of camaraderie existed among the investigators. He even smelled bad, a mixture of oniony sweat and cigarettes. But he wasn't wrong. As much as Radford hated to acknowledge it, a healthy dose of skepticism helped this situation make more sense.

Dickie Gray had told him to ask the right questions. But what the hell was going on? What had he seen? A hole in the roof. Splinters of wood. A mangled seat from the plane. How did those things add up to a passenger surviving such a crash? And why did it bother him so much? What happened in that barn?

The cop sped down the empty highway without turning on the siren. Wheat fields swayed in a light breeze on both sides of the road. Radford wrote down the time and date on his notepad, followed by: *Investigating debris and possible injury in barn; Goddard, KS. En route to hospital to check on victim.* In his training, he'd read about impossible things before. A baby found alive in the burnt wreckage of a Cessna 210. A cargo plane ripped through the roof of a house in Denver but somehow missed the sleeping woman. Could someone have fallen encased inside a piece of the cabin? Might she have floated down on a section of wing? Each scenario he came up with sounded more absurd than the last. No. Whoever the hell they'd found in the barn, she surely wasn't a passenger on that plane.

Kansas's flatlands spread out on all sides. A landscape devoid of contrast. Every few miles, a copse and a few modest homes marked the next town, with its requisite Casey's General Store or the neon lights from a Kwik Shop gas station. After that, only crossroads interrupted the otherwise vast expanses of empty space. They were lucky. Had this plane exploded over Wichita, the destruction on the ground might well have been worse. Instead, the debris rained down over crops, not daycares; metal shards sliced into dark loam instead of shopping malls. A few cars had been damaged on the highway, but with little more impact than a spring hailstorm might've caused. If someone had been hit with debris in the barn, she'd become the first casualty from the fallout.

"Why am I here?" Ellsworth said. "I have real work to do."

"I'm just following orders," Radford said.

"I need a shower," Ellsworth said. "I need a hot meal, a god-damn drink." He leaned forward and spoke to the cop driving. "Hey, take me to the Holiday Inn by the airport. If my friend wants to waste his time, that's his prerogative. I'm punching out for the day."

Radford felt foolish. He wanted to call Wendy. Hell, he wanted to be with her. He'd barely said goodbye to her. They were supposed to meet with a real estate agent this week. She was filling out forms and preference checklists. She'd have to postpone that now or, worse, go it alone and saddle him with more guilt. The cruiser sped east toward the city. He closed his eyes and tried to picture his future with Wendy, but that once-solid idea had become wobbly of late. How had they lost that certainty?

He thought again of his father, and wondered what Martin would say about a woman falling from the sky.

"I'm done too," Radford said to the cop. He wasn't about to become the laughingstock of the investigation on the second day. The Falling Woman had to be a hoax. "Take us both back to the hotel."

15

THE FIRST THING Monday morning, Radford drove to the old Cheney High School gymnasium, where the makeshift morgue was filled with the remains of the dead. A steady stream of ambulances, vans, and buses delivered black body bags from the scattered debris fields into a highly orchestrated maze. The state medical examiner from Topeka slept in the basketball coach's office and showered in the boys' locker room.

Arriving victims were tagged as soon as they were rolled in. On a whiteboard, propped up beneath the CHS Cardinals scoreboard, written in huge block numbers, was 123—the number of passengers and crew on Pointer 795's manifest. Below that number, written in red, was the tally of positive IDs. For Radford, 123 was the only number that mattered. There were 123 sets of husbands and wives, relatives and friends, sons and daughters, all of whom needed closure. Radford saw the number 123 in his sleep.

For everything else, for the growing chorus and clamor of news stories about a possible survivor, Radford simply blocked it out. Only the number mattered, not what had happened at the barn. As far as he was concerned, the woman in the barn was not his problem.

As the head of the survival factors working group, Radford would lead the disaster management team, comprising pathologists, dentists, X-ray technicians, criminal investigators. Several times a day, a body was transported from one of six large white refrigerator trucks parked outside the gym. A tech logged the bodies into the database by numbers: Passenger 1. Passenger 37. Crew member 3. Then lab techs pushed the rollaway gurneys and ushered the bodies through the long, deliberate process of identification. Red Cross volunteers accompanied each body, from the moment it left the refrigerated truck until it returned hours later. The volunteers smiled and wore blue ribbons on their lapels. Except for the grim black bags, the scene might've resembled a blood drive.

Depending on the condition of a body—sometimes only a leg, a section of torso—they moved from dental exams to X-rays to fingerprinting to autopsy, a journey that might take up to three days to complete. Some IDs were easy. Some bodies were in good shape, and photos could be shown to next of kin. Sometimes a body had a distinct tattoo; sometimes a man's wallet was still in his pocket; sometimes an engagement ring was engraved. But if a positive identification couldn't be made within three days, the process became more complicated. At that point, outside labs became involved, and the identification could take months.

By Monday, less than half of the bodies were positively identified, and many more were still coming in from the field. The current red number, 57, on the whiteboard was like a mark of shame.

"The pathologists need to start sending tissue samples out," the state coroner told Radford. "So many of the bodies are burned or crushed beyond recognition. It's going to be a slow process."

"Keep at it," Radford said. "I need that number to move."

Across the street, where the high school's new buildings stood, they'd set up risers and dark blue plastic tarps to block access to the old gym. They also roped off the field house parking lot, and armed sheriffs roamed the old campus to keep the public far away. But to hear laughter at lunch from high school students across the street, to hear the bells clanging on the hour, or coach's whistles during afternoon practices—these things only added to the dreary nature of the work. Radford promised the coroner they would have a better facility soon. Then he thanked the techs, the assistant coroners, and volunteers before he copied the red number on the board into his notepad. That number had to climb, and climb quickly.

He spent the rest of the day in the field, wandering among wreckage and assisting in the gathering of body parts. The day was long, the work grueling and relentless, and the rewards only grim.

As the sun dipped toward the horizon, he climbed into a rental car and headed back to the Holiday Inn, the de facto headquarters for a growing army of investigators, FBI agents, and engineers. For the foreseeable future, this would be the routine. He would awake before dawn, grab a coffee and head out to the morgue, and then to the field. He'd work all day tagging debris, marking locations on maps, collecting the dead. Then each night, he would gather with the others in the hotel's second-floor conference room for the daily progress meeting, or DPM. It allowed the investigators and police to compare notes. There were arguments, questions, frustrations, and complaints, but there was also laughter, stories of home, hints of progress.

"Why are we so far behind with the IDs?" Ulrich asked. He and Radford stood in the hall outside the conference room, called the Birch Room, an incongruous name since there was not a birch tree in sight.

"Most of the remains are grossly deformed," Radford told Ulrich before the DPM began. "Heads and limbs severed, clothes ripped off, serious burns, traumatic crushing."

"That's not useful," Ulrich said. "I can't tell the press that. I need to reassure the public that we are doing everything we can."

"This doesn't happen overnight," Radford said. "There's a process at work here. I need time."

"And I need answers," Ulrich said. "Why was the captain not in his seat? Who was flying the plane? Jesus, Charlie, I don't want excuses."

That morning, they'd found the body of Bill Oakley, Pointer 795's captain, a good two miles away from where the cockpit section had come down. Radford had no idea why the captain had fallen there, nor what the location might mean to the investigation.

"Why was there no Mayday?" Ulrich asked. "Help me out here. I need to tell the press something."

"Tell them the lawyers arrived," Lucy Masterson said, walking toward the conference room with Shep Ellsworth. Their pants and shoes were covered in mud.

"Blood in the water," Shep Ellsworth said, retying his ponytail.

They all entered the conference room, which consisted of three tables in a horseshoe shape. Near the back of the room, a fourth table held plastic cups and a pitcher of water. By now, the investigative team had grown. More than a dozen investigators found seats around the table. Scattered among them were cops, engineers from Boeing, FBI agents, and firemen. They were all exhausted, filthy, and hungry after another fifteen-hour day in the debris fields. Ellsworth stood near the window, his tattooed arms folded across his chest. Ulrich was now on his cell phone at the head of the table. The air smelled like a football locker room after a long and grueling game. Radford was already down to his last clean underwear and socks. He needed to find a laundromat or go buy new clothes. There was just no time.

"Ulrich can't find a few dollars in his budget for a carafe of coffee?" Lucy Masterson whispered to him.

Shep Ellsworth turned on the projector and waited for it to warm up. Ellsworth had discovered several sections of the ruined fuel tank on the sixth fairway of the Cherry Oaks Golf Course.

"Witness marks in the spar line up with similar marks in the fuel tank baffle," he said, a picture of the mangled wing spar now coming into focus on the screen. As much as Radford disliked him, Shep Ellsworth knew his work. "The explosion on Pointer

795 sent this metal beam," he said, pointing a laser, "through the center of the cabin like a supersonic harpoon shot through the belly of a whale. This created an explosive decompression in the cabin, and along with the ignited fuel . . . Boom!"

Ellsworth made an explosion gesture with his hands.

"Data from Kansas City air traffic control radar clearly shows the moment the flight began to come apart," Lucy Masterson said.

She clicked a button and a digital map appeared. A moment later, a blue line tracked Pointer 795 in accelerated time—thirty seconds to the hour. From takeoff in Dulles, across the Appalachians, a slight jog north over the Ohio River, then arcing south again, over Indiana, Illinois, across the Mississippi, Saint Louis, until the blue line disappeared southwest of Wichita. Silence filled the room as the trace slowed and Lucy zoomed in on the avatar of the plane.

Radford loved the way that order slowly reasserted itself after so much chaos. He loved watching an investigation come together because even the worst disaster began to make sense. The process, the way the theories emerged, felt like an orchestra warming up. This was progress, how civilization itself had been constructed. This was the reason he loved this work. It demanded careful attention, energy stretched across months and years, commitment, care, and endurance. One piece at a time. One small step in front of the next. This was the only way to keep chaos at bay, the only way to create a story that would accurately explain what had happened. And Radford now had his part to play. Sitting in this room, with these men and women, he told himself he'd arrived, that he was, at last, doing the work he was meant to do.

"Nothing we will do in this room will bring back the dead," Ulrich said. For someone so obsessed with statistics and data, he sounded more like a politician running for office. "Nothing can do that. But we'll restore balance. We'll make sense of tragedy."

Ulrich looked around, almost like he was waiting for applause. None came.

"In the belly of the plane," Lucy said, "jet fuel combusted, setting off a chain reaction beneath the plane that then spread rapidly toward the cabin, blowing open a gash in the pressurized hull, mixing fuel, spark, and air so that a massive fireball incinerated anyone sitting near the middle of the craft."

Ulrich furiously scribbled notes, even though he should already have known the basic facts.

"You aren't telling me the thing I need," he said. "What caused the boom? Why wasn't the captain flying? The press corps is eating me alive."

"It takes time," Lucy said. "Lightning, a wire arcing in the fuel cell, a fire burn-through."

"A bomb?" an FBI agent asked.

"There's no way to get a bomb into the fuel tank itself," Lucy said.

"Within a few seconds of the ignition, the plane snapped into three large pieces," she said. "The nose and forward third of the plane kept flying for twelve seconds, which explains the relatively condensed debris field near Belmont."

It was staggering to imagine those twelve seconds, most of the passengers in the front of the plane still alive. The noise, the cold, the terror would have been overwhelming. His training had taught

Radford to block out those thoughts, but with each passing hour, he seemed to be bothered by them more and more.

"The bodies from this section of the plane have been almost impossible to identify," he said, trying to insert himself into the conversation.

"What you don't have is a source of combustion," an FBI agent said. "Like a bomb."

"It's still a possibility," Ulrich said, glancing up from his notes.

The FBI agent pointed to a radiograph of a section of left wing.

"That looks like a pretty large fucking hole to me," he said.

Radford still believed that the answer would be subtler than a bomb.

"Anything else?" Ulrich asked.

"Yeah," Shep Ellsworth said. He glanced at Radford and smiled. "Where we at on Sasquatch?"

The room erupted in laughter, and Radford's stomach dropped. He had summarily ignored the story since leaving the barn. He avoided watching or reading the news, distanced himself from the reports. Was he hoping it would just go away?

"Charlie, I need this off my plate," Ulrich said. "Do we have a name at least? A theory as to who she is?"

Radford glanced at his notes and shook his head.

"Jesus, Charlie, help me out on this. I told you, I need to know who she is and why she's telling this story. I'm tired of standing in front of the press with my dick in my hands."

"It's possible, you know," Lucy Masterson said, first glancing at Ulrich, then back to Radford. He was sure he heard her wrong. "The story could be true."

"You're kidding me," Ellsworth said. "We're entertaining this foolishness?"

"I did my grad school thesis on survivability factors," she said. "I stumbled on some strange shit."

Beneath the table, Radford's fists clenched. Why was she talking about this? He didn't want to talk about the woman. He wanted to talk about his work with the bodies. What mattered was the number, 123. What mattered was identifying the dead, getting the relatives the answers they deserved, and then moving on with the more difficult work of reconstruction. Exhausted, hungry, down to his last pair of clean socks, the work ahead relentless. He wanted a drink, time to call Wendy. They were only days into investigating one of the worst aviation accidents imaginable, a million questions he hadn't begun to even ask. The last thing he needed was this distraction. The Falling Woman. *Sasquatch*. Who was she? How was it possible? Was she faking it? Everyone was asking the wrong questions, but Radford didn't know what the right questions even were. He was eager for this complication to go away. He didn't want the nonsense to continue. You take it, then, Lucy, he thought but didn't say.

Ulrich frowned and pointed at Radford. "The story should not be about this woman," he said. "Make it go away."

"I'm just saying," Lucy said, "that it's happened before."

"I'm out of here," Ellsworth said. "Some of us have an actual investigation to conduct."

Ellsworth stood, pushed back his chair noisily, but paused at the door. He glared back at Radford with an almost open hostility. The others in the room glanced from Radford to Lucy and back to Ellsworth.

"From what I can tell," Lucy said, "there have been a handful of reported cases of sustained free-fall survival."

"What are you saying?" Ulrich said.

"The data is murky at best," Lucy said. "But it might have been possible for someone to survive the fall."

Ellsworth groaned and shook his head. Radford wanted to leave too. He didn't want to hear any more. But Lucy continued, talking about at least five other people who had fallen from airplanes without parachutes or wings or ropes, all of them surviving falls that were seemingly impossible to survive. How could this be understood?

"Lucy, you're saying this is possible?" Ulrich said.

"I only know what I've read," she said.

"I've heard it all now," Ellsworth said.

"Enough," Ulrich said. He turned to Radford. "Top priority. I need something definitive on this woman. No more rumors and myths. This isn't difficult. Find out who she is. Find out why she was in that barn. Expose her, arrest her—hell I don't care what you do to her. But get her off my plate."

Outside the conference room, Radford spotted Lucy in the hall. He wanted to scream at her, to remind her that the next time she wanted to throw him under a bus, the least she could do was warn him. But he liked Lucy more than anyone else on the team, and he still needed her help.

"I'm sorry, Charlie," she said. "Probably not what you wanted to hear."

"You could've warned me," he said.

"I didn't plan on saying anything," she said. "I just think we need to keep an open mind."

"That's easy to do when it's not your head on the block," he said.

"Why didn't you go to the hospital Sunday night?" she asked.

"Ellsworth," he said. "Hell, I don't know. Maybe I didn't want to be a part of this nonsense."

"You're a part of it now," she said.

Lucy promised to send him what research she had. "What the hell difference does it make?" he said. "The idea of it is preposterous. A woman falling out of an exploding plane? Shep is right. I am searching for Sasquatch, with a pencil and a flashlight."

Lucy patted him on the shoulder and walked away. Radford was left thinking that he needed a drink and a good night's sleep, but knowing that neither was in his future.

16

Rolling hills and rain east of Columbus. Adam was talking about Ho Chi Minh when they stopped for lunch. He'd been reading a book about the Vietnamese ruler. Adam ordered coffee, a chicken sandwich, french fries. Erin ordered tea, nibbled at a Caesar salad, and pushed the lettuce around the plate with her fork. The food was bland and she had no appetite.

He paid for lunch, helped her back into the car. Walking hurt, and every step sent hellish spasms through her back. He insisted that they stop every few hours, insisted that she get out and move around. It was all so surreal, like a dream. The rain fell more steadily as they moved ahead, the wiper blades beating out a rhythm. They ascended into mountains, and the rain turned colder, and the clouds sank closer to the ground. At a rest stop, he bought her a soda, asked her to take another pill.

"We're about four hours away from D.C.," he said. "We can stop here and finish in the morning. Or we can keep going. It's up to you."

Darkness enveloped them. She had lost track of the days. Was it still Tuesday? She had a vague memory of spending the previous night in a motel; Adam sleeping on the floor, blue walls, an old rotary phone. The ringing in her ears had returned, less piercing than before, less sharp, intermittent, like church bells calling the hours. "My ears," she said.

"They're probably reacting to the altitude," he said.

He took a wrong turn, spent half an hour trying to get back on the highway. She had no memory of the past few days or even getting in the car, no memory of walking or waking or even of being alive, as if a great eraser had scrubbed her thoughts clear, so that only the afterimages remained. Blue walls, straw falling from the sky, and a great fire.

"All those underground tunnels and caverns in Vietnam," he said. "They weren't allowed to make maps. They trained at night, memorizing the intricate turns and twists. The tunnels ran all over the country."

She wanted to ask questions. Who are you? What are you talking about? Why have you erased my brain? But then, a moment later, she recognized him, recognized the car, the song on the radio.

"Ho studied cooking in Europe," Adam said. "But then I guess his life took a dramatic turn. There's no way to predict a person's path. We all wander around like ghosts, waiting for our futures to unfold."

She laid her head back, trying to remember. Some of her memories were scrambled, but others were clear.

She thought back to a year earlier. They had driven out to his hunting cabin in the Blue Ridge Mountains after work. She lied to Doug that day, told him she was going to stay in the city to finish up a series of contract reviews for the Defense Department, a not infrequent occurrence when the work piled up.

"He'll expect you to call," Adam said a year ago.

"I told him I was working. My phone is off. I'm with you. I'm yours. Nothing else in the world matters."

They'd waited more than a month, since the night in Atlanta, where their passion could've been chalked up to the wine, or to being on the road, or to the escape from long hours at the office. But to disappear this way, to run off together, meant they were walking into something much bigger. A full moon had risen. She worried about how she smelled after sitting in the office all day. She worried about her dry skin, but Adam wouldn't let go of her hand.

"I'm not sure about sex," she said. It was a silly thing to say, awful considering how much she wanted him.

Adam smiled and squeezed her hand tighter. They approached the Blue Ridge Parkway. Shadows of mountains loomed. The sky above the car darkened and filled with stars.

"Do you need me to stop anywhere?" he asked. "Can I get you anything?"

She moved in, grabbed his leg, kissed his neck while he drove. At its best, she and Doug and shared a tepid sex life. Her husband's indifference often confused her, seldom aroused her, and never satisfied. She'd been with only two other men before Doug. With Adam, the sex became exalted. He treated her body the way a dervish treats the dance, spinning her into higher and higher planes of joy and ecstasy.

"I would dream about you," Adam said. "I've been half wild thinking about you."

He turned off the highway and curlicued up a switchback road.

"Let's not talk about the past," she said. "Can we concentrate on now?"

What an asinine thing to have said. She was so full of herself, so preprogrammed to respond. Ahead, the cabin was dark, almost spooky. Adam told her that the nearest neighbors were a mile away. Wind whistled through tall pines, which cast moon shadows on the ground. Fishing poles leaned against the porch. An old canoe. Adam lifted a stone that hid the key, opened the front door, and turned on the porch light, revealing the cabin's rustic charm. The air smelled of fireplaces and wet leaves. She held his hand. It felt holy, almost blessed, despite what they were doing, or maybe because of it, like they had stepped into a realm in which the rules no longer applied.

Inside, the cabin was spare, musty, and perfect. She wondered if he'd brought other women here. The thought disturbed her, chilled the radiating warmth inside. Was she just one of many? She wanted to be the exception, wanted his passion for her to be as singular as hers was for him. He opened the blinds, turned on lights. A creek burbled nearby. Forest smells—juniper, last fall's leaf litter, sharp mud, distant smoke from a fire. She opened a window, then another. Inside the small kitchen, with its tiny stove, a cupboard full of pots, pans, and utensils, she discovered a world so different from her own.

"What do you think?" he said.

"Perfect."

"I'll go into town and pick up some supplies," he said.

"It's late," she said. "Just stay."

But he insisted, so she gave him a small list. Was he having second thoughts? Was she? After he left, she showered, changed into clean clothes, and began to tidy up the cabin. With scissors, she went outside in the moonlight and cut flowers, gathered wild grass and autumn's first leaves. The mountain air chilled her skin. By the time he returned, she'd transformed the small cabin. Candles flickered in the windows.

"It looks great," he said.

He carried the groceries into the kitchen and she followed. She stood behind him, wanting to touch him yet resisting.

"Look," she said. "This is awkward enough. We don't have to stay."

Adam turned, reached for her, pulled her close. He took her, right there in the kitchen, shimmying her body up onto the counter. It was over quickly. They were both out of breath, sweating. She wrapped her arms around his waist and turned.

"Jesus," she said, laughing. "The door was wide open."

SHE REMEMBERED THAT as though it had been yesterday, but of course, it was from a different life. Now they were in West Virginia. Rolling hills. Coal country.

Nothing made sense.

What parts of the past few days had she dreamed? What parts were imagined? Was she still dreaming? She didn't know how to locate the line anymore, the line between reality and her imagination. Her memory was fuzzy, a distant static that refused to ease.

"I can't go back," she said. It was not something she knew for certain. But it was more than a hunch. A feeling seemed to take possession of her. No more hospitals. No more doctors. No more overbearing husbands. She had no idea what the feeling meant or what came next. She didn't know where they were going; she only knew she couldn't go back. Not yet. "I can't go home."

"Of course you can," he said. "Your daughters. Your family. You have to go back."

She had no certain memory of children, no sense of home or family. She fell silent. Her thoughts slipped again, moving back and forth like the tide sliding in and out.

Adam changed the subject, kept talking, now about his father, a navy SEAL in Vietnam. "He jumped from airplanes," he said. "He wore a parachute." Was he trying to be funny? she wondered. She didn't laugh.

"What did you do before you became a lawyer?" she asked, attempting to stay focused on their conversation rather than her own drifting thoughts.

"I was a submarine officer in the navy," he said. "Twice we sailed under the North Pole."

"What was that like?" she asked.

"It was dark and quiet," he said. "I felt like we didn't belong there. I wanted to leave."

"It sounds perfect," she said.

Adam kept telling stories, stories he'd never shared with her before. He seemed nervous, maybe even afraid of her. As the miles passed, he slowly became familiar to her again, not as a lover but as someone she could still trust. She reached out and touched the back of his head while he drove. She didn't talk about what would come next because, in part, she didn't know. Everything felt shrouded, confusing, detached. Some memories seeped back into her consciousness as they drove, vivid and lustrous, only to recede a few miles down the road.

"My father," she said, "kept this little plastic statuette of a naked couple in his top drawer. No bigger than a matchbook. I found it when I was a little girl. I couldn't have been more than six or seven. There was a tab on the man's leg. When you pulled down on the tab, the man's oversized penis jabbed inside the woman."

Adam laughed. "What an odd memory. But that's good. You see, things are beginning to come back to you."

"My father died the summer before I started seventh grade," she said.

She didn't know where this memory was coming from, but she told him anyway, how an ordinary August morning broke when she was a child, a morning full of chores, reading, cartoons, and lunch. "My father was a doctor. Each summer, he'd take a week off and spend long lazy days with us. There was no indication that anything was wrong, that he was ill. That morning, he played nine holes of golf with friends and came home and made us lunch. My father asked me if I'd walk to the store and buy a gallon of milk. Those were the last words he ever said to me. While I was gone, he had a massive heart attack and died in our living room."

Adam reached out and touched her hand.

"It all felt so normal," she said.

He flicked the headlights on high beam. Fog shrouded the road ahead and scattered the light.

"The world seems stable," she said. "But it's not. Nothing would feel stable again after that day." Adam craned his neck and looked out the window. Was he listening? she wondered. Had his thoughts drifted elsewhere? Back to Ho Chi Minh?

She wasn't sad telling the story about her father. Darkness replaced light but then light shone again. Life didn't have to make sense; it just had to be lived.

Outside, fog dimmed what little sky remained visible. The irregular cadence of the wheels on the road lulled her toward sleep. The car's engine droned. Adam's slight breaths were barely audible. They crossed over into Virginia. They were close now.

"Take me to the cabin," she said.

He turned, his face showing concern and confusion. "Absolutely not," he said. "Your family needs to know you're okay."

"I can't go home," she said. "I want to go to the cabin."

"You aren't making sense. You need to be seen at a hospital."

"I'm making perfect sense," she said. "Take me to the cabin. I'll stay there. Please."

She knew he would do as she asked. It may have been the only thing she knew for certain at that moment. That was why she had called him. He always listened to her. And so, when they reached the Blue Ridge Parkway, Adam turned north without another word. North toward the cabin. On some level, she knew he would never understand her decision. But she no longer cared. She felt so small, like a piece of dust landing on the surface of a table. If she were any smaller, she could disappear. She wanted to be that small.

17

Tuesday morning, the road adjacent to Wichita's Via Christi Hospital was jammed with news vans, satellite poles, and vendors hawking T-shirts. On opposite sidewalks, zealots and skeptics shouted insults, many with cartoon images of the Falling Woman on posters and signboards. One side celebrated the miracle; the other decried the heresy. The whole scene resembled a sideshow. Behind blue sawhorse barricades, Wichita police stood watch.

As Radford drove past the ambulance bay, he shook his head in wonderment at how the story had turned so quickly into a spectacle. He didn't want to be there. He had 123 bodies that needed his attention, and this unnecessary diversion was just going to make things take longer.

At the barriers in front of the hospital parking garage, he

stopped and rolled down his window. The long hours and the relentless pressures of the investigation had eroded his enthusiasm for distractions, and a deep weariness had replaced the initial thrill of working his first major investigation. A city cop approached his car.

"I need to park," Radford said.

"Sorry, sir," the cop said. "Not without a permit."

"I'm visiting a patient," he said.

"Permits office is back on Topeka Street. You'll have to go back there before I can let you through."

Radford could've simply pulled out his credentials, but something held him back. The fact was, he didn't want to admit why he was there. The cop signaled him to turn around, so he ended up parking three blocks away. He left his NTSB jacket in the car, tucked his badge into his pocket, and headed back to Via Christi.

He walked toward the hospital under a sunny blue sky. Warm breezes shook the poplars that lined the street. Under different circumstances, he might've found a sidewalk café, ordered a coffee, and read the paper or just watched people strolling by, the charm of being a stranger in an unfamiliar city. As he approached the hospital's entrance, another cop stopped him. Radford was impressed, almost taken aback by the layered security. This time, he flashed his badge, but he still had to endure additional scrutiny of two walkie-talkie calls before they allowed him to enter the hospital lobby.

A woman at the reception desk refused to acknowledge what was so painfully obvious to every reporter, street vendor, and kook on the street outside: clearly the Falling Woman was somewhere inside Via Christi.

"Sir," the receptionist said, "I'll need the patient's name before I can direct you."

"I'm part of the investigative team on the accident. You know who I'm here to see."

"Without a name, sir, there's nothing I can do."

After another long delay, Radford demanded to speak to a supervisor. Despite the gatekeepers' obstructionism, he admired their scrutiny. Ten minutes passed before a Catholic priest arrived. The man was lean and muscular in appearance, more like an Olympic sprinter than a clergyman, except for his black shirt and clerical collar.

"I'm Father George Otten," he said. "I'm Via Christi's chaplain."

Radford explained that he wasn't leaving until he had answers, until he'd talked with the woman. He was uncomfortable being so impudent with a priest.

"You understand our concern," Father George said. "Things have been rather topsy-turvy for a few days."

A moment later, a door opened behind the reception desk and another man emerged, this one dressed in a gray business suit. He appeared to be about thirty years old but carried himself with the serious purpose of a much older man. Dark hair, big smile, broad shoulders.

"I'm Jack Liu, an attorney," the man said. "I represent the Diocese of Wichita."

"Why do I need to talk to a lawyer?" Radford asked.

The priest guided them through the lobby and onto the elevator.

The situation had all the makings of a bad joke: a priest, a lawyer, and an accident investigator step onto an elevator. Radford could only hope that he wasn't about to become the punch line. No one spoke as the elevator climbed to the third floor. They walked past several rooms with closed doors before they arrived at a nurses' station. Two women glanced up but kept working. Liu smiled and pointed Radford toward a small conference room.

"I need to speak to her," Radford said, turning to the priest.

"We paged Dr. Lassanske," Father Otten said. "She'll be here soon."

An awkward silence filled the room. Radford resisted the urge to stand up and leave. He was supposed to interview the flight captain's widow today, but if Ulrich wanted a report on the mythical Falling Woman, then he'd give his boss a damn report. He wanted it to be over and done with. He had no intention of becoming the in-house conspiracy theorist.

A few minutes passed. Jack Liu kept his eyes glued to his phone. Father Otten appeared to be praying, his eyelids half closed. Radford jotted down their names, along with the time and date, in his notepad. Don't be smarter than the evidence, he thought, though nothing he'd seen so far qualified as evidence. When the doctor entered the room, Radford stood up.

She was tall and pretty, with long straight hair but tired eyes. She couldn't have been more than a year or two out of training. Radford wondered if they'd sent her on purpose, to distract him with her beauty. She extended her hand to him and forced a smile.

"Mr. Radford?" she said, "I'm Dr. Lassanske."

She was the first person in Via Christi to shake his hand.

"We'd like to go on the record, right now," Jack Liu said, suddenly participating again, "that Via Christi places the utmost care on patient privacy."

"You've seen what's going on outside?" Radford asked. "It's a circus out there."

"We have done everything we possibly can to ensure hospital security," Jack Liu said. "Not a single reporter has been spoken to. Not one has entered the lobby."

The priest asked if they could say a quick prayer. Radford lowered his head while the chaplain asked for peace, comfort to the grieving, and for a resolution about the accident.

"There are all kinds of stories going around," Radford said as soon at the priest finished. "The woman who was brought here on Sunday. I need to talk to her, to clarify all this confusion. I need to ask her some questions."

Jack Liu paused and then nodded at the doctor.

"You understand there are limits to what I can say," Dr. Lassanske said. "We are required to protect patient privacy."

"She's not in trouble," Radford said. "I'm simply trying to clarify what's happened."

"She came in as a Jane Doe," the doctor said. "Her most significant injury was a large contusion on her sacroiliac region. Her hip. Some degloved skin on her hands. Cuts and scratches here and there."

"What did you think happened?" Radford asked.

"I suspected a motorcycle accident upon exam," the doctor

said. "But then one of the ambulance drivers came in and said she'd fallen from the plane."

Jack Liu looked at his notes and the priest closed his eyes.

"Were her eardrums intact?" Radford asked.

"I'd like you to know," Jack Liu said, "that her presence has significantly disrupted our routine operations. With the intense security, the media coverage, our resources are pretty much at the breaking point."

"I want to resolve this just as fast as you do," Radford said.

Jack Liu again nodded at the doctor.

Dr. Lassanske said, "She had persistent amnesia, and some confusion about where she was."

"She's said nothing about the accident?" Radford asked.

"Well," Dr. Lassanske said, "not exactly."

The priest stood. Jack Liu glanced at the priest and then at the doctor.

"Why all the mystery, folks?" Radford asked.

"Are you a religious man?" the priest said.

"I'm an accident investigator," Radford replied. "I'm just interested in the facts. I have 123 families that deserve answers."

"Her scans were clear," the doctor said. "Her tests were all negative. Except for the cuts and bruises, she was, essentially, healthy."

"I just want to talk to her. That's all. Hear what she has to say. I have families that need to stop holding on to false hope that a loved one may have survived. Right now, every second this goes on, my job gets harder." Radford paused. "Most people at my agency think she's lying, probably looking for attention in a very sick way."

The priest shook his head.

"She's not lying, Mr. Radford," the priest said. There was a gravity to the man's voice, and in his conclusion, a kind of solemn prayer. Radford tried to shake it off.

"Let me talk to her then, so we can move forward," Radford said. "She's not in trouble. I just need to clarify some questions."

Jack Liu smiled. The priest folded his hands. Both men turned toward Dr. Lassanske.

"She's not here," the doctor said.

"What?" Radford said.

"The woman who came in Sunday night, presumably the woman you are here to see, walked out the hospital yesterday morning. We don't know where she is."

18

Almost a year before, the last time they came to the cabin, Adam read to Erin from Kawabata's novel *Thousand Cranes*. She was seeing the specialist for the first time later that week, but she had told Adam nothing, only that she was fighting a cold. She curled up in his arms while he read from the book.

The novel, set in postwar Japan, portrayed an ancient culture crumbling in the aftermath of bombing and death. She drifted in and out of sleep while he read. The pain in her abdomen hadn't yet become so acute she couldn't sleep. The passionate story, sad and haunting, reminded her of her passion for Adam. She knew something was wrong with her body, maybe even something grave and life altering, but that weekend she still clung to hope. It couldn't be cancer, at least that's what she tried to convince herself. She had so much life left, so much yet to do. But as hard as she tried to pretend, some part of her knew.

At night, he kissed her forehead tenderly, the way a father might. He placed water by her side, draped an extra blanket over her, and turned off the light. They spent three days that way at the cabin. She loved hearing the wind, the water from the creek. She loved waking up in the morning to birdsong. Three perfect days. Reading. Making love. Laughing. She didn't want to leave, didn't want to face what lay ahead.

And now what lay ahead was here. So much had changed in a year.

At the once-familiar cabin, parts of her past came rushing back, not as memories but as something else, as raw emotion cut off from thought, like a river of smells, sights, and sounds. The wooden front porch. The chirp of tree frogs. Pine resin and leaf litter and the crunch of gravel beneath the tires. The world felt suddenly familiar. After being gone for a very long time, she'd come back.

Outside, wind rushed through white pines and oaks. This time, she told herself, she would never leave.

She slept soundly but alone that first night. The next morning passed quietly. She had trouble placing what day it was, but knew that time had passed. In place of passion, an awkward silence filled their hours together. He did not touch her, did not offer to rub her back, did not read her books. He swore he wasn't angry, only stunned, *flabbergasted* was the word he used. She didn't know if he meant by her or by her decision, or some combination of the two.

"How did this happen?" he asked, over and over.

During the afternoon, he cleared brush from outside, bought groceries, cleaned the grill on the porch, chopped firewood, cut back the weeds growing around the house. She suspected he snuck away to call his wife, because he returned with a guilty look on his face. He was avoiding her, perhaps hoping she'd come to her senses. She knew that he no longer saw the woman he once loved. He saw a freak, a sideshow performer who wanted to abandon her family. She could hardly blame him.

"You have to call home," he kept saying.

She didn't respond. Not with anger, not even with an explanation. Her memory was hazy, detached, as though unmoored from her brain, but she did know that something had happened. She knew that there'd been an accident of some sort, but she couldn't remember the full event. Just flashes of it. The cold. The fire. Debris in the air. Gasping for breath. The smell of rain. Otherwise, there was a gap, a blank space, a portion of her memory scrubbed clean. Was it caused by trauma and shock? Was it self-induced? In the end, it didn't matter.

Adam remained cautious around her. He didn't press but worked slowly on her defenses, trying to guide her back toward a rational path. But it was becoming apparent that rational and reasonable rules no longer applied.

When he came in from outside, he found her sitting at the small table. He stood by the stove, staring down at her with a serious expression.

"What do you remember?" he asked.

She didn't want to answer but knew he would give her little choice.

"I have these flashes," she said, "wind and fire, cold air. I have strange, almost hallucinatory dreams, but I don't know what is real and what isn't."

THE FIRST FULL day passed, and another night, and then the second morning came. He told her he had to leave for home. He was expecting her to leave with him. Late Thursday afternoon, Adam began to pack. They'd been at the cabin since Tuesday night, all but cut off from the outside world.

"We'll leave in an hour," he said. Suddenly, he was back in a courtroom, controlling the argument. Had he forgotten, though, that she too knew her way around an argument?

"I'm not sure I can go," she said.

"That makes no sense. Of course you're going home."

"I think I am home," she said. But Adam had turned away from her and didn't seem to hear.

She loved him so much before she got sick. He had stormed into her life like a tornado, and the wreckage had been exquisite. He challenged her assumptions about what was possible. But then came the questions and the doubts: Was she the kind of woman who cheated on her husband? Could she leave her family? Would she get divorced? The questions were entirely new. Growing up, she was so awkward around boys. She never had a boyfriend, rarely even received a hint of interest. Boys looked past her, at the prettier girls, at the wilder girls who would kiss and, later, do much more. After her father died, she stopped believing in love. It could disappear so fast. What claims she made toward passion arrived later in life, maybe too late since Doug never seemed to notice.

She had been a gangly and awkward teenager who wore braces until graduation, and it was only later that she fit into her body. The body that Adam would worship. The body that cancer would ravage.

She'd met Doug after a nasty breakup with the man she'd been dating her junior year of college. Her ex turned out to be leading a secret life—sex with men in bathroom stalls, and drugs she'd never even heard of. She didn't just feel betrayed; she felt fooled. Foolish. She'd crept out from behind a wall of fear only to be tricked. She took every test available, and somehow, they all came back clean. After that, all that mattered was security, stability, sanity. Doug came along prepackaged, a man so safe and stable he quickly became inert. At twenty-two, she couldn't see into the future, couldn't imagine that someday she'd be the one running off for sex with someone who wasn't her husband. She must have asked herself a thousand times, What am I doing? Sneaking away to a cabin with a man she barely knew. Risking both their marriages, their families. Abandoning the life she'd worked so hard to build. In the end, it didn't matter. Her body decided for her.

Now, rather than staying inside the cabin with Adam while he packed, she walked toward the small creek that crossed the property. A thin bridge, slick with moss, connected to a trail on the other side of the water. She hesitated on unsteady legs. Between the two cycles of chemo, and who knows what other toxic chemicals she'd ingested over the past six months, not to mention the bruises and cuts from her long, long fall, she no longer trusted her body. But she took a first step, and another, and soon walked across the slippery bridge and onto the trailhead.

The trail wound through mountain laurel and milkweed, which gave way to ash, fir, and spruce farther up the hill. She loved the woods. Before the illness, when she still believed in the future, she swore that one day she'd quit the firm and go work for the National Park Service as a naturalist. She dreamed about going back to school, pursuing a degree in ecology or land management. What the hell had she waited for? She knelt and touched a fiddlehead fern before heading up the trail.

Walking loosened her bruised hip. The stiffness in her lower back eased. A morning rain shower had released earthy resins from the forest, the petrichor of musty earth mixing with last fall's decomposing blanket of leaves, spicing the air, now suddenly aromatic. Midges danced in light shafts. Clouds moved above the treetops.

After a few minutes, footfalls crunched leaves behind her, growing closer. She didn't slow, but she didn't speed up either.

"You need to go home," Adam said, catching up to her. "You need to let your family know you are alive. You can't hide out here and think that's okay."

She ignored him, barely hearing his words. He stopped and grabbed her wrist.

"You need to stop this and go home," he said. "Your husband thinks you're dead."

"I am dead," she said. "I've been dead for almost a year. Not that you noticed."

Adam released her wrist. "That's not fair. You didn't even tell me you were sick."

She wanted to scare him, wanted to do something wild to make him run away. And at the same time, she wanted him to promise to stay.

"I can't go back to the world," she said. "I won't."

"I don't understand," he said.

She didn't respond. She was tired of talking.

Back at the cabin, he helped her into the shower. He touched her skin tenderly but without passion. He changed the bandages on her hands, where the fingers remained raw and sore. A persistent bell still rang in her ears, day and night, with little relief.

"You have to come with me," he said, but he was pleading now. And she was aware of a new certainty, aware the argument was settled.

19

For DAYS AFTER Radford visited the hospital, he was more confused than ever. Who was this woman? Why would she have disappeared? He had no answers, and realized now he'd asked the wrong questions. All that week, he dodged the other investigators. He avoided Ulrich and Ellsworth in particular. Ulrich because every hour he spent on the Falling Woman was an extra hour of work away from the bodies; Ellsworth because talk of the Falling Woman only increased his scorn.

He promised that he was working hard, promised that he'd have answers by the end of the week. And now it was Friday morning, and the daily progress meeting loomed that afternoon.

All week he'd retreated to the sanctuary of his hotel room. From there, he'd conducted phone interviews with the EMTs, the firemen, the police officers who found the woman in the barn. He talked to the orderlies at the hospital, the nurses, techs, and doctors, anyone who had even the briefest contact with the woman. No one could offer much of a description. A white woman, middle-aged, who didn't say much, didn't stand out in any way. Radford began to wonder who the hell had been brought into the hospital. When these interviews offered little, he began to examine the archival material Lucy had sent him.

He'd read Lucy's thesis on survivor stories. Most of the report was standard investigator speak: safety recommendations and systems failures. But then at the end, in an appendix, she covered stories that seemed to defy the logic and science: a 757 that crashed into the mountainside in Colombia, killing everyone aboard except for four passengers. The "miracle" girl who survived a crash in the Indian Ocean by floating on a piece of wreckage. A toddler who alone survived a crash in Detroit, a copilot who was the lone survivor of a crash in Kentucky. As staggering as these tales were, Lucy's thesis didn't mention, nor could it explain, a woman falling out of an exploding plane and surviving.

"They were just too extreme," she told him when he asked why she didn't mention the other cases. "They were too far outside the scope of what I was studying."

Ulrich wanted a formal report by the end of the week, and now the end of the week was here—and Radford had almost nothing new. What's more, he hadn't even typed up his notes yet. He hoped his boss would choke on the damn report. The way he figured it, the final judgment on this woman's story would soon be clear. Once they identified all the bodies, the truth would emerge. But as the story of the Falling Woman spread, the media coverage exploded. People stopped talking about the accident, and only wanted to know about the rumor that someone had survived.

As far as Radford was concerned, once this afternoon's DPM was over, and he dealt with whatever shit Ellsworth and Ulrich threw his way, then he'd be done. He had real work to do, and he intended to get back to it.

The number of positive IDs from the morgue had barely moved. On top of the press and the families, insurance agents began leaving him voice mails. Everyone wanted answers.

His report would be little more than a short summary of his frustration and confusion. He had no name, no information. He could reference some of Lucy's research, reference a few other sources he'd found on his own. But he knew he had nothing. It was almost time for the meeting. He couldn't put off finishing his report any longer. But he had to do one thing first: from his room at the Holiday Inn, he called home.

"Charlie, what the hell is going on out there?" Wendy said.

"It's a circus," he said. "I'm heading in now for a meeting, and they're going to tear me apart."

"Is it true?" Wendy said. "Did someone really survive?"

Wendy never talked about his work. She never asked questions, never cared about the details. He wished for her apathy now.

"I don't know," he said. "I don't think so. But whatever, I've done my part. It will be someone else's problem soon."

"What do you mean you 'don't know'?"

"She's gone," he said. "Whoever this woman is, whatever happened to her, she's not at the hospital. She's nowhere."

"So now what?" Wendy asked.

"I don't care," he said. "I'm done. I'll stand there tonight and take the criticism. And then I get back to work."

He thought of Wendy's freckled skin. How wonderful to be home, to watch a movie with her, to take her out to dinner.

"Charlie, can we please talk about the other thing?"

He knew what she meant, knew that she still wanted to discuss their future family.

"I can't now," he said. "Wendy, I'm getting killed here."

The line went silent.

"I miss you," he said.

"I just want you here," she said. "I know the work matters, Charlie. I know you are dealing with all that misery and death. But I'm all alone here. I can't depend on you, can I?"

He wanted to say more, but he wasn't sure how. She hung up without saying goodbye.

AFTER PUTTING IT off all week, he tackled the report in his hotel room an hour before the DPM. He'd mentioned the security, the crowds across the street, the wait for information, the lawyer, Dr. Lassanske. He'd written up the entire conversation. Jane Doe. Injuries to the woman's hip and hands. Persistent amnesia. Injuries consistent with a motorcycle accident. There was no medical reason to keep her. He typed up the last paragraph.

The attending physician made no determination about the source of her injuries. Nor the extenuating circumstance of her arrival. The woman managed to leave the hospital on Monday morning, undetected. She had carried no identification, and gave no name. No

further evidence exists at this time to support the claim that this
woman was involved, directly or indirectly, with the ongoing inves-
tigation. Recommendation: closure of inquiry until further evidence
presents itself.

The report was cold, rational, devoid of context or speculation.
He omitted any mention of the priest's ominous statement, *She's*
not lying, preferring to stick with the facts and the science. The
story already had too many sharp edges; the last thing Radford
intended to do was add another by talking about priests. After
printing out the report, he spotted Lucy Masterson in the lobby.

"So, what now?" Lucy asked. The DPM was less than thirty
minutes away.

"Let me buy you a drink?"

"Charlie, you know I don't drink," she said.

"Then come watch me drink."

In the bar, Lucy read his report. The investigators began arriving from the field. A week had passed since Pointer 795 exploded,
and the small lounge had become an oasis, a protected space
where normal life could go on for at least a few minutes. The brutal
fieldwork—the relentless gathering of body parts, aluminum, and
despair—exacted a heavy toll.

Lucy finished reading and shook her head. "Charlie, this is
pretty sparse," she said. "I mean, I get that you don't have answers,
but I'm not sure Ulrich is going to take this as a conclusive
summary."

"I don't care," he said. "I did my part. I'm not trained to find a
missing person."

She glanced at the report again and sipped a club soda with

lime. He liked Lucy, trusted her in a way that he didn't trust Ulrich or Ellsworth. He respected her work too, respected her instincts as an investigator. She didn't wear the job on her sleeve like the others did. But once again, the affirmation he needed was not arriving.

"The priest said something," he said. "It was strange. He said she wasn't lying. But it was the way he said it. I just can't get the sound of his voice out of my head."

"Why didn't you put that in the report?" she asked.

"I'm not sinking my career over the hunch of a priest," he said. "Not until I know something concrete."

"But you know it's possible," she said. "You know this woman might really have fallen and survived."

"It's possible," he said. "It's possible the sun won't come up tomorrow. But why would she disappear? Why run away from such a thing?"

"You have no thoughts?" Lucy said.

"I don't care," he said. "I can't spend my time speculating. I have real work to do too."

Shep Ellsworth, his jeans splotchy with mud, entered and went straight to the bar. Radford hoped he wouldn't come over, but Ellsworth had an instinct for fouling another person's good mood. He didn't ask to join them; he just sat at their table and lowered a sweating cocktail. One look at his eyes revealed this was not his first drink of the day. His forehead was sunburned, except for the raccoon coloration from his sunglasses. He squeezed lime into his gin and tonic.

"How's the hunt for Sasquatch?" Ellsworth said.

"Don't start on him," Lucy said. "He drew the short straw."

"I don't get what Ulrich wants from me," Radford said. "This is way out of my zip code."

"Douchebag wants cover," Ellsworth said. "He needs someone to eat this."

"It doesn't matter now," Radford said. "The woman is MIA."

"You only wish it were that easy," Ellsworth said.

What he didn't need were opinions. He'd take small talk about the weather, stories from home, any subject but the Falling Woman. He'd rather lock himself away and drink in his room than listen to more talk of that.

"It's a bad beat," Ellsworth said, almost reading his mind. "I'll give you that. But your partner here screwed you by talking about the other cases. She gave the whole thing plausibility."

Radford nodded. "That did make everything harder."

"What was I supposed to do?" Lucy said. "What does your hero, Dickie Gray, always say? Don't be smarter than the evidence."

"Except there is no evidence," Radford said.

Their camaraderie, however intended, masked relief, a better-you-than-me gratitude. "What's the next step?" Lucy asked.

"Ulrich can do what he wants with it," Radford said. "Tomorrow, I'm back on the bodies."

Ellsworth laughed. "I'll bet you a hundred dollars that you'll be back in D.C. this weekend. This is turning political. Someone has to carry the ball, and they aren't letting you fumble it."

Across the bar, Gordon Ulrich sat alone, scribbling into a notebook without looking up.

"Fuck you, Shep," Lucy said. "You sure know how to kick a guy."

"Next round's on me," Ellsworth said, raising his arm over his head to signal the waitress. "I'll take it out of my future winnings."

Radford finished his drink, but rather than waiting for the next one to arrive, he stood and walked over to Ulrich's table. He pulled out a chair and sat down. Ulrich glanced up over a pair of wire-framed reading glasses, low on the bridge of his nose.

"I'm nowhere," Radford said. "The woman, whoever she is, wherever she came from, is gone. Checked out of the hospital four days ago."

Ulrich continued to scribble notes. Then he clicked the pen and placed it in his shirt pocket. Radford slid his report over the table, and Ulrich skimmed the document. He looked like a college professor, ready to correct grammar and footnotes. Radford glanced back at Lucy Masterson, surrounded now by four other investigators.

"This tells me nothing," Ulrich said.

"It tells you what I know," Radford said. "Read the whole thing, and then let me get back to work. I'm not trained for this."

"I asked you to find her. To give her a name. I need this settled. Jesus, Charlie, I had higher hopes for you."

"I have fieldwork to do," Radford said. "Instead, I've spent four days chasing down rumors."

"There are families out there," Ulrich said. His voice was sincere. For the first time, Radford understood some of what his boss was up against. "Families wondering if this woman is their wife or daughter. Little kids crying on the six o'clock news, saying prayers that she's really their mommy."

"She's gone, Gordo," Radford said. He wanted to offer more

but couldn't. Was it the gin? The sheer exhaustion? He couldn't keep up the act. "I'm not a private detective. I don't know anything about tracking down missing persons."

"You're making excuses," Ulrich said. "Look. Something like this, it could really set you apart. You'd make a name for yourself if you do this right."

"I've done my job," Radford said. "Read my report. Every hour I spend working this story is an hour that's taken away from the real work. Give it to the FBI. They do this shit for a living."

For a moment, Ulrich seemed to ponder the idea. He slipped Radford's report into a pile of others. "I'll read it this weekend," he said.

Above the bar, on the television, reporters were discussing Pointer 795. Serving as a backdrop was a photo of the tail section of the ruined airliner. Radford cursed the muted television. Across the bar, Ellsworth stirred the now-slushy contents of his drink, grinned, and took out his wallet. On Ellsworth's forearm, a tattoo of woman with huge, bulging breasts stared straight at Lucy Masterson.

20

ADAM MADE ONE final plea that Erin let him take her home. Then he left, returned to work, went back to his wife and kids, but on Sunday morning, he drove back to the cabin. She welcomed him with a growing list of demands and favors. She sent him to town for groceries, for new clothes, for DVD rentals, books, bottles of wine. She apologized for nothing and expected everything. And with each request, each demand, she felt more empowered. His will buckled. The day passed this way, until he stood in the cabin's small kitchen on Sunday night and began issuing his own ultimatums.

"It's time to go home," he said, sounding more like a stern teacher than the man who once shared her deepest passions.

"Stop being an ass," she said. "Just let me be."

"You need to be in a hospital," he said. His tone was hurt, angry, confused. "I can't care for you here. I'm worried about you."

"Stop talking," she said. "Go make us dinner."

"This could be an incredible opportunity," he said. "Do you realize what you could do with this? The entire world wants to know what happened."

"I don't care," she said. "Leave me alone. And change that—I don't want dinner. Make me a drink."

Her anger and its tyranny felt strange, new to him, newer still to her. Solitude had changed her, softened her in some ways, hardened her in others. He couldn't seem to understand it, to locate its origins or unpack its implications, but ultimately his submission was complete and absolute. The truth was, she had come to realize this urgency Adam seemed to feel was not about her or her family. She had become a problem, a complication, one that could explode in his life. He wanted to get his life back to normal. Getting Erin to go home would take the pressure off him.

In the small kitchen, he burned the loaf of garlic bread he'd prepared to go with dinner. The cabin filled with the acrid smell of char and burnt garlic. He paced around the cabin, opening windows to release the stench. He fiddled with his phone, rearranged the furniture. For the first time, he reminded her of Doug.

"We need a plan," he said. "We need to discuss what happens now."

"A plan of what?" she asked.

"Your daughters," he said. "God damn it, they need to know you are alive."

All day, she'd resisted his entreaties, his kindness, finally breaking his spirit. She'd done the same thing to Doug when she was sick, making unyielding demands. Her recognition of this pattern came as something of a shock. She was not the giver, not the nurturing mother, not the glue that held the seams together. Adam was right. She should have rushed home, thrown her arms around her girls. Instead, for reasons she didn't fully understand, she was hiding out in this cabin, refusing to do the only rational thing.

"How much do you remember?" he said again, circling back to the original questions.

"I don't want to talk about it," she said. "I can't. Why can't you just leave me alone?"

She wanted to sleep, to remain still. She'd spent most of the previous three days in bed, resting, barely moving. And then she'd awake and go for an afternoon walk in the woods. What the hell am I doing? she'd think, but then she'd come back to the cabin and fall asleep again. She tried to forget about everything that existed outside this small patch of land.

"The accident," he said. "That's how you ended up in Kansas. Jesus, I don't know what you remember. How do I tell you any of this?"

"I don't care," she said.

"Your plane blew up," he said. "Do you remember? You called me. I came and picked you up and brought you here. Do you remember any of that?"

The words he said felt as distant and remote as the Kawabata novel he'd once read to her. The details, the facts, the sheer outlandishness of what happened, about these things she didn't understand, or chose not to believe.

"What do you remember?" he asked.

"Everything is jumbled, hazy," she said. "I don't know who to trust. I don't know what to believe."

"You can trust me," he said. "You need to go home. You need to see a doctor."

"No. No more doctors. No more hospitals."

The only thing she knew, the only steady, consistent thought that kept running through her head was the one that told her she had to stay here until she could figure out what came next, or maybe to accept that nothing came next.

"You called me from a hospital. You asked me to come get you." He explained how he'd flown into Missouri, rented a car, crossed the river, and that they left together. "I must be out of my mind."

She knew what he said was true. She knew none of it made sense. She didn't care. He pulled a sheaf of newspaper articles from his briefcase and threw them on the table.

"You need help," he said, unfolding the papers. "You're not acting rationally."

She read the bold headlines: "Plane Explodes!" "Bodies Falling across Kansas." She read further, about the speculation over bombs and lightning strikes. In the first articles, there was no mention of a survivor.

"So what?" she said.

Adam tapped on his phone and passed it to her.

"SURVIVOR?" the headline screamed. She skimmed the article quickly, her eyes glancing over the account of a woman rushed to a Wichita hospital. She knew it was the truth, the facts of what had happened, but still she didn't believe it. She did not feel a part of it, as though it had happened to someone else.

"None of it matters," she said.

"You need to call home," he said. "Tell your daughters you're safe. That's the first thing. We can work out the details as we go." He started pacing again. "You can tell Doug you called the firm. There are enough legal issues involved in this whole thing that it will make sense. We walk the story back through that lens."

She closed her eyes, tried to concentrate on what he was saying for a moment, but still she couldn't make the pieces fit. Her daughters, Doug, her home, her life, it all floated somewhere far away, hers but somehow not hers.

"I've never been very good at letting go," she said. "Claire used to sleep with a stuffed blue dog."

"What are you talking about?" Adam said. His voice was cold, angry. He refused to sit down.

"Just listen to me," she said. "I've been thinking about that stuffed dog since you left. It's all I've been thinking about in some ways. I can still feel its faded blue fur, the scratchy place where the fur had worn down to plastic mesh. God, Claire loved that damned dog. She was always my sensitive one, always the one who reminded me most of myself.

"I woke one morning, went to check on her, and discovered the dog wasn't in her arms. Her father had taken it away from her in the night. There'd been no argument, no tedious pleas, no gnashing of teeth. My sweet Claire simply awoke and found her beloved dog gone."

"I don't get the point," Adam said. "How is this connected?"

"Parents have instincts about their children," she said. "Doug knew I'd never take that dog from her. He was right too. I'd have protected her innocence for as long I could. What he did, it seemed an oddly cruel act, and yet, somehow merciful too." She paused, looked up at Adam. "Doug was protecting Claire from me. Well, this time I'm going to protect them. I'm going to protect them from me."

Adam touched her back, but she felt nothing, only confusion.

"Let me take you home," he said. "You have a lot to sort out, but you can't do it out here, all alone. You would've called the firm first. That's an easy explanation. Blame the rest on your memory loss. No one will care about the details."

"No," she said. "I have to let go this time."

He began to gather her clothes and to stuff them in a small suitcase. Then, as if a switch were flipped to off inside her, she collapsed onto the bed and lay staring up at the ceiling.

"I used to shit myself," she said. Her voice was hollow, devoid of emotion. Adam finally stopped packing. He turned toward her, as if remembering she was in the room. "After they ablated my pancreas with radiation, I'd carry around extra underwear, adult diapers, wet wipes in my purse."

He reached for her hand, but she pulled away.

"You're going to be okay," he said. "You just need to go home."

"I'm going to die," she said. "You know it's true. Tell me I'm wrong."

"Did you hear what I just told you? Do you realize what's happening? You fell from a fucking airplane. Do you even realize what that means?"

"I don't care," she said. "Please go. Leave me alone."

"You have to go back," he said. "I wasn't thinking straight when I brought you here. That's over now. I'm taking you home."

He gripped her hands and pulled her up and off the bed. They were face-to-face, like two boxers before a match, ready to attack. Then, out of nowhere, he let go of her and she collapsed back to the bed, as if her knees gave way, as if she swooned. I've never fainted in my entire life, she thought. And then she did.

A moment later, she came to. Adam sat on the edge of the bed, frantically tapping her cheek.

"I'm so tired," she said.

"You aren't well," he said. "You need to be checked."

"I've been explaining myself to people for too long. Justifying. Rationalizing. Please tell me I'm going to wake up and this will all be a dream."

"Just trust me," he said.

"No, I have to trust myself on this. I can't leave."

Then he curled around her and she closed her eyes. She needed his caresses, needed to feel safe and warm and protected. She never wanted him to stop.

"The crash." His voice was soft now, soothing, like when he used to read to her. "There are legal issues here. They will recover the bodies and ID them. They won't find yours and they're going to come looking for you. Let me take you home."

"I just want to sleep," she said

"I'm taking you home," he said. "You aren't thinking clearly."

"I'm not going anywhere," she said.

In spite of the deepest exhaustion she'd ever known, deeper

than that caused by the chemo, deeper than anything but death itself, she was utterly resolved.

"Your family thinks you're dead. Erin, just imagine your daughters."

"That's how it should be, Adam. That's how it has to be. Just lay here and hold me and let me sleep."

21

Ulrich had wanted answers on Friday, but Radford didn't have them. In fact, by the end of the weekend, he had run out of questions to ask. All the evidence pointed in contradictory directions. Pure logic said that surviving such a fall was impossible. Common sense and physics rejected the notion. The rational brain flailed at the very possibility. Such a story, were it proven, would be a profound miracle of escape, an incomprehensible near miss with death that science couldn't explain. For days, Radford had waded through debris fields littered with broken bodies. He'd witnessed the most horrific injuries—severe burns, crushed heads, injuries that confirmed the violence of the crash. But he'd also seen relatively intact bodies too, dead passengers with no visible trauma, still strapped in their seats. He'd found a young child's body in a muddy bog with hardly a scratch. And then there were the crowds in front of the hospital, and the news reports of a possible survivor. And he could not forget the priest's comment: *She's not lying.* Didn't these things point to the possibility of an anomalous event? A freak occurrence? A miracle? And what of the other cases Lucy had researched?

With each day that passed, with each positive ID of a body, it became clear that something most unusual had happened the night Pointer 795 exploded. And if he could find this woman, if he could untangle the facts of her story, he'd make a name for himself at the agency. They'd still be talking about this investigation twenty years from now. But the risks were weighted the other way too. The laughter at the DPM would be nothing compared with the humiliation he'd face if he went after this story and it turned out to be a hoax. The world was watching. If he screwed up, there'd be no coming back. If he decided to try to find her, he'd have to take on the search with full effort.

The fallout from his report and Friday's meeting had been less painful than he'd expected. Ulrich was reading the report and would have a response soon. The weekend passed with an unexpected but welcome silence—a truce was how he thought of it. Radford did his part to avoid conflict too. He mostly stayed locked in his room, wrestling with his thoughts, and by the time he returned to work Monday morning, he felt resolved but unsure of what he was walking into. Instead of chasing down any further leads on the Falling Woman, he intended to concentrate on identifying the remaining bodies. He just didn't know if Ulrich would agree with his plan.

He left the Holiday Inn early and headed out to McConnell Air Force Base, which had become the permanent morgue. The bodies, the whiteboard, and all the equipment had been shifted from the high school gym over the weekend. Pieces of the plane were being hauled there too. Radford passed through security, flashing his ID to an airman and entering the hangar. It was the middle of May in Kansas, but the heat made him think of an August morning.

An outline of the 737-600 was taped to the floor of the cavernous hangar. The ghost plane—102.5 feet long, 117 feet wide at the wings, almost 12 feet wide at the fuselage—was partially filled in with pieces of the destroyed aircraft. A long section of the plane's keel beam bisected the middle of the white outline. The metal, bent and charred, ran at least twelve feet along the center of the outline. The aft air-conditioning pack lay crushed on its side. Running aft to fore were sections of stabilizer ribs, wing panels, fuselage windows, upright seat rows, motor windings, engine cowls, two sections of landing gear, arrester tubes, low pressure compressors, a rubber tire, a piece of radome. The whole place smelled of jet fuel, smoke, mud, and terror.

Radford's thoughts flashed back to a fox carcass he had come across in the woods last winter. He and Wendy had taken their dog for a walk. A dusting of snow covered the trail, and when Yeager began sniffing and scratching at the white earth, Radford spotted the fox's rotting remains, identifiable only by the thinnest tuft of red fur along the decomposing spine. It was the contrast that was so stark; the pieces of plane, like the bones on that fox, just hinted at what was once real.

"It's jarring, isn't it?" Lucy Masterson said.

"It looks so different in the field," he said. "You can't see the pieces connected."

"I'm glad you're back," she said. "We have the tower tapes from the FAA. I haven't listened yet."

"Investigating a crash," Radford said, "is one part archaeology, one part guesswork, and one part origami."

"What was that?" Lucy asked.

"Something that Dickie Gray told me a while ago," Radford said. "I wish the hell he were running this instead of Ulrich."

"I don't know the man well," Lucy said. "But Ulrich isn't all bad. He wants the same outcome we all do. Did he bless your report?"

He shook his head, surprised to hear Lucy defend their boss, and more surprised that he almost agreed with her.

Along the hangar's south side, two large bulletin boards leaned against a metal wall. At Ulrich's insistence, someone had tacked up photographs of the still unidentified victims. As each new positive ID was made, the victim's photograph was removed. They were entering the second week of the investigation, and more than forty photos still hung from the boards. Good, steady progress had been made, but there was much more work ahead. Lucy had helped by taking over some of Radford's duties while he investigated the Falling Woman, but she hadn't moved the number. He needed to get all those photos down. That was all that mattered now.

They crossed through the hangar and into the small office where the NTSB investigators had set up shop. Three cluttered desks crowded the room, along with stacks of aviation manuals. Lucy cued up the first tape and hit the play button. The recording came to life.

Indy Center, Pointer 795 with you at flight level 3-3-0.

Radford recognized the copilot's voice. Jack Delacroix. His résumé was on the desk: Six years with Pointer Air. Almost eight thousand hours of flight time. Radford remembered his lifeless body in the destroyed cockpit, the bloodied spike of femur tearing through his uniform trousers. He thought of the man's wife and three young kids.

The tapes were scratchy but the voices clear. Lucy took notes as she traced the plane's flight path across a chart she had laid out on the small desk. As the plane crossed the Mississippi River, the first potential signs of trouble appeared on the tape.

Pointer 795, Indy Center, turn left to a heading of 230. Will try to get you higher to avoid weather at your eleven o'clock.

"How bad were the thunderstorms?" Radford asked.

"Bad," Lucy said. "Two different weather fronts converged. Cloud tops climbed to fifty thousand feet."

Outcomes turned on such things. What seemed stable could suddenly come apart, and the routine nature of flying often hid the risks. Life was the same. Radford had spent his life building defenses against such chaos, yet the chaos found its way to him anyway. The heart condition in college that ended his flying career. His shattered dreams. Wendy's depression. And now this.

The ill-fated flight was now fifteen minutes from destruction, but, of course, no one on board knew. Radford imagined the routine of it all, inside the cockpit, in the cabin. The end of a four-day trip for the crew, they would've been excited about coming home for Crock-Pot meals and Little League games and piano lessons. He imagined the passengers, some on the plane for business trips, others going on vacation. As much as he could, Radford tried to filter out emotion. But hearing the pilots' voices in real time was always disturbing, like looking down on a tragedy from above, knowing its inevitability. He had the urge to warn them, wanted to tell Delacroix to call his wife, wanted to shout at the captain.

Kansas City Center, Pointer 795 requests either higher or a way around this cell.

Pointer 795, KC Center, hold for vectors. Traffic ahead at same flight level.

"Crowded skies," Lucy said.

"Less than a minute now," he said.

Then came the last call from the doomed craft: *Kansas City Center, Pointer 795 requests two-niner-zero to avoid weather.* He thought of Delacroix's wife, probably getting the kids to bed in San Francisco. And that storm, surging up into the troposphere, a spring cold front colliding with tropical air streaming up from the Gulf of Mexico. It must have been a monster, part of a system that spawned tornadoes in Iowa, flash flooding in Nebraska. The lightning would have flashed in the tops of the cloud. Radford imagined the pilots' final seconds. When did they know? After a long pause on the scratchy tapes, the tragedy became apparent.

Pointer 795, KC Center. Could you check your transponder, sir? We have lost your Mode C.

Mode C was the airplane's altitude reporting transponder, a radar signature on the controller's screen. It meant that the plane had already come apart. Radford startled when Lucy clutched his hand, the same way a child might grab a hand in a scary movie, looking for reassurance that they were not alone.

"The controllers know something's up," he said. Lucy had closed her eyes.

The air traffic controller sent three more requests, none of which got a response. Ten seconds of blank tape followed before another aircraft called. *Kansas City Center, Cactus 1185. Sir, we have a large explosion at our three o'clock. Very bright.* Lucy squeezed his hand. Charlie wanted to pull away, but he didn't.

A few seconds later, another flight, this one eastbound, reported seeing a similar flash of light. By now, the controller saw Pointer 795 coming apart on his radar screen, the single blip dissolving into grains. *All aircraft with Kansas City Center, be advised we have a possible explosion. Standby for vectors.* Remaining remarkably calm, the controller's voice betrayed no panic. Given the magnitude of what was occurring in his sector, a series of commands followed that turned all approaching airplanes away from the disintegrating jet.

"All those bodies," Lucy said. "It's painful to think about it."

Radford learned in training not to look at the bodies as a whole, not to see them as people but to concentrate on sections. Study the leg. Inspect the shattered abdomen. You had to think about the implication of the injuries, not the life of the person. But as they sat there, listening to the tapes, he could envision the passengers whole again, experiencing the final few moments of their lives. That plane hailing down, and the bodies, 123 of them, falling through the night. How long did the passengers live? How many were still conscious when they started to fall?

In spite of himself, he imagined a woman falling through the sky and heading toward the barn. He pictured her dropping, imagined what she felt—the cold air, the speed, the rush of wind. In all likelihood, she would've lost consciousness, which, given the circumstances, was a gift. Did she wake up at some point? Did she see the ground rushing toward her? What did she think in that moment?

"Could someone really have made it through?" he asked.

Lucy looked up. Their hands were still touching.

"Charlie, I don't know, but you need to find out. We need to be certain. You can't let all these questions just float out there unanswered. There are families waiting to hear. There are people who need to know."

"Listening to these tapes," he said, "hearing the voices of the other pilots and the air traffic controllers, everything seems so grounded. With all the work ahead of us, a miracle seems hardly plausible."

"You think you'll be able to ignore it then?" she asked. "You think you can just wait for someone else to solve it?"

"I've done my part," Radford said.

Lucy tapped the power button and took out her headphone jack. A door closed in a nearby room just before the lights flicked on, seeping through the door's glass window. They both turned. Shep Ellsworth stood at the door.

"Isn't this fucking poignant," he said. "Do you two want me to turn out the light?"

"Grow up, Shep," Lucy said. She seemed unfazed by the intrusion, but Radford felt his cheeks flush. Their hands came apart.

"Asshole wants us," Ellsworth said. "Downstairs in five, if you can tear yourselves away."

"I need to call my wife," Radford said.

"I bet you do," Ellsworth said, laughing.

Lucy touched his shoulder lightly and smiled. Then she stood, grabbed her notes, and walked out of the room with Ellsworth. Radford admired her confidence, her cool response. He pulled out his phone.

"I only have a minute," he said to Wendy. "I wanted to say good morning."

"My doctor just called," she said. "Everything looks good. Charlie—she said there's no reason for us to wait. We can start trying. I just need to know where you stand."

He missed Wendy more acutely than he ever had. When they were first married, and sexual passion filled their days, he thought it would never change. But all this talk of children made a difference, caused a shift. He wanted her back, the woman he loved, the woman he fell in love with.

"I've got to go," he said. "I'll call you later. I love you."

"Wait," she said. "A reporter called the house. She asked about you, about the Falling Woman."

"What?" he said. Anger swelled. How had his name leaked to the press? How did someone get his home phone number? The investigators weren't supposed to be part of the story.

"Don't say anything," he said. "Please, Wendy. Just don't talk to them. I'll handle it here. Call me if they bother you again. I'm serious. Anything at all. Call me right away."

"Is it true?" Wendy asked. "Did she really fall from that plane and survive?"

"Listen, I have to go."

"Did she, Charlie?"

"I don't know," he said. "It doesn't matter anyway. I'll be back on the pile today. No more of this foolishness."

"I don't understand," she said. "It's not natural. A person isn't supposed to just fall out of a plane and live."

22

ADAM LEFT SUNDAY night for the second time, and Erin awoke early Monday morning, excited about the prospect of the day ahead: long hours of solitude, birdsong, the sunrise, a hike into the woods, a fire if the spring evening turned chilly. Or she could roll over and go back to sleep. Stay in her pajamas until noon, drink coffee on the patio, and listen to the sounds of nature for hours. How long since she'd been truly alone? How long since she'd had a day without work, appointments, emails to answer, calls to return? This is where she wanted to be. She felt no need for company, no real desire for contact with the world.

Did she think about what she was doing? Did she consider the consequences of her actions? Did she feel any responsibility to anyone? Not then. She still couldn't unsort the scramble of memory and fact, her past a patchwork of disconnected stories and forgotten events. But during those first quiet days at the cabin, she simply allowed herself to be still. Everything slowed down. For the first time, she stopped trying to figure out what it all meant.

But soon solitude yielded to loneliness. The morning was manageable, but by lunchtime, she became restless. The afternoon loomed, and the evening ahead suddenly felt empty, sad, lonely. She needed company, something to break up the monotony.

Adam had left enough supplies to last a month, but she had to get out of the cabin, to do something, so she made a grocery list, put on a pair of running shoes, and decided to venture out.

Behind the cabin was an old bicycle. She oiled the rusty chain, adjusted the seat, and then pedaled the four miles into town.

During their affair, when she and Adam escaped to the cabin for an occasional weekend, they spent little time in the village. With its gas station, its hunting supply store, and grocery market, there wasn't much to see or do. They preferred privacy, preferred the intimacy and anonymity that the cabin offered. But sometimes they'd go out, and of the two restaurants in town, she favored Sandy's over the Mexican place with its oily empanadas. Sandy's was a quaint country kitchen that doubled as a biker bar on the weekends. Today, it was the first place Erin stopped when she reached town.

Her legs burned from pedaling the hills, but the smell of meat-loaf on the afternoon breeze made her forget her discomfort. The gravel parking lot in front of the restaurant was mostly empty except for a couple of pickups and an old Harley. By nine o'clock on any given night, there might be fifty bikers inside, drinking and howling at the moon, but at one-thirty, Sandy's ample wooden deck also sat empty. The patio furniture remained in winter storage despite the balmy conditions. Inside, kitsch adorned the walls: black-and-white photos of miners and lumberjacks next to glossy eight-by-tens of Virginia Tech jocks turned pro. Above the bar, the head of a stuffed moose shared space with a beaver. To the right, in the main dining room, a young kid was setting tables in anticipation of the evening rush.

After college, she had worked in a place much like this, while Doug finished his dissertation work at Penn State. Back then, she squirreled away her tips while he researched complicated packet-switching algorithms and taught linear algebra to undergrads.

Behind the bar, an older man—handsome in a rugged way, with white hair, a thin beard—smiled at her and slid a menu in her direction. Without even looking, she ordered a beer and a burger with french fries. The man reached for a napkin and silverware and introduced himself.

"Hazard," he said.

"That a name or a job description?" she asked.

"Little a both," he said.

She liked him immediately. When he returned with a beer, he asked if she was on vacation. Not having thought to prepare for questions, she found no answers readily available.

"My friend has a cabin on the Middle River," she said after a pause. "I'm staying out there." She stopped, unsure how to proceed with this emerging story.

"Who you hiding from?" Hazard asked. The man gave no indication either way if he was kidding or serious.

Twenty minutes later, emboldened by the beer and by Hazard's quiet charm, she asked him if they were hiring.

"You don't look like you need a job."

It was the first time in six months that someone had commented in a positive way about her appearance. It was the first time in twenty years that she asked someone for a job.

"Well, I do. And if you know of anyone in town who's looking for help, I'd appreciate it if you'd let me know."

She had not walked into Sandy's that day with a plan. She didn't expect to lie, or hide, or ask for a job. She never planned to reinvent herself. Because she had very little control over what happened to her in the past year, she felt a profound freedom in this new situation, as if she'd become a child again, free to do whatever she wanted.

She pulled a book from her bag and placed it on the bar. Hazard glanced down at the cover.

"You a reader?" she asked.

He shrugged. "I used to like Hemingway. Read the occasional whodunit."

"I read once—I think it was Susan Sontag who said it—that people used to hope for tuberculosis," she said, finishing her beer. "They wanted to get sick so they could go to a sanatorium and escape from their routine lives. They could read books and go for walks or just be still."

Hazard looked at her as he thought about her remark. "We're all running from something," he said. "If you've stopped running from something, you've probably stopped living."

Was that her? she wondered. Was she running? Did she even worry about why? For the first time in her life, she did not. She still sensed darkness in the void, still felt the sinister beast lurking in the shadows, but in that moment, she was profoundly happy. She felt the sheer joy at being cut loose from life.

She ordered another beer. She and Hazard chatted about their lives in a general way. He told her that, years ago, he'd served time for armed robbery. She told him that she'd left her husband but said nothing about the accident as she picked at the last of the fries.

"We were so strict with the girls," she said. "I always made them get fruit for dessert when we went out to dinner. We never allowed McDonald's or ordered pizza just because."

Hazard smiled. "Something's gonna get ya," he said. "My mother lived till she was ninety-seven, and smoked a pack of cigarettes a day until the hearse pulled into her driveway."

"All those years of worry and calorie counting," she said, feeling a little drunk from the second beer. "I treated my body like a goddamn shrine. Shouldn't there be a reward for such diligence? Shouldn't someone else get cancer? Someone who smoked and drank too much and ate processed cheese and antibiotic-loaded beef?"

Hazard nodded and asked if she wanted another beer. In a few more hours, the evening crowd would begin to arrive. She hadn't meant to spend this long in a bar and certainly couldn't stay longer. Soon headlights would shimmer through the front window. Soon country music would come on, lightly over the din of chatter, and elderly waitresses would shuffle between the tables, delivering plates of meatloaf, fried chicken, catfish, all served with mashed potatoes and gravy. It was a wonderful image, but she knew she couldn't stay to see it. Above the bar, the mounted moose head stared down while she settled the tab.

"I didn't know you had moose in Virginia," she said.

Hazard glanced up at the trophy.

"Came with the place," he said. "Damn thing frightens me, to be honest, always staring down."

More than anything, she wanted to stay longer, to be around people. She knew better than to order another beer but didn't want to go back to the cabin yet, just to be alone. Suddenly, the cabin seemed a sad and desperate place. She thought about her girls. She wanted to see them so much, and wished they were sitting here with her.

"Hi, sweetie," a drawling voice said. "I'm Sandy. This little gem is my place."

A woman appeared, wearing jeans and a flannel shirt, the spitting image of a saint. Her bleached golden hair fell in soft curls down her back, and thick glasses magnified the wrinkles beneath her eyes. She was beautiful, a vision in a green apron, with a yellow pencil tucked behind her ear. Gravy stained the apron, and she smelled of lemon soap, bacon fat, and home. Sandy looked like she could shoe a horse, sling a mean hash, and put the grandkids to bed with a tender lullaby. "Hazard tells me you're looking for a job."

23

RADFORD MADE HIS way to the hangar early on Tuesday morning. He was still waiting for an answer from Ulrich on his report. On the tarmac outside, an air force flight crew was preflighting its cargo plane. Radford envied them as well as their mission. He wanted nothing more than to climb into the plane to fly away. But he was resolved now, and ready to get back to the investigation. He'd lost over a week chasing the Falling Woman and had nothing to show for it. As he clomped down a metal staircase toward the remains of Pointer 795, a forklift's horn beeped. The sound reminded him of diligence, of the hard work ahead, but also of certainty, of linearity. Enough is enough, he thought. The forklift lowered a pallet of debris to the floor.

"I'm reviewing specs on the thermal fuses," Ellsworth was

saying to Ulrich as Radford approached. For the past two nights, Ellsworth had slept in the hangar. What the man lacked in social graces he made up for in dedication.

One thing Radford had already learned, eleven days into working his first major, was that no amount of talent or reputation mattered. The only thing that mattered was hard work. You put in your hours and you didn't complain. *Ass-in-chair time*, Dickie Gray called it. The job demanded far more than it returned. And he was dug in now, committed to the outcome, but toward what end? Back in D.C., before this whole thing began, he thought a major investigation would change the stakes. He assumed there'd be teamwork, camaraderie, some sort of wonderful harmony of effort. But with each passing day, the truth came into clearer focus. This work was no different, only more complex, from the work he'd done on *Yankee X-Ray*. Dot the i's, check the boxes. He realized now there was nothing heroic about this work, and he felt foolish for assuming there would be. They were little more than specialized bureaucrats, engineers with bad table manners and short tempers, and all of them together with one hell of a puzzle to piece together. The most interesting personality on the team was Ellsworth, and Radford could barely breathe the same air with him.

"Charlie, I can't accept your report," Ulrich said, turning to Radford. "I'm not running that upstairs. We need something conclusive. This doesn't even give me a name."

"A reporter called my home yesterday," Radford said. "My wife answered. This whole goddamn thing has become a circus. I have to get back to the investigation. I've already wasted enough time on this."

Ellsworth, tattooed forearms folded across his chest, a mocking grin on his face, stood there watching Radford suffer.

"You see that?" Ulrich said, turning and pointing toward the press tent just on the other side of the security fence. "You answer to me. I answer to them. They tell the public, and the public calls their congressmen. Shit doesn't roll downhill, Charlie. It rolls through a complicated maze of politicians, businessmen, bureaucrats, and lawyers. And then it rolls downhill."

Was he trying to be funny? With his thin nose, his wire-rimmed glasses, his skinny tie and rolled-up shirtsleeves, he looked more like a high school guidance counselor than an accident investigator. Was this the picture of success? Was that what Radford wanted to be one day? Was Gordon Ulrich the end of the line?

"When I head over there in ten minutes, what do you think they're going to ask me about?"

"I turned in my report," Radford said.

"That's not a report," Ulrich said. "That's an apology for a report. She's gone? She disappeared?"

"Look," Radford says. "I don't know what you want from me. The woman left the hospital. We have no idea who she is or where she went. And we especially don't know if she has any part in our investigation. I have work to do. I have interviews to conduct, lab reports to chase down. I was supposed to meet with the widows of the two pilots—instead, I ran to the hospital to talk about ghosts."

"We're all overworked," Ulrich said. "Everyone here is maxed out. Twice a day I stand out there making a fool of myself."

Outside, the cargo plane taxied by. The low rumble of the

plane's four turboprops filled the hangar and shut off conversation. The three men stood waiting for the plane to pass.

The plane's round fuselage crawled past the hangar door, its nosewheel tracking a precise line. Lights blinked on the wings. In so many ways, flying had betrayed Radford, had broken his heart, but he was still intrigued by it. The mythology. The science. The codes. He still read Saint-Exupéry and Tom Wolfe, still loved watching planes in flight. No one at the agency ever talked about flying. Their work was so grim and grounded. If these people had private dreams, they'd all been stashed away. At times, Radford felt asinine clinging to his love of flying. Most days, he didn't dwell on the past, didn't wonder if this was the work he was meant to do. But then, like a love-struck fool, he would be flooded by the dream all over again. Fate had dealt him a different hand of cards, and it nearly broke him, but he'd landed on his feet. The problem was that it just wasn't what he wanted. No, this will never be enough, he thought.

The cargo plane turned left, the deepening rumble of its turboprops spooling up. He felt something raw and unformed growing inside him. His whole life, he'd followed the straight path, but where had it taken him? He'd walked into the hangar this morning with new resolve, ready to put the Falling Woman behind him. But while he watched the cargo plane, something broke in him. The plane accelerated down the runway. He didn't even consider what he was saying before he said it.

"Take me off the working group," Radford said. "Put Lucy Masterson in charge of the bodies and put me on the Falling Woman full-time."

"What the fuck are you talking about?" Ellsworth said.

Ulrich's expression crinkled, but then he seemed to grasp what Radford was saying.

"You can tell the press you've put on a full-time investigator," Radford said. "Say you are taking the story seriously."

"Give me a break," Ellsworth said. "We're turning this into the goddamn *X-Files* now?"

But Ulrich shook his head and held up his hand.

"It will only cost a few hundred man-hours," he said. "But it will shut everybody up."

And the risk, Radford thought, as well as the potential reward, will all fall on someone else's shoulders. On mine.

"This is ridiculous," Ellsworth said. His face was flushed with anger. "I'm sleeping in the hangar, counting fuses, and he's getting off the pile?"

"No," Ulrich said. "Charlie, this is good. The public hearing is in ten days. I need a name. I need an answer. Figure out what happened. Don't screw me, or I'll reassign you to the goddamn highway investigations unit."

"I need full discretion," Radford said. "I don't know what the hell I'm looking for yet."

Ulrich placed his hand on Radford's shoulder and forced a smile.

"Get me something I can use," he said. "Give me a plan of attack. Where you take it from there, that's up to you."

Ulrich's phone rang and he answered, crossing the hangar and leaving Radford alone with Ellsworth.

"You slick motherfucker," Ellsworth said. "You can't hack it on the pile, so you slip out by chasing a goddamn ghost. What's your master plan? Write a book about the woman?"

"I'm nowhere," Radford said. "I have no leads. No clue what I'm looking for. I just shot myself in the kneecap."

"You're a hack," Ellsworth said. "You're not cut out for this work."

In spite of Ellsworth's ire, Radford felt that for the first time since he'd joined the agency, he'd stood up for himself. He realized what he needed and he went after it. He'd be on his own now. He'd get no help from the other investigators. He worried that Lucy might never speak to him again. But he'd acted. Decisively.

All he needed now was a plan.

Ellsworth shook his head and walked away. In the distance, the cargo plane's engines droned off into silence.

24

TUESDAY MORNING, BEFORE her first shift at the restaurant, Erin stood, unlocked the desk drawer, and removed the phone Adam had left. He was so certain she'd crack, come to her senses, and give in. She tucked the phone into her pocket and pedaled out toward a small pond not far from the cabin.

Starting the job felt significant, a step toward permanence. Was she really doing it? Was she really going to walk away from her life?

The morning air warmed her skin. Shadows and light danced over the road. A wooden dock jutted out into the lake's silver water. A rope swung idly from a pine tree. Finches chirped along the shore. Adam would be coming back. She was confident of that. He'd keep trying to convince her to go home. And of course, it was an option. Maybe even an inevitability. She could explain to Doug. Tell her diligent husband how she'd needed time to sort out what had happened. He would understand, and the parts he couldn't understand, he'd simply file those away.

She turned on the phone. The world was close. She dialed the first numbers. A few more, and she could press send and the signal would bounce. Doug would answer. The enormity of that simple round button. She closed her eyes, listened to the sounds around her, and pressed down on the next number. She imagined her bed, billowing spinnakers on the river, the view from the upstairs office. She wondered if Doug was still raising the flag every morning, her grandfather's forty-eight-star flag. Doug loved that silly old flag, almost as if he'd fought in the Battle of Leyte Gulf himself. Or was Doug grieving her death now? Had he cried? No. She knew better, knew he was orchestrating the events that gathered around her death: insurance claims, memorial services, goddamn honey-glazed hams for the mourners. What of the girls? Did Claire, so much like her father, throw herself into her studies? Would Tory drink to mask her grief? She'd never loved anything or anyone more than she loved the girls. Even then, even as she took those tentative first steps to erase herself, her own logic baffled.

One flick of her thumb, and it all would all come back, her lies, fears, hopes, passions, and dread. A few seconds for the call to find the cell tower, and then for the signal to bounce toward space at light speed; the miracle of instant communication, like so many other miracles, daily taken for granted. She spent most of her life going through the motions. Asleep. Habituated by routine. Unable to notice life surging around her. A few more seconds while the house phone rang. She imagined saying the words. *I'm alive*. Imagined hearing Doug's voice.

I'm alive, she'd say, and then everything would change. Maybe the shock of her resurrection would snap Doug out of his obsessive behavior. Maybe at last he'd see her as more than a problem to solve. Maybe he'd pay attention to her again, not just to her disease. Could she go back and retain this feeling? Could she, by the sheer force of her story, awaken others too? Was this the temptation of the prophets? *Yes*, she'd had a spiritual awakening, as silly as that sounded. She saw the angle of her journey, which had started long before boarding the plane, had started, in fact, the day her father died some forty years ago. That was why she married Doug, why she'd led such a safe and predictable life. That was also why she had the affair with Adam. One man to feel secure and safe, the other to *feel* again.

After her father died, her mother stopped showing her love. A vital piece of her mother's heart had been removed; Erin understood that now, understood that parents weren't invincible, that they made mistakes, had lives, had desires and passions that reached beyond the ordinary. She wouldn't go home. Standing on the dock staring out at the water, she knew a similar piece of her heart had been removed too. For the first time, she finally began to understand what had happened to her mother. She didn't forgive her, but she saw that forgiveness was possible.

She was tempted to push the remaining numbers. The decision was not final until the split-second she lifted her thumb from the keypad, gripped her hand securely around the phone's spine, and heaved it into the pond.

25

U.S. HOUSE OF REPRESENTATIVES PANEL INVESTIGATING
POINTER AIRLINES FLIGHT 795 (FOURTH SESSION):

"DAY AFTER DAY, I buried myself in research," Radford says. "I made three more trips to the barn."

"You did more interviews?"

"Yes. Paramedics, nurses, Dr. Lassanske again. I spoke with the chaplain again. Everyone who'd seen her, everyone who encountered the woman said the same thing—there was no way she was faking it."

"Such testimony hardly counts as evidence."

"It reinforced my belief," he says, "that the work mattered, and needed to be done."

"What happened in Goddard? What happened at the barn?"

"I hired a cherry picker truck and crew," he says. "Up in the bucket, I retraced the trajectory of the seat, running strings from stakes in the mud, up through the loft, the roof, into the top of the trees. I shot laser pointers through the branches."

On-screen now, photographs and diagrams of his work appear. He goes through them slowly, allowing each image to register before moving on to the next.

"In the hangar," he says, "I scrutinized the seat. Its braces were bent but intact."

"How do you explain that?"

"The explosion in Pointer's fuselage could've cracked at just the right angle to release the brackets. On the ground, we'd found at least a dozen seats with similar damage. Assuming a rapid decompression, the seats essentially ejected out of the crumbling plane."

"There are still huge gaps though. Still inexplicable odds."

"Yes," Radford says.

"The first public hearing was still days away. Did you think you'd have a compelling argument by then?"

"If I made the right impression with the other investigators," he says, "and if they conceded it was plausible, then I could take that as confirmation."

"Confirmation of what?"

"That I wasn't just wasting my time."

"But you still had no identifiable name, no lead on the woman?"

He shakes his head. He remembers the shame of not solving the mystery of the Falling Woman, for not having a lead, or a theory, or anything he could present.

"What did it mean?"

"The possibilities," he says, "felt endless."

"At this point, what was the agency consensus?"

"They continued to call her Sasquatch," Radford says.

Laughter ripples over the speakers in the hearing room. Radford thinks about how, back in Kansas, they'd all teased him about his work. Then he thinks about Dickie Gray investigating TWA 800 in 1996. Missiles and bombs and secret plots; it turned out that a single piece of electrical wiring misfired and the plane's fuel tank exploded. For months, they'd investigated outlandish conspiracy theories that all turned out to be bullshit. What became of the guy who investigated those theories? Radford wondered. Where did he end up?

The congressional conference room is humid, fetid, like a locker room after a game. Why had he created so much anger and spite among the other investigators? Hadn't he just followed the evidence? Wasn't he simply doing his job? It is after four now. He's been testifying for almost six hours. His back aches. His throat is sore. When he flips open the report again, he thinks about Kansas. Lucy stopped speaking to him after he dumped his workload on her. Ellsworth openly mocked him. He was on his own then, working, focused, driven to get to the end.

"No one took me seriously," he says, unprompted.

26

FIRST, HE NEEDED to get to the barn and reexamine the roof. He wanted to measure and inspect the rafters in the loft, to take samples of the tiny crater in the ground. He needed to talk with the family that owned the farm, find out what those people had witnessed. If he followed rational constraints, collected evidence, applied logic, he could file a detailed report. After all, Ulrich was a self-described data man. The trick was to stop judging the story. Investigate this as if it were a separate accident. Gather the evidence. Ask the right questions. He didn't have to worry about the answers. Wasn't that what he'd been taught? He still had no idea where the woman had disappeared to, much less if her story was true, but it didn't matter. The barn wouldn't lead him to the missing woman, but it was something tangible, something to put in the report.

Clouds formed on the distant horizon. Another warm spring day settled in as Radford drove west toward Goddard. In the haze, the red prairie barn appeared almost blue as he approached. No police cars idled along the country road this time. There were no fire trucks, no news crews. The barn's gambrel roof was more pitched than he recalled, higher off the ground, a good forty feet up. The dual-pitch roof slanted at a steep angle before slowly descending into sidewalls. A rusted hay track extended from below the roofline. The building looked weathered but sturdy. Two heavy sliding doors were locked with a chain and bolt. He also took note of two massive bur oak trees that grew along the southern facade.

What Radford couldn't initially see from the road was the odd memorial crawling up the east side of the red-clapboard walls. A few days after the news broke, a slow, steady procession of the curious made the daily pilgrimage to the barn. They were mostly locals at first, but by the third day, the dirt road adjacent to the farm became crowded with out-of-state cars bringing people who took selfies in front of the barn doors. Photographs, flowers, handwritten notes, crosses, empty whiskey bottles, helium balloons, paperback novels, and votive candles now littered the side of the barn, spilling out across hay bales and rusted hitching posts, all the way back to an old swine trough. Many of the photographs and notes had started to fade in the sun. As with roadside memorials for accident victims, the attention waned after an initial surge of interest. The pilgrimage for the Falling Woman had also disappeared from the sidewalks in front of the hospital. Life was returning to normal.

From his car window, Radford snapped a few photos of the barn and then drove to the farmhouse a hundred yards past.

The farm had been in the Werner family for almost a century. Like most Kansas farms, it had gone through several iterations since old Hannibal Werner had planted his first field of rye wheat. The family had come west from Cincinnati when the Depression forced the closure of their business. Once there, the Werner brothers cobbled together a few acres of viable crop and eventually made a modest go of it.

All this Radford learned sipping iced tea on Norbert and Mildred Werner's front porch, before he gently steered them to the subject of the Falling Woman.

"We had to hire a damned private security company to keep these nuts away," Norbert said. His hearing aid was misfiring, so he often shouted despite the near silence of the afternoon. Millie smiled and offered Radford more tea.

"I'd really just like to see the barn," he said politely.

"Well, I don't have the key," Norbert said. "And the security guard didn't show up this morning."

"You know where the key is," Millie said.

"Don't tell me what I know," Norbert said. "What's your name again?"

Radford smiled. He found their zaniness compelling, an almost welcome relief from the strain of the work. They reminded him of his grandparents.

"I'll get you the key, son," Millie said. "He likes to tell stories."

Millie stood and went inside.

"Who found her?" Radford asked.

"Who found who?" Norbert said.

"The woman in the barn," Radford said. "Did you find her?"

"I don't get out to the barn much anymore," Norbert said. "Rheumatism in my knees. No. Millie feeds the cats. Damn things could starve as far as I'm concerned. But she went out there that morning and came running back screaming blue bloody murder."

He stretched one leg out in front of the chair and groaned softly.

"It scared me about half to death," Millie said, returning from inside with the key. "That poor woman, all bruised and naked, out there all alone for more than a day. I'll take you over."

A thick alloy chain secured the doors. Millie struggled a bit with the lock before it gave way. Radford hadn't spoken with the Werners when he was there earlier, an oversight that now seemed glaring. He'd interviewed the paramedics, cops, and firemen, but not the woman who stumbled onto the scene.

"We don't get many visitors, and then all those people started showing up," she said. "I'll need some help with these doors."

He pressed one door to the side, its hinges stiff with rust and silage.

"How often do you come out here?" he asked.

"To the barn?" Millie contemplated the question. "Well, before all this hoopla, not more than two or three times a week. I feed the cats a little milk, in case they come up short on the mice. The barn's not much use to us these days. My grandsons store their motorbikes out here in the winter."

Radford stepped inside. A shaft of light beamed through the hole in the roof. Standing there, in the middle of the barn, the story seemed more impossible than before. There was no way someone fell through the roof, crashed through the hayloft, and landed on the dirt floor. No way that a woman could survive that fall, never mind sustain only minor injuries.

Through the hole overhead, he could see where branches had been snapped off the top of the oak trees. Based on the angles and the arc line, whatever came through the barn roof hit the trees first.

"Can you tell me what you saw?" Radford asked.

"Well, like I told the police, I didn't hear nothing. Sheriff Johnson had stopped by that very morning. Told us about the plane crash. Wanted to make sure we were okay."

"You hadn't seen the news?"

"Norb reads the paper still," Millie said. "But we don't watch the TV much these days. All that violence and sex."

Millie pointed toward a spot below in the mud.

"The woman was just lyin' there," she said. "Naked as the day she was born."

"Was she awake?" Radford asked. "Was she conscious?"

"Mister, I didn't stick around too long. I ran inside and called the sheriff."

Radford circled the spot, looking up at the loft. Was it possible? Did some uncanny mix of oak branch, pitch tar, rotting timber, hay, and muddy ground act as a cosmic shock absorber? He thought of Alan Magee crashing through a French train station's glass roof. He thought of Juliane Koepcke falling from ten thousand feet into the waiting rain forest canopy.

"Did you come back outside?" Radford asked. "After you spotted her and called the sheriff, did you come out after?"

"We're simple folk, Mr. Radford," Millie said. "We aren't looking for attention. You need to understand that. Some fancy magazine editor called and offered us five thousand dollars to do a photo shoot here. You see what I'm saying?"

Millie smiled but seemed irritated by all this curiosity. She'd probably never expected to be at the center of so much attention, especially this late in her life. Radford wondered if secretly, despite the security guards and the chain, the Werners welcomed it. He didn't ask her if she'd accepted the magazine's offer.

"I just need to understand what you saw," he said. "Or what you thought had happened."

Millie paused and seemed to contemplate his question. "I'm a Christian woman. I don't get to church much these days, on account of my husband's health, and, well, I'll just say it—I don't like all this happy horseshit that goes on these days." Radford laughed. "But I've led a reasonable life. I think I've been, on balance, a decent person."

She paused and looked up at the roof.

"Mr. Radford, I've never seen anything like that in my life. I don't know that I've ever been more frightened either. That poor woman was just lying there, helpless. I didn't know what to do."

Radford took out his notepad and began to make some preliminary observations. He circled around the spot where they found the seat and glanced up at the hole in the roof. Millie stood near the door.

"Do you think she fell from the plane?" she asked.

Radford put down his notepad.

"I don't know," he said.

He wasn't sure what else to say. He asked Millie if he might climb up on the barn roof. Thunder rumbled in the distance, and the wind had picked up.

"May I ask you something?" she said. "What are you going to do with that woman, assuming you find her?"

"I just want to talk to her," he said. "I just need to hear her version of the story."

"Trauma changes folk," she said. "If you find her, be kind. Make me that promise, will you? Whatever her story is. She deserves someone to look out for her."

Radford asked Millie if he could spend some time alone in the barn taking measurements. He told her he'd lock up, and that he wouldn't touch anything without her permission.

"You're invited to stick around for dinner," Millie said. "I'm making chicken and dumplings."

HE SPENT MORE than an hour in the barn. The storm passed overhead while he took detailed notes and measurements. Lightning flashed as he bagged samples of hay, timber, mud, and dirt. By the time he climbed onto the roof, the sun had come out again. Water dripped from the trees. The longer he worked, the less likely the story of the Falling Woman seemed. But he reserved judgment, forced the improbability to the back of his mind. When he finished, his shirt was soaked with sweat. He latched the heavy chain through the barn doors and waved to Norbert Werner, who still sat on the porch. From inside the house came the aroma of sautéing onions. As tempting as it was to stay for a home-cooked meal, he had to get back to the hotel to clarify his thoughts.

He spent the rest of Tuesday afternoon in his room typing up notes. What he needed now was research. He needed to compare the data he'd retrieved from the barn with other cases. When he finished, he had less than an hour until that day's DPM. He showered, put on clean clothes, and headed down to the lobby bar for a drink.

The bar was empty. Radford hadn't expected a warm reception from the rest of the investigators—after all, his new assignment shorted the team, and that slack would have to be made up, mostly by Lucy. Still, he felt like he'd done solid work. He ordered bourbon on the rocks, his father's drink. Without much thought, he dialed his father's number.

"I thought maybe you'd died," Martin said. His voice slurred from his afternoon cocktails. Radford resisted the urge to judge his father's drinking. Soon enough, Radford would be into his second whiskey.

"Just busy, Pops," Radford said. "I'm in Kansas, investigating the plane crash."

"Mr. Big Shot," Martin said, laughing.

Over the years, the script of their conversation changed little. His father would launch into a litany of complaints that usually began with liberal politicians ruining the country and ended with his latest medical ailment. Radford tried to be a sympathetic son, tried not to react to his father's often-incendiary words. Reacting only made Martin shout louder.

"You coming out this weekend?" he asked.

"Dad, I'm in Wichita. I can have Wendy go if you need something."

"Just be nice to have company once in a while."

When his father drank, which was every day since Radford's mother had died four years ago, Martin teetered between maudlin anxiety and outright hostility. Radford had navigated this minefield enough times to know where to step, but sometimes he wanted to alter the script. Sometimes, he wanted to assert his own opinions.

"You flying at all?" his father asked.

"No, Dad. You know I have a heart condition. Listen," he said. Just once he wanted to have a normal conversation with the man. Just once he wanted his father to give him some fatherly advice. "Wendy wants to have a kid. She thinks she's ready, but I don't know."

"Who is?"

His father was too far gone. Radford pointed at his glass, and the bartender filled it with another shot of bourbon. He then spent the next few minutes trying to extract himself from the conversation with his father, after which he smacked his phone down on the bar, wondering why he'd called in the first place.

"Long day?" a woman said.

Radford hadn't noticed her sit down. She smiled. She was young, attractive, well dressed. He never picked up women, not even when he was single, but at that moment, he rather welcomed the company if only to get his mind off troubling thoughts.

"Several long days," Radford said.

"You waiting for someone?"

What was this woman's angle? he wondered. Sex? Was she trying to sell him kitchen cleaners? Convert him to follow Jesus? On the television, the news came on; the bartender turned up the volume. Radford and the woman looked up at the screen.

"We're going to go to Liz Rash," the male anchor said, "who has live reactions from local Kansans to this incredible story."

The screen cut to a young reporter standing outside the McConnell hangar.

"Sedgwick County residents continue to express strong opinions about this mysterious story," the reporter said. "And they are wondering why investigators haven't been able to confirm or deny the rumors of the so-called Falling Woman."

"It's a miracle," a woman said as her husband nodded. "We've been praying ever since that plane exploded. And now, God has answered those prayers. There is a survivor."

Radford sipped his drink. On the screen, a teenage girl appeared. "It's creepy. You know?" she said. "A plane blows up like that, and now they're saying one woman lived. It's just so weird."

Radford glanced back at the woman sitting next to him.

"What do you think?" she said. "Isn't this the strangest story you ever heard?"

Radford shrugged. When the news report cut back to the studio, Radford reached for his wallet. He couldn't listen to this another moment.

"Hers too," he said to the bartender, handing him a twenty. The woman smiled at him. He didn't look back to see her remove a small notebook from her purse. Had he turned before entering the elevator, he might have seen the woman scribbling in the notebook in the wake of his abrupt departure.

27

THE DAYS PASSED quickly and Erin fell into a rhythm. Loneliness continued to visit, but only in the margins of her days. When she was first told she had pancreatic cancer, she knew what the diagnosis meant. Her chances of being alive in five years were abysmal. She'd look around for other faces, for smiles from the girls, for words, even for Doug's predictable habits—his nightly news, clopping work shoes on the kitchen tile, his grins and grimaces. In their place, she saw people still living their lives while she was dying. She resented them all, resented especially the very people who loved her the most. Their ingrained habits became one more reminder that she was alone. But in the midst of that depression, a strange comfort started to grow, in silences and shadows. She'd never paid attention to it before, how tuning out from the world allowed peace to enter.

Once again, at the cabin, she discovered a familiar tug-of-war taking place. Solitude, the lack of connection to the world, loneliness—these things would start to weigh heavily, but then, just as quickly, a bird's song would snap her out of it. Or the way the afternoon light fell across the cabin's porch. Or the smell of a spring afternoon. The simplest things offered incredible, bountiful gifts. She once spent a whole morning arranging small sticks into intricate shapes, in some primitive expression of art that called to her. Another day, she made a great swirling vortex out of white and gray pebbles. How long since she'd been able to play like that? To sit and think. To read and be still. Or even just to let go and cry. Alone, in the cabin, she could lament her life properly, and she also could celebrate her good fortunes.

One morning, the memories that had disappeared after the crash returned, in one large dump, like a massive file that finished downloading. She awoke and remembered everything, from the day her father chased her with a hose and she fell and skinned her knee, to the time in fourth grade when Dean Markarian tripped and knocked out his front teeth, to sixth-grade camp in the New Hampshire pines, to her father's funeral, to the first day of high school, to college graduation, to law school exams, to her wedding night, to the birth of the twins. That morning on the trail, she flipped through the past as if reading a book, searching for and finding missing pieces. Her amnesia, such as it was, was cured. Her whole life returned, even pieces she hadn't thought of in a long, long time. Something had reorganized the lapse in memory, collated the moments for efficient retrieval.

She remembered her grandmother's house, the hutch where she kept scented candles organized in precise rows. How the hinges squeaked when she pulled open the door to sniff inside. The summer her father died, she went to live with her grandmother. Two weeks of love and attention. She'd forgotten about that time, about the scent of the candles.

She also remembered that day in the departure lounge at Dulles, that tension in her bowels, the phone call with Adam, the sandwich she ate. She remembered standing on the walkway talking to a handsome man, and she remembered the sapphire color of his shirt. Her memory no longer had gaps. No more missing hours. No missing facts.

She remembered falling. Every sight, every sound, every second. The rush of wind. Fire. Blackness. Air thick with the smell of fuel. The ground.

When she went to work at the bar, she told Sandy and Hazard very little about herself, only the barest of facts. An injury. Head trauma. They didn't need to know the details, and they never pried. Intentionally vague, she was sparing them as much as herself because the truth of her life, its reality, was not something she was prepared to face.

"It's just nice to feel normal again," she said at some point.

That evening, after her shift, Hazard handed over her first paycheck, almost $400. The Pay To line was left blank.

"She only knows your first name, sweetie," Hazard said. "You want it in cash?"

For a moment, she was trapped in her own lie. Were Sandy and Hazard and the others here onto her? Would the slipperiness of her new identity curse her in the end? At any moment, she expected to be exposed. She'd look up and see the police, Doug, her daughters walking in the front door to haul her away.

"It's okay," Hazard said. "Half them guys in the kitchen get paid in cash too. You just don't look like someone hiding from Immigration."

"It's complicated," she said.

"I'll have cash for you tomorrow," he said. "You just be careful carrying all that money home on that bike of yours."

Her last year at the law firm, she pulled down close to $400,000, but the work was tedious, soul crushing. The contrast with this job and this pay was almost laughable. Doug believed in wealth as an article of faith. Hell, maybe she did too. She could've quit her job at the law firm. She could've gone off and chased her dreams. But every dollar in the bank account was another brick to strengthen their lives—Doug and hers, and Claire and Tory's too. But at the same time, every dollar was also another brick to wall them in.

She thanked Hazard, went and found Sandy in back, and told her how much she appreciated their patience, their decency.

"You don't need to thank me," Sandy said. "How else do you treat people?"

28

FRIDAY'S DAILY PROGRESS meeting was a dry run for next week's public hearing. At the DPM, only the insiders would be present. But in a week's time, the cameras would roll, and there would be reporters, lawyers, insurance agents, and family members. Radford knew that those people would demand answers.

He spent the afternoon in his room, finishing up his new report. In the conference room that evening, attendance was thin. Lucy showed up a few minutes early and avoided him. Conspicuously absent, much to Radford's relief, was Shep Ellsworth. Ulrich opened the meeting with the usual remarks, reminders to fill out time sheets, to communicate with the local liaison for travel vouchers, to log miles driven.

"I'm going to turn it over to Charlie Radford first," Ulrich said.

"As most of you know, he's running a special investigation into reports about a possible survivor."

A faint chuckle of laughter spread through the room while Radford passed around the copies of his report.

"This two-page summary details what I know," Radford said, trying to sound composed and serious. For the moment, everyone at the table at least did him the courtesy of listening. "On or about 0900 on Sunday, May seventh, Mildred Werner entered the barn on her property in Goddard, Kansas. Upon opening the barn doors, Werner spotted the subject lying on the floor, naked, unconscious, lying next to a seat from the Pointer plane. ID on the seat is positive."

"What do we know about the seat?" an FBI agent asked.

"We know the seat came from row twelve, forward of the port wing," Radford said.

"So not to ask the obvious here fellas," the agent said, "but why don't we just match up the passenger manifest with the seat and get back to the real work?"

Radford was always amazed at how shortsighted the FBI agents could be. He wondered if their polygraph tests somehow screened out common sense along with the lies.

"Pointer Airlines has an open seating policy," Lucy said. "Seat numbers tell us very little."

"So where does that leave us?" Ulrich said.

Radford pulled up pictures of the barn, the hayloft, the hole in the roof. He'd taken almost two hundred photos of the two bur oak trees that grew adjacent to the barn. He zoomed in on a few photos that showed the obvious path of the seat through the now-broken branches. A perfect trajectory from sky to tree to barn to ground.

"There are indications that debris hit both trees before entering the barn," Radford said, careful to use the word *debris*, and to avoid attaching any human characteristics yet. "Such impact could've dissipated energy. And the chair passed cleanly through the roof. From what I could see, it only scraped one of the roof beams. The combination of impact forces had the potential to slow the seat rapidly and to significantly diminish the impact forces."

He hated the sound of his own voice. He felt he sounded like a televangelist, exploiting half-truths and evidence to document the supernatural. What he wanted to say was that he had no idea what had happened at the barn in Goddard.

"Jesus-H-Tap-Dancing-Christ," Shep Ellsworth said, bursting into the conference room. "We're really going to do this?"

Radford's stomach heaved as Ellsworth took a seat, but he allowed the laughter to settle before pushing the button for his next digital slide: a black-and-white photo of a train station in France. Between two stone-block buildings with dark trim was the large glass atrium. The triangular roof, even in the photo, looked sharp, its iron beams and spars hardly suggesting a soft place to land.

"This was the train station where the American airman landed during World War II," Radford said. "Notice the pitched angle of the roof."

Lucy Masterson nodded.

"But Magee got tangled in the rafters," she said. "He didn't fall into the mud."

"I don't have a theory yet," Radford said. "I'm not even suggesting that this happened the way it's being reported."

Several men shook their heads. Others whispered, or jotted notes and laughed. What the hell was he thinking by doing this?

The mood had turned from comical to skeptical, then to downright hostile. He wanted to tell them, *I didn't go looking for this story*, but of course, now he had. He'd stuck his neck all the way out, and now he had to let them hack away at it. He wanted to share in their skepticism, to sit there and laugh at this quackery. Who would try to convince a roomful of engineers, pilots, federal agents, and scientists that the laws of physics had temporarily been set aside? Who would defend such a ludicrous claim? At the same time, he couldn't forget the look on Millie Werner's face or the certainty of the priest when he said, "She's not lying." Neither of those people had a motive to protect anything, nor did they try to convince him of anything. They'd simply seen something they couldn't rationally explain. No, the hostility in this room had nothing to do with truth. These people just wanted this crazy story to go away. They wanted him to erase it, and the longer he defended it, the more arguments he made, the more they resented him.

"I'm going to say this once more," Ellsworth said. "I'm not sitting through any more of this nonsense. I'm here to investigate an accident, not to listen to stories about Henny Penny."

"Shep, enough," Ulrich said. "Charlie's almost done."

"Charlie should've been done a long time ago," Ellsworth said.

An awkward silence followed. Radford waited for more to be said in his defense, hoping that Ulrich would explain that this investigation had been blessed—had been demanded, in fact—by the folks in D.C. But no such explanation came.

"Lucy, you're right," Radford said. "In each of the other cases, there were unusual circumstances that helped increase the chances for survival. I'm not making a case for the Falling Woman. I'm simply looking for possible explanations."

"Maybe she's a bird-woman," Ellsworth said, evoking more laughter in the room. "Did you scour the place for feathers?"

"Look," Radford said, "the timber in that barn was soft from rot. The debris fell through a three-foot stack of wet hay. The ground was muddy. I don't know if that's enough to make a difference. I don't even know who to ask."

Ellsworth mumbled something low, and a nearby FBI agent almost spit out his coffee.

"Shep, that's enough," Ulrich said.

Ellsworth made a mocking salute.

"Is this woman a hoax?" Radford asked. "Maybe. Maybe she was in that barn and the seat hit her on the head. If so, where the hell is she? Why not step forward and tell her story?"

Ellsworth shook his head.

"Where are we now?" Ulrich said.

"I need Lucy to push the IDs on the bodies," Radford said. He hated saying it, hated calling her out for not making progress. But the IDs were the best chance he had, the fastest, simplest way to resolve things, one way or the other. Account for all the passengers on the plane, and this whole thing would go away.

"Lucy?" Ulrich asked.

"It could be weeks," she said. "Hell, it could be months."

THAT NIGHT, RADFORD barely slept. He'd run out of options. He had no leads, no credible direction to take the next day. He had nothing beyond what he'd presented at the meeting. He remembered the days after he was told he couldn't be a pilot. How lost he felt. How empty. His whole world had been crushed, his very identity shattered, but on the surface, to the outside world, everything looked the same. It was similar now. On the surface, he was still an accident investigator. He still wore the same uniform, carried the same credentials. But inside the meeting room, he was a pariah. They only wanted him to debunk this story. Each day his investigation continued, each day he kept doubt and uncertainty alive, each day his research pulled the team away from the credible work of the investigation, Radford's reputation sank.

Hell, he'd felt the same way two weeks ago. If this woman really survived this fall, if she really broke all the rules, then they'd never figure out how. No amount of rotten timber, wet hay, and mud was going to satisfy their skepticism. He needed to find the woman. He needed to march her into the conference room. It was the only way this story would make sense. These people believed in things that could be seen, measured, and documented. The lone way to prove or disprove this woman's story was to find her. Short of that, it came down to Lucy and identifying the remaining bodies. Dickie Gray had told him to ask the right questions and trust the evidence. Radford had followed that advice. But this time, the evidence had walked out of Via Christi Hospital, and the right questions pointed in the wrong direction. No matter what questions Radford asked, no matter how many pieces of data he gathered, a story like this was too far off the charts. Only two questions mattered now: Who the hell was she? And where had she gone?

29

After tossing and turning most of the night, Charlie called Wendy on Saturday morning.

"I'm looking at another house today," she said. "Charlie, tell me this isn't pointless. Tell me that we have a chance."

"Of course, we do," he said. "How can you say that?"

"You know what I mean. You know why I'm looking at houses. You know why this matters to me. If you can't at least acknowledge what I'm saying, then what's the point?"

"Slow down," he said. "Can't you just slow down a bit? Can you wait until I'm through with this craziness? The whole damn thing is blowing up around me."

"It always is," she said. "It will never change."

"It may not matter anyway," he said. "I'm out of ideas. I have nowhere to turn. If something doesn't pop loose, and soon, I'll be home for the duration."

"It's that Falling Woman, isn't it?" she said. "It's all over the news. Something about that feels wrong. Why do you have to be mixed up in it?"

"If anyone asks," he said, "reporters, even friends, please don't tell them anything."

"That reporter keeps calling,"

"Don't talk to her," he said.

"What would I tell her?" she said. "I don't know anything more than what's on television." She paused, then sighed. "Tell me you love me, Charlie. Tell me you want to have a family with me. I need to hear you say it."

"It's weird," he said. "The more they don't believe in it, the more I think it really happened."

"Did you hear me?"

"Nothing has changed for me," he said. "I love you. I will always love you. I will always want to be with you. I'm sorry that can't be enough. It used to be."

Someone knocked on his door.

"I love you," she said, "but you need to hear me. I've never felt this way before. I need this, as much as you need your damn job. I want to be a mother, Charlie. I'm ready to start. I just want to know if my husband is going to be with me."

"I have to go," he said. "I love you."

He pulled on a shirt and opened the door. Lucy Masterson stood in the hallway, already dressed for the field, her khaki pants tucked into her work boots. She held a stack of files in her hand.

"I need to go over these with you," she said. "I need to have my facts straight before the public hearing."

"I need movement on the bodies, Lucy."

"Charlie, you dumped all this on me and haven't even said thank you yet."

He reached out and squeezed her hand. As an apology, it was a feeble one, but he was grateful she didn't pull away.

"Give me a minute," he said, but as he turned to go back inside, Ulrich raced down the hallway.

"Downstairs, now," he said, not even slowing as he passed.

Radford looked to Lucy for an explanation, but she shrugged. He grabbed his windbreaker, stepped into his shoes, and closed the door behind him.

"What's on fire now?" he asked.

"No clue," Lucy said. "Listen. I need to transfer some of the remains from the morgue to a D.C. lab. Double-check this paperwork for me. This is my first hearing too."

"Lucy," Radford said, "you know they're going to eat me alive."

"You deserve it," she said, but a smile creased her lips.

When they arrived at the conference room, Shep Ellsworth stood outside the door, grinning and back-slapping everyone who entered. He looked more smug than normal. The son of a bitch had even shaved this morning, and he wore a starched shirt, creased and clean khakis. He'd tucked his ponytail tightly behind his head.

"Jesus," Lucy said. "He's such a prick."

Radford looked down as he approached. He tried to slip past Ellsworth, but a tattooed forearm blocked the entryway to the conference room.

"This is what real investigators do," he said. "Maybe you'll learn something today."

Radford pushed Ellsworth's arm aside and with Lucy went into the conference room. Whatever was happening, it attracted a lot of attention. The room was packed. Government officials, engineers from Boeing, reps from Pointer Airlines, and investigators all jockeyed for a spot. Ulrich stood by the pull-down screen, talking into his cell phone. Energy buzzed in the room. In his confusion, Radford felt outside of everything.

"Let's find seats," Ulrich said. He sounded eager, excited, almost giddy. Light streamed in through the windows. A few stragglers entered the room smiling and shaking hands. Radford didn't recognize half of the people. Clearly, there were many competing interests in the investigation.

"Well, folks," Ulrich began. "After two long, exhausting weeks, we finally have some genuinely good news to share."

Radford leaned in and whispered to Lucy, "What the hell is going on?"

"Beats me," she said. "Maybe Ellsworth won the lottery."

"Without further ado," Ulrich said, "let me bring in Shepherd Ellsworth to fill you in. Shep."

Radford felt like he might throw up. At the same time, he envied Ellsworth's entrance, envied the moment. This was the moment Radford had dreamed would be his.

"As part of our ongoing investigation into combustion sources for Pointer 795," Ellsworth said, "we've inspected fifteen more airframes in the fleet. Twelve of those planes showed degradation of thermal bonding in and around the center-wing fuel tanks. Of those twelve, at least six planes showed significant degradation."

"What does this mean?" an FBI agent asked.

"It means," Lucy whispered to Radford, "Shep Ellsworth just cracked the fucking case."

The knot in Radford's gut tightened. Ellsworth explained how a gap in the bonds could, given the right electrical conditions, lead to an arc between two pieces of metal. "A short circuit," he said, simplifying his explanation for the sake of the nonengineers. "Right now, it looks like the probable cause of the explosion was a combination of lightning, degraded thermal bonds, and fuel vapors in the center tank."

The man's arrogance was unchecked. Even if he was right, a conclusion was still far away. "You buying this?" he asked Lucy.

She shrugged, but the look on her face suggested that indeed she was buying it.

"Ladies and gentlemen," Ulrich said, "we have a lot of work ahead of us. Make no mistake. Based on Shep's excellent work, we are making a recommendation for a fleet-wide inspection of all fuel tanks in the 737-600. We will decide soon about the 400 and 500 models. We will continue to investigate alternative combustion sources, but I believe everyone in this room will agree that this has brought us all one step closer to an answer."

There was applause, and Ellsworth beamed. A moment later, on the conference room video hookup, the NTSB director appeared on-screen. A wide smile broke across her face.

"Just heard the good news," Carol Wilson said. "Great work, Shep. Everybody out there too."

Radford quietly slipped out of the conference room, letting the excitement cover his absence.

FOR THE NEXT two days, Ellsworth's theory dominated the conversation. Structural engineers and metallurgists spent hours combing over the ruined pieces of the plane, seeking to confirm that somehow, because of improperly bonded metal components, a lightning strike could've led to a spark in the fuel tank that ignited the fuel and brought down Pointer 795. Experts arrived in Wichita: college professors, meteorologists, along with aerospace engineers and Boeing's lawyers. Tests were run in adjacent hangars. Pieces of aluminum skin and iron baffles were jolted with electricity. Pictures were taken, X-rays, magnetic images. A section of the fuel tank was shipped to a lab at the Air Force Academy for further tests.

Shep would get to announce his findings at Friday's public hearing. This was a breakthrough, the first major one so far. The investigators would show the press, show the families, show the politicians and the public that they'd made great progress.

But rather than taking the pressure off Radford, Ellsworth's theory only intensified Ulrich's demand for answers. He became obsessed with Radford's findings, checking on him constantly. "What are you looking at now?" he'd ask over breakfast. "What have you found out?" he'd ask at lunch. "Where are we at now?" at the evening DPM.

Radford felt stymied. If anything, his investigation regressed. Locked away in his hotel room, he did research day and night, trying to find a plausible explanation. He had stacks of papers now, reams of data, but none of it added up to anything. There were no experts in this field, no scientists to call, no free-fall consultants.

He was stuck in place, and he knew it. And the hearing was now only days away.

His hotel room began to resemble Dickie Gray's office. Stacks of files covered the floor. When not conducting interviews, or attending meetings, he holed up inside, letting the maid enter for only the most cursory cleaning. He'd obtained a printer, boxes of file folders, pens, markers, poster boards, maps, photo paper, and tape. He pored over the information he had, but it pointed nowhere. There were only dead ends, uncorroborated sources, myths and legends. From what he could tell, historically a handful of people really had survived incredible falls, but no legitimate explanation existed for how.

Meanwhile, the furor over the Falling Woman continued to grow. Rumors began to spread, tales of miracle cures in Via Christi Hospital. A diabetic patient who'd tossed her insulin. A woman with lung cancer claiming to be cured. An inveterate alcoholic sobering up. As ridiculous as these stories were, as utterly absurd, the press kept reporting them. Almost daily, there was a story that associated some miracle with the mystery of Pointer 795. Radford was sick of the whole thing, plus he was out of ideas, out of explanations, and soon he'd be out of time.

On Monday morning, four days before the public hearing, Radford went down for breakfast. Lucy had asked to meet up to discuss the paperwork from the morgue. When he exited the elevator, Radford felt a strange twinge of anxiety. A moment later, before he had time to maneuver away, three people approached him in the lobby. A man and two women stood before him, a look of desperation on their faces.

"Are you an investigator?" the man asked.

"My sister was on that flight," one of the women said. Her face was flushed and angry. "Please, my god, tell me that she's the one who survived."

"I'm sorry," Radford managed to say. He started to back away and glanced around for hotel security.

"Why aren't you releasing more information?" the man asked. His tone was harsh, not just angry but sharp and hostile. "You goddamn people are holding us hostage. We need answers. We deserve the truth."

"Stop, Jack," the other woman said. "Don't make it worse."

Finally, a hotel security guard appeared. He grasped the man on the elbow, but the man spun around.

"My daughter. Why won't you tell us anything? You people are monsters."

Radford's heart pounded. The security guard reached for the man's elbow again, and this time, the man relented, holding up his hands and allowing himself to be led away. The two women followed the security guard toward the door, the man still shouting.

A moment later, Lucy emerged from the elevator, but the commotion was now over. She looked at Radford.

"What's up?" she said. "You look like you just saw a ghost."

He didn't know what to say. This was what he'd feared all along. The chaos was starting to circle around him. Those people didn't even know he was the one leading the investigation into the missing woman. They were just desperate, grasping for some glimmer of hope, praying for an answer.

"You okay?" Lucy poked his shoulder. "I've been thinking

about Ellsworth's lightning theory. How did six decades of engineering work somehow fail?"

Her question shook him out of his trance.

"Airplanes are struck by lightning all the time," he said. They walked toward the small bar now converted into a breakfast buffet. He'd lost his appetite.

"These families deserve a private meeting," she said.

"What the hell are you worrying about that for?" she said. "You seem to have enough to do to get ready by Friday."

"I'm nowhere," he said. "I'm one hundred nautical miles east of nowhere and I'm running out of fuel."

"Can't you get any information from the hospital?"

"No one saw her leave," he said. "And no one can seem to remember with any certainty what she looked like. The descriptions vary. I've interviewed everyone who had contact with her. I've interviewed many of them three times. They're dodging my phone calls now. They think I'm nuts."

"I'm worried about you," she said. "When was the last time you took a shower?"

"It's the families that get to me," he said. "Seven female passengers still unaccounted for. Seven families still clinging to hope. Seven!"

Under Lucy's leadership, the forensics team had identified ninety-eight passengers and crew, but that still left twenty-five without IDs, and of those, seven women fit the potential profile for the woman who'd been admitted to Via Christi and disappeared. That meant seven families still didn't know what to believe.

"I need those IDs, Lucy."

"You know as well as I do that I can't make that happen any faster."

"Then my only choice is to start interviewing those families."

"Why haven't you before?" she asked.

"Because as soon as I do, I legitimize their hope. I make it real."

"What then? What are you going to do?"

"I'm going to tell Ulrich to keep me out of the hearing," he said. "I have no evidence. He'll have to see that."

"I don't know, Charlie. After pulling you off the working group. After putting you on full-time assignment to find that woman. I'm not sure that will fly."

"Then I'm going to end up splashing down in spectacular fashion," he said. "I hope you enjoy the show."

AN HOUR LATER, Radford entered the hangar at McConnell. The reconstruction team had been working day and night to attach pieces of the ruined airplane to scaffolding. The eerie site of the shattered plane coming back to a recognizable form reminded him of a broken child's toy repaired with glue and tape.

The reconstruction team had made a solid start. Several sections of fuselage now hung in place. Waiting to be lowered, the starboard wing spar dangled from a gantry crane. Rows of passenger seats had been placed in the forward compartment. Radford thought again of the human costs. Real people's lives wiped out. Whole families forever changed. Near the center of the plane, dark char marks—burn-through from the explosion—stained the white aluminum panels.

Ellsworth's theory—that a lightning strike had caused the fuel tanks to explode—wasn't holding up. The various experts brought in to confirm the theory were instead ripping it apart. Secretly, Radford took a small measure of delight in how quickly the mood had changed for Ellsworth. As the hearing approached, the tension grew.

Overnight, someone—almost certainly Ellsworth—had punched a hole in the victims' bulletin board. A gaping maw in the corkboard screamed trouble. Radford bent and gathered the victims' photos from the floor. Smiling, clear-eyed mothers and sons, sisters and husbands, each photo captured a moment when these people still harbored dreams and desires. He flipped through them slowly, trying to memorize their features. Then he stacked the photos neatly on a chair and bent to pick up the scattered pins.

As he repinned the photos to the cracked board, he set aside the seven photos of possible female victims. One of them might be the Falling Woman, assuming there was a Falling Woman, assuming her story was true and not some wild fantasy. The photos reminded him that a lot of people were still holding on to hope, people whose lives and families were in limbo. On Friday, Radford would stand before reporters, lawyers, and some of the family members of those seven women, and he'd present his meager findings. The thought of it made him feel nauseous. It would be a public shaming. A repudiation of his work, of the path he had chosen. It was one thing to stay alone in his Wichita hotel room, quietly doing research and assembling stories, and quite another to step into the arena of a public forum with a story that had no substance. He wanted an answer, but one hadn't appeared. Ellsworth openly mocked him. The other investigators ignored him. The only friend he had left, the only person he could still count on, was Lucy, and she was inadvertently making it worse. Without a body, without a name, Radford would look worse than foolish up there; he'd look incompetent.

Upstairs, Shep Ellsworth cursed and slammed a door. They passed each other on the staircase, almost colliding, Ellsworth coming down, Radford going up. Ellsworth mumbled something as they passed, but Radford no longer cared. He entered Ulrich's office without knocking.

"I'm nowhere," he said.

"I don't want to hear it, Charlie."

Ulrich was at his computer and barely glanced up.

"I need those bodies identified," Radford said.

"At this point, I don't care if she's alive or dead, real or fake," Ulrich said. "You have one job. One. You will stand up there on Friday and you'll own this."

"I have nothing new," he said.

"You've shown pictures to the witnesses?"

Radford nodded. He'd shown over thirty pictures to every witness. He'd gone back three times with the charge nurse at Via Christi, four times with the paramedic who rode in the ambulance. Not a single person could say for certain if the woman they'd seen—in the barn, in the ambulance, at the hospital—was among those in the photographs. For more than two weeks, he'd wrestled with every implication of this story. He'd kept an open mind. He'd asked all the questions he could think to ask. But he had no control over any of it now. It no longer mattered what questions he should ask.

"I'm done," he said. "I have nothing to present. Don't put me up there on Friday."

"I can't accept that," Ulrich said. "Stop making excuses. Do your job."

"What am I supposed to do? Stand in front of the cameras, in front of those families, and tell them what? That a girl fell almost fifty years ago into the rain forest? That a goddamn tail gunner may have survived a fall in World War II? That's my evidence?"

Ulrich stopped typing and rolled his chair around so that he could face Radford.

"Charlie, I'm going to say this once and not say it again. I don't care what you do on Friday. I don't care if you make shadow puppets onstage. But you asked for this, and so now you own this story. You're going to stand up there and take responsibility."

Then his boss stood, grabbed a stack of files, and slammed them down on his desk. It was almost comical, as if this skinny bureaucrat's tirade would somehow intimidate him. Radford turned away.

He needed a break, something to fall his way for a change.

"I might as well be writing fiction," he said to Ulrich on the way out. Charlie Radford had no way of knowing that at that very moment, the break he'd been waiting for had just walked into the lobby of the Wichita Holiday Inn.

30

—

ERIN HAD BEEN thinking about betrayals. How she betrayed her husband. How Adam betrayed his wife. How cancer betrayed her body. How that plane betrayed its passengers, including her. How every act toward salvation was also an act of betrayal. She needed to be free, needed not to become part of a world that would turn her private life into a spectacle. But to do that, in order to be free, she had to imprison herself in a cabin in the mountains of Virginia, holed up like some fugitive.

She tried to convince herself she wouldn't regret her decision to disappear. She knew that when the truth came out, people would judge her harshly, and that even the people who loved her most would never understand. She wondered if she could she accept that judgment. She wondered what choice she had.

Adam had come back to the cabin one last time over the weekend. Erin had returned from work and found him sitting on the couch. The sight of him made her furious. She'd begun to think of the cabin as hers, not his, and now his presence felt like a violation. Her anger was raw, new, and something she couldn't explain. Rage welled up and erupted out before she could stop it.

"Why the hell are you here?" she said. "Why can't you just leave me alone?"

"This might be a good thing," Adam said. "This delay has given me time to think. You did the right thing by coming here."

"Get out," she said. "Leave me alone."

He stayed calm, made her a drink.

"You need to talk about what happened," he said. "Put it out there. People want to hear your story."

"What am I supposed to say? Why would people want to hear from me? I'm no prophet."

She wanted to talk and wanted him to listen the way he used to. She wanted to tell him about her job, about the books she'd been reading, about her thoughts and the rhythm of her days. She wanted to talk about anything except going home.

"You're all alone out here," he said. "It's not safe. Not to mention that none of this makes sense."

"Stop. I'm not in the mood for a lecture."

Once again, Adam tried to persuade her to go home, but she wasn't listening. Perhaps if he made love to her instead of talking, perhaps if he swept her up with the passion she craved, perhaps if he looked at her with something besides pity and disgust, perhaps then she'd entertain his notions about what she should do.

"This isn't sustainable," he said, "not to mention the fact that there are people out there who are suffering because of you, wondering if you're their mother, or wife, or daughter. Your disappearance has created so many questions."

"I can't help them. I can't answer their questions," she said.

"No one is looking for you to answer their questions," he said. "They just want to know who you are. You owe it to the others, and you especially owe it to your family."

"Why don't you answer a question for me. Why me? Why am I the one that's still here?"

He didn't answer, but she didn't expect him to.

By the end of the night, Adam said he had no idea what to do with her.

"You could murder me. That may be your only viable option," she said playfully. "The perfect crime. You could literally get away with it."

"This isn't funny," he said.

"On the contrary, it's fundamentally hilarious."

She was angry, unyielding and unreasonable. He tried one last time to sway her with reason and logic.

"Look, Erin, you have to go home. This makes no sense."

"Every morning," she said, "for the last twenty years, Doug would come downstairs and go through his rituals. With his puffy half-closed eyelids, he'd turn on a light and glance down at me, forcing that crooked half smile of his in my general direction before grabbing a white mug and a Lipton tea bag from the cabinet. There were so many times I wanted to shake him. So many times, I wanted to scream in his face and say, 'Don't you feel this?

Don't you feel anything?' Our lives were slipping through our fingers, and he didn't even notice. He seemed to feel that he had his part to play, and he'd be damned if he wasn't going to play it. Well, that's over now, thank god."

Adam just stared at her, silenced by her passion.

"He's a good person. I see that. Never once did Doug question my irrational moods. Never once did he ask for an explanation about my missing weekends. Never once did he object to my constant bellyaching. But his ambivalence, however much it may have verged on saintliness, made me feel paralyzed, comatose. Every morning, those two minutes while he warmed his tea felt like a century."

"They're just little life patterns," Adam said. "Everyone falls into them."

"That tea was the highlight of his day. That was the only time he seemed awake. How can I go back to that? Please tell me."

Adam explained how he and his wife fell into patterns too, but Erin tuned out. She hated the sound of his wife's name coming from his mouth. She hated him for dismissing her pain so easily.

"I don't care," she said. "I reject them all. I've been granted immunity from patterns. I reject the mundane too. I'm awake, at last, and I won't go back to sleep."

"You have two daughters who need you," he said. "My god, have you considered them?"

"I think about them all the time," she said. "Should I go home so they can watch me waste away again? Should I come back from the dead so I can shrivel and die with them weeping at my bedside four months from now?"

"You need to see a doctor," he said. "You've stopped making sense."

"A doctor can't help me. There's no cure for what I have," she said.

"You're going insane," he said. "I mean it, Erin. I think you're losing your mind."

She shook her head. "But then again, maybe I'm finding it. Maybe I'm rediscovering what matters." She finished her drink and sat on the bed, realizing suddenly that this was where they last made love, almost a year ago. Adam's presence only served to remind her of what she'd lost.

"Watching his morning routines, I used to pretend Doug was a fortune-teller, and that my fate would appear in the tea leaves left at the bottom of his cup. But if he saw my future, he never shared it. Surely, if he had seen all this, he would have told me. Or maybe not. I feel now like I never really knew him."

"You're being unfair," Adam said, his voice sharp with anger.

"I don't care," she said before he left for the last time. "I'm not going back. I won't."

31

THE MEETING WITH Ulrich left Radford frustrated and defeated. He had nothing to go on, nowhere to look, no more interviews. He was standing in the hangar, in the shadow of Pointer 795's ruined engine cowling, when his phone rang. He saw the hotel's number and assumed someone was calling with another urgent plea to allow a cleaning crew to enter his room, so his first instinct was to ignore the call. But on the fourth ring, he yielded.

"There's a man here who's asking to speak with you," the day manager said. The employees long ago dropped their polite customer-service voices when talking to him. He understood how they saw him. Were he not holding the room with a government credit card, in all likelihood a local would've already broken down his door.

"I'm busy," Radford said. "Have him leave a message."

"The man says it's urgent," the manager said. "He says he needs to speak to you in person."

On a different day, Radford wouldn't have cared, but with his investigation at a standstill, with his career in jeopardy, he had nothing to lose.

"Tell him I'll be there in twenty minutes," he said.

COMING FROM THE humid morning air into the cool hotel lobby, Radford wiped the sweat from his face with his shirtsleeve. Three days since his last shower. He'd worn the same khakis for a week. A ketchup stain smudged his shirtfront like a battlefield wound. An oniony scent now wafted from his armpits.

The man sat in the lobby, reading the *Wichita Eagle*. The hotel clerk rolled her eyes at Radford's approach. The man stood awkwardly, dropped the paper, and turned to face Radford.

"I'm Charlie Radford."

"Is there somewhere we can talk?" he said without introducing himself.

Radford gestured toward the bar and the man followed. Except for a woman sipping a cup of coffee, the bar was empty. It wasn't even eleven o'clock. Radford took a booth near the door and invited the man to sit.

"I hope you're not looking for an interview, because that's not going to happen," Radford said. "But I'll listen to you if you'll have a drink with me."

"I'm not comfortable talking about this," the man said.

"Then why are you here?" A waiter approached, and Radford

ordered a gin and tonic. The stranger checked his watch but ordered a beer anyway.

"She's left me no other choice," he said. "But first, I need assurances from you. Nothing can happen to her."

"I don't even know what you're talking about," Radford said.

The waiter brought the drinks to their table. Radford realized he'd been drinking earlier and earlier each day, sometimes, like today, starting before noon. For a man with such a firm grip on reality, he was surprised how he embraced his own free fall. At the end of the week, he'd be publicly humiliated. However debauched and degraded things had become, they were only going to get worse. But he felt he'd cracked through something. Dealing with this investigation, this woman's story, his own descent into obsession, something had snapped. It was as if he could see himself from the outside now. After years of trying to live up to everyone else's version of him, Radford had begun to trust his own instincts. The only problem was, until now, that trust had gotten him nowhere.

Radford watched as the man fiddled with his beer bottle. Whatever he'd come here for, he was clearly having second thoughts. Could this guy really be talking about *her*? Was it possible this man had information on the Falling Woman? Had he really just walked in off the street, into the lobby of the Wichita Holiday Inn, with the precise information Radford needed?

"I need to know that you aren't going to exploit this," the man said. "I loved her. I still love her, but she doesn't have any idea what she's doing anymore."

"Slow down," Radford said. "Start at the beginning. Start by telling me your name."

"My name is Adam Moskowitz," he said. "And I know where the Falling Woman is."

Stunned, Radford reached into his pocket for his notepad, but his pocket was empty. He knew he must have left the notepad in his hotel room, yet another symptom of his ongoing decline. With no alternative, he began scribbling notes onto bar napkins. Adam spoke fast. Before long, Radford was on his fifth napkin.

Adam explained that he and the woman had worked together. That they'd fallen in love and had an affair. He explained that she still possessed a strange power over him. "I don't act rationally around her," he said. He had known that she was going to California, knew what flight she was on, knew the plane blew up. He watched the news, saw the footage of the burned and shattered plane. "And then she called me," Adam said. "Two days after the accident. My phone rang and it was her."

"What did you think?" Radford asked.

"I thought it was a goddamn joke," Adam said.

Some small part of Radford didn't want this story to be true. Some tiny corner of his obsession preferred uncertainty, doubt, the mystery of it all. Yet now it appeared that the shades were about to be thrown open, and everything illuminated. Was he ready for that?

He put the drink down and tried to focus. Adam told him how she asked him to come to Wichita to get her. And though he doubted the truth of what she said, Adam booked a flight to Kansas City, rented a car, and drove toward the hospital. "As I approached the hospital, I saw the crowds outside and realized that something incredible had happened."

Radford reached for more napkins. He tried not to judge the fact that this man admitted to cheating on his wife. He tried to separate his feelings about what they'd done with his need to find this woman.

"But now she won't go home. She's not seeing this thing clearly. I've tried and tried to convince her she has to contact her family at least, but she's not listening to reason." Adam took a sip of his beer. "I don't want to betray her like this, but I don't have a choice. First, I need you to agree to a few terms."

Radford listened while Adam outlined the framework of his terms, which included the stipulation that she could not be charged with any crime, and that she had the right to refuse to cooperate.

"The NTSB isn't a law enforcement agency," Radford said. "Besides, she's committed no crime that I can see."

The waiter came by and offered to bring another round, but almost surprising himself, Radford declined. He needed to be clearheaded.

"She won't go home," Adam said. "She's been very sick. She has pancreatic cancer, Mr. Radford. She's not going to beat it, and I think she wants to disappear. To go off into the woods and live out her remaining days. But she has a family. I can't stop thinking about her daughters."

"What's her name?" Radford asked, trying not to reveal his excitement.

"I need you to understand," Adam said, "there's a lot at stake here. She will be exposed. Frankly, our affair will be too, which means that a lot of people we both love will be hurt."

"I need to talk to her. I need her name. There are seven families still holding out hope."

"I'm not sure I can do this," Adam said. "I thought I could. I came all the way out here to find you. But I love her, Mr. Radford. I don't know if I can betray her."

He didn't doubt the man's sincerity, but he wondered about his character, and this was still a negotiation. Radford didn't want to yield his advantage by revealing his own desperation.

"I'm not selling her out. I will never go to the press. If she decides to come forward, if she decides to do what's right and come home, then that will be her choice." Adam stared at Radford. "You have to promise me that."

"I'm not playing games here," Radford said. "I need a name. There's a world of people out there wondering who the hell this woman is. This whole thing has been a media circus from the start."

Adam fiddled with his beer and seemed uncertain about what to say or do next. He looked at Radford, at his watch, at his phone, and then up at the television above the bar. Radford waited patiently, not wanting to provoke the man, not wanting to say the wrong thing and turn him away.

"Her name is Erin Geraghty," he finally said. A great weight seemed to fall from his shoulders. The man visibly slouched in the chair. "She's staying at my hunting cabin in Virginia. If you go there, you'll find her."

Radford recognized the name immediately, third on the list of seven passengers who fit the profile of the Falling Woman. Hearing it spoken out loud felt like a shot of ice to his spine. He wrote the address of the cabin on a napkin. He was too stunned to feel anything at that moment, too shocked to register what the man was telling him.

He pressed Adam further, asking for more details, but he got nothing.

"I have to catch a flight back to D.C. in two hours," he said. "I've told you more than enough. I've been half out of my mind since this started. Find her. End this."

Adam paid for their drinks and left Radford sitting alone in the bar, the ice melting in his drink. For a moment, he was paralyzed, unable to move or think.

Twenty minutes later, he'd showered, shaved, donned a fresh pair of khakis, and was on his way back to the hangar. He failed to notice the blue Chevy that followed him out of the hotel parking lot. Had he been paying more attention, he might have seen the car trailing him all the way to the base. He might also have noticed the woman from the bar, the same woman whose drink he bought a week ago, the same woman sipping coffee that morning. Now that woman pointed a telephoto lens at his car as he drove onto the base.

ULRICH AND ELLSWORTH turned when Radford entered the office. It was just after one on Monday afternoon.

"I need a travel voucher," he said.

"Abso-fucking-lutely not," Ellsworth said. "If I have to put up with this nonsense, then the Sasquatch hunter does too."

"Shut up, Shep," Radford said. "I'm done listening to you."

Ulrich pounded his desk.

"Enough," Ulrich said. "What are you talking about, Charlie."

A surge of adrenaline made it hard for him to breathe. He hated showing any hint of fear in front of Ellsworth, but his legs pulsed and threatened to buckle. He hadn't wanted to hit anyone this badly since Wendy told him about her abusive ex-boyfriend.

"I just got a lead," Radford said. "A solid lead. I think I found her."

"Sit down," Ulrich said.

"This cocksucker gets a free pass from the investigation," Ellsworth said, "and you let him come in here and demand a travel voucher?"

"You're out of line, Shep," Ulrich said. "You've been out of line since day one. Let's start acting like goddamn professionals around here. We don't have time for this childish crap."

Radford hoped that Ellsworth would take the hint and step out of the office, but Shep didn't move.

"I have new information," Radford said. "From a credible source."

"Sweet Jesus, tell me you have a name," Ulrich said, folding his hands into prayer.

"Not a name," he said. He wasn't going to tell them everything, not yet. He had to see her first, had to verify that this information was true. "I need to run this down. I need to go see."

"I'm not inclined to send you off on a wild-goose chase this close to the hearing," Ulrich said. "We are in an all-hands-on-deck situation here."

"This could be the break we've needed," Radford said.

Ulrich shook his head. "I need more than that. Shep isn't

wrong. We've granted you an awful lot of leeway. And so far, your results have been less than stellar."

Radford had no intention of revealing the source of his new information. Adam provided enough details, he seemed credible, and it was clear he was conflicted about coming forward. Radford believed his story.

"Look, I have nothing to add at this point," Radford said. "But I might soon if you give me the voucher."

"You don't belong here," Ellsworth said. "Cut him loose, Gordo. Earn your pay for once."

"If I want your thoughts, Shep, I'll ask for them," Ulrich said. "Charlie, I can't let you go. Not without more information. I can't chip into the budget so you can satisfy an itch."

No one trusted him anymore. All the investigators had backed away from him because of this story. No one wanted the stink of the Falling Woman on them; no one wanted to be smeared by it, to have their professional reputations tainted. *Oh, were you one of the ones who chased down that crazy story? A woman falling out of the sky!* Radford understood such reluctance. Until this morning, he'd even shared it.

"I have a location," Radford said. "I know where the woman is."

"There is no fucking woman." Ellsworth shot up, coming quickly across the room toward Radford until the two men were face-to-face. "And every goddamn day you keep going on like this means we're one day further from solving the whole thing. A plane exploded. People died. And you're out chasing fairy tales." He put his hand on Radford's shoulder.

Radford smacked Ellsworth's hand away and pushed him

backward, but the man came right back at him, his body braced for violence. Ulrich quickly moved between them and then shoved Ellsworth out of the office.

"I'm sorry," Ulrich said. "That shouldn't have happened. You can file an incident report."

"I don't give a shit about him."

Radford realized he was shaking, and made a conscious effort to calm himself.

"What do you need?" Ulrich said.

"I need to resolve this," Radford said. "I need to run this one out. That's why you put me on this case, isn't it?"

"But I can't let you just disappear. That will send the wrong signal."

"I'm going," he said. "I'll take leave if I have to. I'm doing no good here. I'm holed up in my room like a goddamn psychopath. The maids don't even knock anymore. You want this too. You want me up on that stage with answers. I think I can get them, but you have to let me go."

Ulrich shook his head, but the image of the hostile hearing room must have been enough to sway him. He held out three fingers.

"Three days, Charlie," he said. "I'm serious. You have three days. The hearing is Friday. I want you back in town by Thursday night. With answers. With a name. Don't tell me you couldn't find her. Don't come back and ask for more time. This is going down on Friday, and you will be up there, with me, in that hearing room."

Once outside, Radford spotted Lucy Masterson. With her were two women, both wearing dark coats and sunglasses. He remembered that Lucy would be conducting the rescheduled interviews with the pilots' widows today. He wanted to introduce himself, to offer condolences, to look each of them in the eye and promise that they'd solve this mystery, that in time, somehow, all of it would make sense. He also wanted to share his news with Lucy. But there simply wasn't time. He sped away as the three women entered the hangar.

Radford didn't notice that the same blue car followed him back to the hotel. He went to his room to pack. Time was moving fast. He had a purpose now, and he was eager to get going. But there were delays getting his travel approved, and Radford missed the last flight out of Wichita. He would not leave until Tuesday morning now, precious hours wasted on red tape.

In the early morning, on his way out of the hotel, he removed the hanging Do Not Disturb tag from his door. In the lobby, he asked for a shuttle to the airport.

"You heading home?" It was the woman from the bar. She was sitting near the hotel's sliding doors, casually reading a newspaper.

"Back to D.C.," Radford said. She seemed familiar, friendly. Radford smiled. He tried to place her, to see if she was one of the many investigators now working the case, but nothing came to him.

"Have a nice trip," she said.

32

THE BLUE RIDGE Lanes sign glowed in red neon, even in bright sunshine. The bowling alley had become Erin's office of sorts, with its posted boasts of League Discounts, Kidz Parties!, Friday-Night Karaoke & $2 Pitchers, and Cosmic Bowling. She never bowled, but Blue Ridge Lanes had the only reliable public wireless signal in town. Adam left an old laptop, and it worked well enough for what she needed today. Erin ordered a coffee from the bar and sat near the pool tables, away from the overweight and elderly men in rayon shirts who risked herniated discs from their efforts to knock down pins.

That morning, she went online to her hometown newspaper, the *Capital Gazette*. Adam's email had directed her to the link. In the body of his email, he wrote only three words: "I'm so sorry."

On the web page, her family posed on the front porch of their home. She was struck by Doug's stern expression, his gray cardigan sweater and slacks. He looked handsome. She was always attracted to him, but for the first time, she genuinely missed him. Tory leaned on his shoulder, head down, her mascara running just a bit from her eyes. Claire stood to the side, somber, stoic, aloof, and yet so very pretty.

From the depths of her heart, she wanted to comfort them, to tell them all that their lives were better this way. With her gone. With that finality.

The caption beneath the photo reported that a local family was holding a memorial service for their deceased wife and mother. A short quote from Doug followed: "We appreciate the outpouring of support and love from our Annapolis friends and neighbors." She imagined him rehearsing those lines before he spoke them. Even his grief felt modulated.

She clicked to a photograph of herself, precancer, smiling, her head tilted to the side. It had been taken when she and Doug went to a wedding on the Eastern Shore. She remembered making love to him that night in their hotel, one of the last times they did. Was she sleeping with Adam then? The past already blurred. The woman in the photo looked like a stranger.

The short article went on to say that the family requested privacy in this difficult time. An adjacent article speculated on "The Falling Woman," a title she found ridiculous. *Falling* was only one small part of what she did that night. The oddness of juxtaposing those two stories in the same paper struck her, the way the one teased at the other. What did the girls think? What about Doug?

She knew he was far too pragmatic to place any faith in such a fantastical story. But the girls? Had he convinced them?

When she became sick, Doug fought fiercely on her behalf, but she understood he was fighting her disease, the insult that introduced such chaos in their lives. He fought for a return to stability. He fought for clarity. For Doug, news of her death must've been a clean razor cut through the skin of his confusion. Such clarity could never be threatened by something as preposterous as a woman falling from the sky.

In the obituary, Doug's careful prose excised emotion. His sterile words were precise but cold:

Erin (Walsh) Geraghty was born in Worcester, Massachusetts, in 1969. She attended Holy Name High School and Georgetown University. She graduated from law school at Duke University and passed the bar exam in the state of Maryland. For twenty years, she worked as an attorney at Hawkins, Lemenanger, & Walton, specializing in contracts law. In 1993, she married Doug Geraghty. Their twin daughters, Victoria and Claire, were born in 1998. Erin was an avid runner, a talented gardener, and a loving wife and mother.

Her life reduced to a few lines of text. The facts were all there, but surely she was more than the mere facts. Her life must have had more to it than statistics. She resisted the urge to call the paper and print an amendment. Jesus, Doug. Really? This is what you think of me? She wanted to write him. For a split second, she contemplated returning, not to embrace him but to scream at him one last time for his cold, rational passivity. But then, the girls. What would they think? What would her return do to them?

After Erin's father died, she believed, for a long time, he would come back. She used to awake in the morning and expect to see him downstairs. This went on for months after his death. At times, it felt like he was simply in another room, or the basement, or out of town. Her father's absence felt contingent, reversible, and unreal. His presence radiated long after he was buried. In high school, in college even, she held on to that faint flicker of expectation, not as strong as hope but far sturdier than a fantasy. Maybe she still did. And now, after reading the obituary, after seeing the girls in the *Gazette* family photo, she wondered if her daughters would feel that way too.

She replied to Adam's email: "What the hell are you sorry for?"

33

WHEN RADFORD LANDED at Dulles Tuesday morning, a steady rain was falling. He deplaned in Concourse B but took the AeroTrain over to Concourse D. He wanted to pass by the gate from which Pointer 795 departed. The airport was crowded, and he didn't have much time, but this stop felt important. An odd flicker of hope had slipped into him, an unfamiliar optimism.

He spotted the sign for the gate ahead. There was still so much work to do, still so much he didn't know. He tried to imagine the people who'd walked this same hallway on the night Pointer 795 departed. Tried to picture their lives running out ahead of them. They deserved answers. Standing by the otherwise ordinary gate, D28, he tried to find some context, some meaning for all this.

But nothing at the gate indicated what had occurred there.

Travelers hurried past. On a glossy poster behind glass, the smiling faces of a tanned couple in swimsuits advertised sixty-nine-dollar fares to the Bahamas.

He resisted the urge to stop and eat. He had to stay focused now because he thought he could see the end of his investigation. He didn't know what he'd do if he found the woman, much less how he'd convince her to come forward. For that matter, he didn't know what he'd say in three days at the public hearing, but for the first time since the whole thing began, he had formed a plan that should enable him to reach the end. Above his head, tiny porcelain cranes directed him toward the baggage claim.

Outside, the bustle of the big airport felt so different from what he'd left behind in Wichita. Here crowds of people waited for rides. Taxis and buses passed. He wanted to call Wendy, wanted to stop by their condo to surprise her. But he knew that he needed to finish this first, to find this woman. No part of him wanted to hide from his wife, but right now, he had no other choice. First, he needed to get over to the NTSB headquarters, check in, and grab a vehicle.

"It's criminal that you aren't running this investigation," he said an hour later, peeking his head into Dickie Gray's office door.

"Mr. Radford," Gray said warmly. "Come to pay tribute to the village elder?"

Radford could only imagine the insult, being left off the team during a major investigation, left behind to sift through paperwork and mishaps of little import.

"We sure could use you out there," Radford said.

"Fieldwork is a young man's game," he said. "Besides, I've never been fond of the prairies."

"Ulrich and Ellsworth are tearing each other apart."

"The great lightning debate," Gray said.

"The theory makes sense, but the evidence isn't breaking their way."

"Do you have time for a drink?" Gray asked.

"I'm afraid not," Radford said. "I need to get on the road before traffic starts."

"Such urgency. Shouldn't you be preparing for Friday's hearing?"

Radford hesitated. How much should he tell this man? He wanted to share his news, share his excitement, but he didn't want to face more ridicule.

"I have a lead," Radford said. "On the woman."

"Oh, dear god," Gray said. "Please tell me you aren't mixed up in that foolishness. What are they calling her? Waltzing Matilda?"

A bolt of shame and doubt shot through Radford's chest.

"You told me to follow the evidence. You taught me to ask the right questions. Well, in spite of everything, I've been asking those questions. I've taken enough shit already. I think this all may be true. There may really be a 'Falling Woman.' Will you just look at my initial report?"

"Charlie," Gray said lightly, but with a hesitant edge to his voice, "I thought I'd taught you better than this."

"Will you please look? I only have a few minutes. I need to turn in some paperwork before I get going."

Gray motioned with his hands, but Radford was reluctant to leave his files—they might get lost among the other stacks on Gray's desk.

"She may have hit the trees coming down, and the barn roof was rotting, and the hay was three feet thick. There was soft mud below the hay."

Gray shook his head but opened the first file. "Where is she?"

Radford felt safe around this man, in contrast to how he felt in Kansas. For a moment, he was tempted to invite Gray along for the ride, but the next few hours were filled with so much uncertainty. He told Gray where he was going, and what he hoped to do when he arrived.

"This kind of thing has happened before," Radford said.

"I know," Gray said. "I've done some research. But listen to me. Be careful with this. You've stepped into a shit storm here. This isn't about investigative work. Just be careful. Too many eyes are watching."

As Radford left Gray's office, a department head waved him down and told him to get up to the ninth floor.

"The Director knows you're here," the man said. "She wants to talk."

Carol Wilson became the NTSB director six months earlier, and so far, Radford had not been within fifty feet of her. She had come to Wichita a few times, but he'd only seen her from a distance, usually with a group of reporters in tow. Wilson was a political appointee, with no investigative experience, but so far, she'd done well. She had a reputation for being scrupulous, keen, and direct, and she listened and learned. But Pointer 795 was her first real test, and such scrutiny often brought out the dark side of politicians.

Radford tucked in his shirt and swiped at his hair. When he

arrived upstairs, a secretary asked him to wait outside the executive suite. He didn't welcome the delay, but such proximity to power was rare, and he intended to make the most of it.

Twenty minutes later, the secretary directed Radford from the waiting area to a smaller inner office. The thick oak doors opened into a large anteroom, with a pristine blue couch, hardwood floors, and two polished chairs. On the eggshell walls hung framed photographs with thick matting, pictures of aircraft in flight, trains, buses, plus one of Wilson shaking hands with President Obama. Bright sun streamed through windows that faced north, toward the National Mall and the city's classic bone-white architecture. He was touching the inner core of power. A different secretary offered him water and produced a bottle of mineral water. He knew he should feel more nervous, should be thinking about how he'd address the director. But instead, he felt light, almost at ease. His mind was elsewhere, thinking about the work ahead and how he'd approach the Falling Woman once he found her.

"The director's available now," the secretary said. She knocked lightly on the oak door and then opened it slowly.

Carol Wilson stood when he entered and walked around her elegant mahogany desk to shake his hand. Her skin felt cool, almost delicate, but her handshake was firm. She was tall, lean, attractive in a rather standoffish way. Dark hair, strong eyes, a pretty smile. She possessed charisma, an almost palpable charm. Within a few seconds, Radford felt outmatched. She invited him to sit.

"Catch me up," she said.

He wasn't sure how much she knew, so he talked at first about how they'd stalled with body identification. "So many of the passengers in the blast zone were severely burned," he said. It seemed strange to talk so openly about such violent, intimate details.

"The families are applying pressure," she said. "And the insurance companies are having a field day with this story. They have a right to some closure. How many possible matches are there among the unidentified bodies?"

"Seven," he said.

"So, we still haven't moved that number?"

He shook his head.

"I'm preparing a portfolio for each family," he said, "with painstaking details about what has been done, what's being done, and what will continue to be done to sort out the possible matches among the still-missing victims."

It was a lie. He'd had no plan to make a portfolio until the words came out of his mouth. For the first time, he felt an uneasy kinship with Ulrich, as if he understood the man's behavior a bit better. Understood the need to please, the desire for approval.

"No amount of data," she said, "no assurances or speeches or direct access to my cell phone will make up for the fact that more than two weeks have passed and we still don't have the name of the woman who was taken to the hospital."

She was sharp, direct, just like he'd heard.

"Mr. Radford, what did you think when you were reassigned?"

"I thought this was a goat fuck," Radford said. The words came out of him before he had time to pull them back.

Wilson laughed.

"I know that you're under a lot of pressure," she said. "But it's going to get worse until we resolve this open issue. We need something concrete before Friday."

"I have a lead," he said. "I'm on my way now to check it out. If it's true, if this information pans out, we will have answers very soon."

"I believe in transparency," Wilson said. "My father was an air force pilot. He was shot down in North Vietnam. For six months, the air force wouldn't tell us anything. I won't run my shop that way. You have complete agency support on this, Mr. Radford. Whatever you need. But this woman, whoever she is, can't have just disappeared. Find her, but keep me in the loop."

Radford took this last remark as his cue to leave, so he stood up. But the director wasn't done yet.

"Don't fuck me on this," she said. "Whatever her story turns out to be, bring her in. Get us her name, and you can stand up there on Friday and be justifiably proud."

"May I ask you a question?" he said.

She nodded, already reaching for a pen and the files on her desk, moving on to the next problem.

"What happened to your father?"

She glanced up at him and put down the pen.

"He was dead, Mr. Radford. The air force knew within hours of his plane going down. He'd crossed the wrong line on a map, and so they held back that information. For six months, I held on to false hope."

She didn't shake his hand when he left.

On the elevator, he wondered about the term "agency support." The words felt double-edged, suggesting cooperation but also retractability. Agency support meant that as long as they liked what he was doing, they'd have his back.

Radford stopped back by Gray's office to gather his notes and hear what the man had to say.

"It's pretty thin," Gray said. "Speculative at best."

"What choice do I have?" he said.

"If you find her, if her story is true, you'll look like a genius. But if this is all a hoax, well . . ."

Radford knew the risks, though it didn't matter. Soon he'd be on the road, on the way to a small town in the Shenandoah Valley, where, if his instincts were right, he was going to find the woman who fell from the sky, and then he would end this, once and for all.

34

THE TOWN APPEARED squalid in some places, in others quaint. The tiny Main Street shops had begun to decorate for Memorial Day. Red-white-and-blue bunting hung from shop windows and over doors. It seemed like a good place to spend a holiday weekend, away from D.C. with its crowds and constant buzz.

Radford remembered the smell of white pines from his childhood. He hadn't been to the mountains in years, and the instantaneous familiarity—of light, of sound, and space—surprised him as he drove through the town. He had grown up in a place much like this, and he understood the kind of people who lived here, which he hoped would yield an advantage. If Adam's story proved to be true, and if this woman really was hiding out, she shouldn't be hard to find. At least that was his hope. If Erin Geraghty was here, he wasn't leaving without her.

The post office seemed like a good place to start, but he took a cautious approach. One thing about small towns: they didn't welcome interrogations from outsiders, especially investigators from the federal government. Sitting behind the counter in the post office was a heavyset woman in a puckered blue-denim postal shirt. She smiled at him as he approached the counter.

"Getting ready to close up, hon," she said.

He asked if she knew a place where he could grab an early dinner.

She suggested he try the restaurant up the street. "Sandy's is open," she said. The woman spoke with a thick drawl, something that always surprised him. He was only a few hours outside the D.C. suburbs, but it seemed like an entirely different world. He thanked the woman and headed toward the restaurant on foot.

The steady, piercing chirp of frogs sang from the fields. As a boy, Radford had loved days like this the most, when the first spring heat wave hinted of the long summer days to come. He thought of his older brother Patrick and how they would ride their bikes over to Swan Creek. Sometimes the Miller girls would be there, swimming in their cutoffs and bikini tops. Patrick would climb the oak tree that stretched over the water, attracting the attention of the girls. Then he'd hurl himself off the tree and jump toward the center of the creek. In those days, young Charlie stayed on the shore, always too shy to take off his shirt, too concerned about appearances to run around in his boxers like his brother did. Every part of him envied his brother's freedom and confidence. And he had to admit to himself that little had changed. There were still many things he lacked the courage to do.

Would finding this woman, and bringing her in, would that

make him stronger? Would he prove them all wrong back in Kansas? Would Dickie Gray be there to shake his hand? Because he was doing this whole thing on his own, absorbing all the risk, he hoped he'd also receive all the credit when it was done. That at least would be a bit of redemption.

He was sweating as he approached the restaurant. A cowbell jingled above the door when he entered. An older man stood behind the bar reading the paper.

"What you drinking, captain," the bartender said.

"How are your Bloody Marys?" Radford asked.

"Best in the commonwealth."

Radford nodded and peeked at the menu. He didn't notice the woman who entered, didn't see her place her purse on the bar or reach for a menu from a stack on the corner. But when he glanced over and spotted her, he knew who this woman was: Erin Geraghty. The Falling Woman.

He resisted the urge to rush over and grab her.

After two weeks and three days of searching, after days and nights of hopelessness and ridicule he'd endured, she stood no more than ten feet away, carrying no sign of all that had happened. Panic swept over him. The moment felt surreal. Try as he might, he couldn't reconcile the utter ordinariness of her appearance, of her demeanor. To steady himself, he took a sip of his drink, and nearly choked on the spice.

Casually dressed in jeans, a loose sweatshirt, and with a base-ball cap on her head, she ordered a beer. He did note that there was something distinctly patrician about her carriage, something that set her apart from the locals, the way she held herself at the bar with an erect posture, the way she gripped the glass. She was thin, too thin, he thought, and a bit pale. Her hair was very short. His hand trembled. He'd come all this way to find out if she was real and there she was.

Now what? He had no idea. All along, Radford had expected the whole Falling Woman story to be a hoax. Even as he found evidence to suggest that something like that really could have happened, even after Adam walked into the Wichita Holiday Inn and gave him a name—a verifiable name, one of the seven on his list—even after all that, he still hadn't expected it to be real. Hadn't expected her to be real. But there she was, close enough to reach out and touch. Now, of course, he had to make sure her story was true.

Be careful, he thought, don't draw her attention. But he couldn't stop staring at her. Erin Geraghty. A hundred times he'd studied her picture. Excitement surged through him like electricity.

When the bartender returned, Radford ordered a beer. He didn't want another drink, but he needed to blend into the background. Slowly, his investigator instincts returned. He noted the time and marked it down in his notebook.

Behind the bar, a mirror held half of her reflection, enough for Radford to study her without being obvious. Absolutely, the woman sitting at the bar was Erin Geraghty. She was alive!

But an encounter in a bar? Her sudden appearance was jarring, unexpected, like lightning out of a blue sky. Radford barely touched his drink, just watched as she casually flipped through a book. She seemed so calm, while his pulse was racing.

What had he expected? Something much more dramatic,

certainly. Nothing about the woman at the bar stood out, nothing to indicate that the world was clamoring for her story, her name, her whereabouts. What was she doing here, out in the open, acting as if nothing had really happened to her?

Oddly, he thought of his father. Every year, when his dad called to say thanks for the customary Christmas gift—one hundred dollars' worth of Powerball tickets—Martin would say, "Charlie, if I win this fucking thing, you won't see me for a month. I'll go rent a cabin in the woods and not tell a soul." Protect your interests, that was his father's point. Maybe that's why this woman had come here, to let the dust settle, to work out her plan. Was she collecting offers for a book? Waiting for a movie deal? But if that was the case, surely word would have leaked. And why would Adam have offered her up? And why was she sitting ten feet away from him now, drinking a beer and reading a book, seemingly without a care in the world?

Radford didn't want to confront her here. Obviously, they knew her in this place. She had allies. He glanced at his watch, asked for the check, settled up his tab, and went outside. But he had no intention of going far. He noticed a side door near a large dumpster. He'd have to watch that door too, so she didn't slip away.

He sat on a bench outside at the patio bar, trying to formulate a plan. His car was a good ten-minute walk away, and she might bolt if he went to retrieve it. He couldn't risk it. Though if she'd been this easy to find, what was the risk? He figured that whatever else this woman was up to, she was settled here for a while at least.

The minutes crawled past. He wanted to call Wendy, to share

this incredible news with someone, but he'd neglected to tell her he was in town.

As he waited, time seemed to stop. The longer he sat there, the more he questioned his judgment. He should've just approached the woman in the bar and taken his chances. Ten minutes passed, a half hour; the shadows lengthened around him.

Sandy's parking lot began to fill as the dinner crowd arrived. Radford kept an eye on the front door, but the woman still didn't emerge. Was she a lush? How long would she stay in there drinking? An insect bit his ankle, and he shifted to another spot amidst the trees. That was when he spotted that the side door to the restaurant was now open.

"God damn it," he said as another bug bit into his flesh, this time on his neck. She may already have left, and he'd missed her.

He crossed the street and reentered the restaurant. He expected her to be gone, and sure enough, the woman was no longer at the bar. He walked up to the bartender, and this time pulled out his badge and credentials.

"The woman who was sitting over there," Radford said. "I need to talk to her."

The bartender either didn't register the request or was being hostile, because he didn't respond. Radford braced for a fight, but instead, the man put down his drying towel and motioned with his head toward the main dining room. A tray in her hand, an apron wrapped around her waist, Erin Geraghty was taking dinner orders.

"She works here?" Radford said.

He stood near the hostess stand at the front of the restaurant and watched. After a few minutes, he'd attracted the attention of the other waitresses and a few diners, but Erin hadn't seen him yet. He studied her as she delivered a plate of food to a table of three silver-haired women, pausing a moment to chat with them. She was attractive, despite her frail appearance and close-cropped hair. She had almost flawless skin, strong legs, a pretty smile. But she was incredibly thin too. Her arms, her wrists, what he could see of her ankles beneath her jeans, looked like skin wrapped around bone. And the haircut seemed imposed, not chosen. Try as he might, he couldn't picture her on the plane. He couldn't imagine her falling from the sky. As she walked across the restaurant, he kept trying to piece together the unfathomable circumstances that brought her here. She didn't look like someone who could fall down a set of stairs and be okay, much less come screaming out of the sky, crash through trees, a barn roof, a hayloft, onto the earth, and not only survive but walk away.

The bartender kept a close eye on him, as did most of the wait-staff. Erin Geraghty took two more orders, talking for a long time with a large group seated in the middle of the restaurant. Then a waitress approached her and whispered in her ear. Radford's pulse raced again. He saw the woman's expression change as she glanced around the restaurant before spotting him standing by the kitchen doors.

He stood still, though internally he was ready to give chase. But she didn't run. She didn't look for help, or panic, or turn white. She smiled at her customers, continued to write down their orders, and slowly moved toward him.

"I'd rather not do this here," she said. Her voice was pleasant, her demeanor easy and light. Professional, he thought, like she had just apologized for the slow service and promised to be back to get his order.

"I'm not leaving," he said. "I don't want to make a scene, but you need to understand that I'm not letting you out of my sight."

She smiled. If he thought he was intimidating her with his authority, he realized quickly that was not the case.

"Well," she said, "I work until nine. You can sit at the bar or you can come back in two hours. Tuesday night is the meatloaf special. We always pack 'em in."

Technically, he lacked the authority to do much. He couldn't arrest her because she'd broken no laws. He had a legal right to question any witness involved in the accident but no enforcement authority. If a witness didn't show up, if a passenger refused to cooperate, there was little that Radford could do. She didn't have to speak to him. He couldn't drag her out the front door.

"Where then?" he asked.

She wrote down her address on an order slip and tore the sheet off her pad. Her calm demeanor, her casual attitude about the whole thing confused him. She handed the paper to him.

"I'd prefer to do this in the morning," she said. "But I'm guessing that's not an option."

Radford took the paper, glanced at the address, and shook his head. "I'll be there at nine."

"Well, I won't be home until nine thirty," she said. "I don't have a car."

"I'll pick you up," he said.

"I don't get into cars with strangers," she said. Her tone was playful, lightly mocking, almost flirtatious. What the hell was her angle? With that, she stepped into the kitchen.

He waited a few more minutes near the bar. If she was nervous, if she feared the worst, if she planned a mad-dash escape, nothing about her behavior indicated it. He watched her for a while, but nothing changed. He glanced at the address again and typed it into his phone. The location was nearby.

"You ordering anything?" the bartender asked.

Radford waved his hand and moved toward the door. Outside, he wanted to call Ulrich. He wanted to call Dickie Gray. The urge to share the news was overwhelming. But he still had work to do, and alerting the agency now might backfire. As he walked back toward his car, he knew the only person he could tell, the only one he trusted, was Wendy. She answered on the third ring.

"Where have you been?" she asked. "I called the hotel. I called your cell. I was so worried."

"I'm in Virginia," he said, unsure how to proceed.

"What?" she said, a hint of surprise, maybe anger too, rising in her voice. "You're home?"

"No," he said. "Listen, I'll explain later. I found her. I found the woman."

"You found who?" Wendy asked.

"The Falling Woman. She's alive, Wendy. She's real and I found her."

35

As soon as Radford left, Erin asked Sandy for an advance on her next paycheck. Her only thought was that she had to flee. But where would she go? She had no car, no viable plan, hardly any money. For an instant, she imagined grabbing Adam's tent and camp stove and heading out into the woods. But how long could she last?

Without a question, Sandy brought her an envelope with cash.

"You okay, hon?" Sandy asked.

"I may not be coming in tomorrow," she said.

"Why don't you let Hazard take you home?" she said. "You shouldn't be going alone."

"I'll be okay," she said. "Whatever happens, I've made peace with my choices."

She was tired and was having trouble trying to think straight. Pedaling back in the dark, she tried to reconcile the contradictions of it all.

Once at the cabin, she sat on the porch waiting for Radford. Since the crash, time had slowed down, sped up, gone around in circles. Only in the past few days had she started to feel normal. She thought, for the first time really, how much she missed the girls. Running from them was something she could never fully understand. Had she somehow abandoned her faith in love? How had she so callously severed the bonds with her family?

When Claire was in high school, she hit a rough patch. Depression. Anxiety. Eating issues. Erin watched as this sweet, tender, serious girl, who used to embrace life, turned into a gloomy, hollowed-out shell who wouldn't leave her room. Erin suggested they start running together. On the weekends, she would set an alarm, don her shorts and shoes, and then go quietly into Claire's room to wake her daughter. They'd stretch in the front yard before the sun rose. How long did this go on? A few months maybe. No more than a dozen or so runs. But Erin loved the sound of her daughter's running shoes slapping the pavement. She loved those quiet miles along the river. She loved the closeness. They didn't even talk that much; mostly, they ran in silence. When they got home, Erin would make butter toast and carry it on a tray to Claire, who began to eat again, eventually began to smile. Erin didn't remember when they stopped running together, but she knew she'd done something important, something that mattered. Of all the things in her life, those quiet, intense hours with Claire stood out as among the most important.

Sitting on the porch waiting for Radford to appear, she had almost convinced herself she was ready to go home.

Yet another contradictory force gnawed away at her. It was the certainty of her death. But she wasn't afraid anymore. It was as if fear had been vanquished. All fear. She wasn't afraid of dying. She wasn't afraid to live out her remaining days on her terms. Liberated from fear, all that remained was acceptance.

It had started to rain when she heard tires crunch on the gravel driveway. Frogs croaked from the creek behind the cabin. The headlights shone on the porch and the car stopped.

36

WHATEVER THE HELL this woman's angle was, she'd done a damn good job at staying gone. It seemed like the whole world had been searching for her, yet somehow, she'd just slipped away. Radford knew such a feat required not only cunning but also patience, support, and a great deal of will. He'd be straight with her, transparent. That's how he'd start.

He approached the porch slowly. A steady light rain released forest smells. Lightning flashed in the distance, too far away to hear thunder. Whip-poor-wills sang in the woods. He understood why a place like this would be appealing.

No reason to startle her, he told himself. He would knock gently.

"Do you want a drink?" she called from the porch. Then she lit a candle and placed it on a table next to her.

"Yes," he said, unsure of himself as he approached.

"I just have wine," she said.

Radford stood near the porch. He heard the gurgle of wine being poured into a glass.

"You can come up," she said. "Get out of the rain. I don't bite."

Radford wore his blue NTSB windbreaker. He hadn't worn it in days, but he had it on now, despite the heat and humidity. He was here as an agent of the government and could no longer hide that. But now, the blue coat and its implications of power, of official business, felt burdensome, like somehow, he'd violated protocol.

"Let me try this again," he said. "My name is Charlie Radford. I'm an investigator with the National Transportation Safety Board. Where would you like to begin?"

"My name is Erin Geraghty," she said, "and I think we say cheers."

He sat down and raised his glass.

"Was it Adam?" she asked. Then she shook her head. "Never mind. I don't want to know."

"I have about a thousand questions," he said.

"I'm tired," she said. "I'd prefer if you skipped the caveats and begin."

"What do you remember?" he asked. "What happened on the plane?"

He waited for her to talk. She began by describing the day in general: passengers at the gate, a handsome man on the walkway, a slightly queasy feeling in her gut. "I don't remember much after that," she said. "The medicine made me drowsy. I probably passed out before we took off."

The more she talked, the more he realized he needed some means of getting her story down on paper. He had not come prepared, and regretted letting his emotions get ahead of his work. Still, he couldn't stop her. He asked her about the minutes leading up to the explosion.

"Was anything strange happening? Did you see the captain? Smell fuel or smoke in the cabin?"

"It was bumpy," she said. "People began to make noise. There was a lot of lightning too. The clouds around us were all lit up. It was, oddly, quite beautiful."

He thought of Shep Ellsworth, and how much he would love to hear about the lightning. He let her talk without trying to direct her, asking the next question only when she finished. He listened carefully to every word, and quickly realized she was funny, smart, serious, and charming. But he also knew that very little of what she told him would help with the accident investigation. However, when she began to talk about the moment the plane came apart, and then said she didn't want to linger there, he pressed her anyway.

"What happened next?" he asked. "What do you remember?"

"I'm tired," she said. "I need to sleep. I need to take a shower and get to bed."

Radford hadn't touched the wine, and he had at least fifty more questions he needed to ask her. But right now, of primary importance, he had to convince her to return to D.C. If they left soon, he could have her back in D.C. tonight. He'd get her a hotel room. In the morning, he'd interview her on the record and tell Carol Wilson to call a press conference for the Wednesday evening news cycle. He would call Ulrich on the drive in, alert the duty officer at L'Enfant Plaza. He could do all that in a day and be back in Wichita on Thursday, as Ulrich had demanded, to prepare for Friday's hearing. He wasn't entirely sure how it would all go down, but he felt the gears beginning to grind.

"You can sleep in my car," he said. "Grab a pillow and blankets."

"I'm not leaving with you," she said.

"You have to understand," he said. "This doesn't end with me taking down your story and you disappearing into the woods."

"I do understand," she said. "But I also know you have no legal authority. I've broken no laws, done nothing wrong. I've done my research. What you decide to do with all this, how you decide to spin it back in D.C., that's your business. But I'm not leaving until I'm ready. Not with you or anyone else."

How far could he push her? She knew the law; he couldn't arrest her, but he could have her held on a material witness order. Though technically no one had found one piece of evidence to indicate criminal proceedings with Pointer 795, he could stretch it. The investigation remained open and ongoing.

"I'm not leaving here without you," he said. He tried to sound firm but not angry. The woman was an experienced lawyer and no doubt on firmer legal footing than he was.

"That's your choice," she said. "But if you set foot on this porch after I say good night, you're trespassing. And I'll call the sheriff. He likes me. I bring him extra gravy for his meatloaf."

Had he really expected this to be easy? This woman had unplugged from the world. Why did he think that finding her, and talking to her, he could suddenly convince her to plug back in? She stood and picked up the wine bottle and the two glasses. The rain had stopped and the moon was above the cabin, glowing in the muggy evening sky.

"I don't understand your plan here," he said.

"I don't have a plan," she said. "I told you what I know. What I remember. I need to sleep on this. I need to unpack what's happening. I'm not going to run, Mr. Radford. I'll be at Sandy's tomorrow. You can come by there and we can talk. Please," she said, her voice softer now. "Please don't do anything tonight. Please don't call anyone. Can you make me that promise?"

Reluctantly, he agreed. He wouldn't call anyone. He wouldn't report in. And with that, Erin Geraghty turned and went inside the cabin. A bolt slid through a lock behind the door. Radford stood on the porch a few moments longer and then stepped off, heading back toward his car. The prospect of spending the entire night staked out in front of her cabin didn't seem pleasant, but he had little choice. He hadn't booked a hotel.

What had she told him, exactly? What had she revealed? Nothing more than what he already knew, or what he could surmise. General truths. Nothing specific about the flight, about what she may have witnessed. But he'd found her, the Falling Woman, and he could now prove to everyone involved that his search hadn't been in vain. Maybe a good night's sleep would bring her to her senses, make her see the futility of her situation. In the end, whatever she decided, however she chose to act mattered very little.

Seven families were waiting. Soon, six of those families would have to be contacted, each of them then giving up hope. He'd be the one making those calls. But Erin's family? She'd be back from the dead. A wave of exhaustion hit him. The night was warm, but the rain and the humidity had made the car feel chilly. He pulled on a sweatshirt and climbed into the passenger seat, reclining it as far as it would go.

He thought about what his late mother used to say whenever his father would rant and complain: *Don't worry, Charlie. God works the night shift. In the morning, your problems will look different.* His mother, the eternal optimist. And more often than not, she'd be right. In the morning, his father would have sobered up, and his mother would have cooked breakfast. She was so blindly obedient, so much a coconspirator in the wrack and ruin that was Martin Radford's anger and addiction. Were she still here, what would his mother think and do about all this? She'd pray, that's what she'd do. Find the supernatural explanation. In some ways, it would be easier to believe in miracles, to chalk this story up to angels and divine intervention than to try to piece together the science behind the truth. But Radford needed to make sense of this in the rational world, to understand it on its own terms.

He simply had to bring her back. What she was choosing to do with her personal life, running away from her family, that was of no concern to him. He needed her to get her into a room, to take her formal statement, to get it down on paper, have her sign and verify that statement. He couldn't worry about what happened after, what happened to her. He would take her statement back to Friday's hearing and be able to say that he'd found the woman. What she chose to do, whether to stay out of the spot-light or embrace it, that was not his concern. He'd expose her, but he wasn't responsible for that. Maybe he could buy her some time, help her contact her family so she could make those personal choices privately. The night grew still. A cool breeze carried the smell of the forest. It was past midnight, and he hadn't slept in almost two days. He wouldn't sleep now. His mind still raced.

What would happen after he filed his report? What would he do next? His emotions were shifting, not just about this crazy story but also about his work. He'd been baptized in the fields of Kansas, in the waters of his first major investigation. He'd been tested, and he knew he'd done well. Still, the gnawing inside remained. The work that sometimes felt like everything was turning out to be less than enough. Hadn't that been Gray's message? What did that leave? What would he need to do to quiet the voices? I'm wasting my life, he thought as he finally drifted off to sleep.

Four miles away, a rental car pulled into town. The car drove slowly through the town center, and circled back twice before pulling into the bowling alley parking lot and turning off its head-lights. The car stayed there overnight, inconspicuously parked in the back corner of the parking lot.

RADFORD AWOKE TO knuckles rapping the car window. Erin stood before him in a long bathrobe cinched at the neck. His back hurt and he had a difficult time finding the latch to raise the seat. She held a steaming mug of coffee in her hand. He rolled down the window.

"You're persistent, I'll give you that," she said.

"I have a plan," he said.

"But I told you my plan," she said. She handed the coffee to him.

"I don't need to make a spectacle out of this," he said. "What I need is a detailed statement from you. I need you to answer a questionnaire. I'll play it by the book. Standard accident witness questions. I won't be able to shield your name from this, but you had to know that was inevitable."

She stood near the car with her arms folded. The bathrobe slipped open at the neck, enough to expose the soft curves of her breasts. For the second time, he noticed how pretty she was.

"I don't want to make a statement," she said. "I don't want to answer your questions. Haven't I been through enough?"

"You have," he said. "But there are families out there holding on to false hope. Children who think their mother might still be alive."

"I have children too," she said.

"You're making a choice," he said. "But there are six families other than yours who are still clinging to hope. They have no choice."

"My name will be exposed?"

He nodded and sipped the coffee.

"That was going to happen eventually," he said. "You had to know that. Your family already knows that you are a possible survivor."

"I'll answer your questions," she said. "But that's all I'll agree to at this point. I don't know what comes next for me. Mr. Radford, I'm sick, dying actually, and I don't have much time. I can see nothing good coming out of my return—my family has mourned my death several times over."

Radford realized there was so much he didn't know, so much he might never understand. He told himself not to let those things get in the way. He reminded himself: don't be smarter than the evidence. He had a plan of sorts, now that she'd agreed in part. She'd at least answer the standard questions. He'd have to let go of the rest.

Radford swallowed a sip of coffee and looked around at the cabin and the forest.

"It's beautiful here," he said. "I can appreciate why a person might want to come to a place like this and never leave."

She glanced around and nodded.

"It's funny," she said. "I never liked being alone before. I always had to have people around me. But then I came here and just listened to what the world had to say. Does that make any sense?"

"Something extraordinary happened to you," he said. "It may take a long time to understand what that means. But going home, going back to the world, that doesn't mean you won't be able to escape. You can come back. Make it a priority."

"Your father was an alcoholic, wasn't he?" she said, smiling.

"How did you know that?" he said.

"Psych major in college," she said. "No. I just know a thing or two about compensation, about people who spend their lives smoothing over rough edges. I appreciate what you're saying, Mr. Radford. I do. You are a decent man, I can tell. But if I go back to the world, I'll be going back to sleep. The world makes few allowances for being awake."

She took a deep breath and took the empty coffee cup from his hand. He hoped she might invite him inside, but she made no such offer. He sensed that the conversation was over.

"Come by the diner at two," she said.

"I'm not letting you out of my sight," he said. "Sorry, no way."

"Mr. Radford, if I wanted to slip away from you, I'd be gone already. I'll have time to answer more of your questions between my shifts."

Let me be clear. I possess no secrets. No messages from the great beyond. I'm just an ordinary woman who passed through an extraordinary chain of events.

Normal. Everything appeared utterly normal. Dull engine sounds. Uncomfortable seats. A service cart pushed down a cramped aisle. How utterly unaware I was of all that space below me. All that emptiness. The great illusion of reality is how unreal it all feels. How does one hurtle through the sky at five hundred miles per hour without so much as a ripple on the surface of a glass of water? How does one zoom through the sky and not notice?

I wish I could say I had a premonition. Some hidden, internal inkling of the disaster ahead, but I did not. I've read that Lincoln knew. They say King sensed his death before the shot in Memphis. Me? I thought about San Francisco, about home, about the remaining three olives in my "Mediterranean Snack Box," an $8 bounty of bland hummus, flavorless crackers, a hunk of cheese, and a plastic tin of briny olives. I regretted my decision to purchase the snack box instead of ordering Pringles and M&M's off the à la carte menu. These were the profound thoughts I was having right before all hell broke loose.

Then the plane's floor shuddered, a feeling not unlike hitting a gaping pothole, not so much a crash but a crunch, as if the bottom of the plane had clipped a mountain peak in the middle of Kansas. There was no explosion. There was no great boom. Only a thud, and then cold, black space.

You've heard the rumors about me? People who were in the same hospital as me in Kansas experiencing miracle cures? Total bullshit. Not a stitch of truth to any of it. If my story gave hope to the hopeless, then great. But I had nothing to do with cures. No laying on of hands. No crutches in the basement. Seems to me, people make their own miracles.

What really happened to me? At the end of the day, who will care? In five years, I'll be a footnote, a $400 answer on Jeopardy. What happened to me was a mistake. A random act in a random world floating along in a random universe. The more I try to make sense of it, the more I try to distill meaning and purpose, the further I get from the truth. "Don't expect this to be pretty," my cancer surgeon said to me before slicing into my abdomen the first time. And while I appreciated her honesty, her humor, her skilled hands and years of training, I'd have appreciated her a lot more if she'd put me out of my misery. Cut it all out. Heart and soul.

I was driving through traffic once, on my way into the office, before I was sick, when the world still seemed to adhere to the rules. I was listening to a program on public radio. They were talking about stochasticity. Randomness. How the miracles we experience can only be seen backward. Defying the odds only applies to prediction, not to outcomes. A golf ball lands on a particular blade of grass in a fairway. The odds against that ball landing on that single blade of grass are astronomical. Ten trillion to one if seen from the tee. But the certainty of the ball landing somewhere, on some particular blade of grass, that's a given. Maybe that's my story. It only makes sense when seen in reverse.

The most extraordinary moments in life are often the most ordinary ones. Why is that so hard to see?

37

RADFORD NEVER INTENDED to actually stay overnight, but now he found himself in desperate need of a shower, a change of clothes, a decent meal. Don't think about what this means, he told himself. The Falling Woman was real. He'd found her. In a few hours, he'd be heading back to Kansas with definitive answers. What had Ulrich said? A case like this would open doors.

The way he figured it, he'd simply get her to D.C. and depose her first. Get as much of her statement on the record as he could. It might take a few hours to type up a report. Then he'd catch an evening flight back to Wichita, leaving him the majority of Thursday to prepare for the public hearing. It would be tight, but he had every reason to think that his plan could work.

He needed a place to shower and grab some sleep, but the nearest hotel was an hour down the road in Staunton.

He drove through town, passing the bowling alley. He didn't notice the woman standing outside the rental car, the same woman from the bar, the same woman from the hotel lobby. Nor did he notice the woman's camera pointed at his car as he drove past. Running on adrenaline and coffee, he was aware only that he was exhausted and that his clothes smelled of sweat.

He drove five miles out of town to a truck stop along the highway. He paid ten dollars for a trucker shower at the Sit & Sip Rest Stop, and ignored the black mildew in the grout as he enjoyed the steam. After a short nap in the car, he went inside the truck stop, ordered coffee, bacon and eggs, and began to write up the initial field report. He described Geraghty's physical condition, her behavior, her reluctance to seek attention. He reported as many facts as he could. Then he turned his attention to the NTSB's witness document.

The boilerplate form carried the agency's letterhead and four paragraphs of bureaucratic language, followed by five pages of standardized questions. Designed for people who'd witnessed an aircraft accident, everything from minor mishaps to major tragedies, not one section applied to a woman falling out of an airplane that came apart in midflight. But the questionnaire provided a framework for structuring his interview. He downloaded a copy of the form to his computer and then set to work modifying its contents.

Working through the form, Radford understood the extreme nature of this woman's experience. No form, especially one with routine questions, covered the fall she had experienced. After an hour, he'd whittled the form down to a single page. He checked his watch. It was just after noon, and while he wanted to be on time for their two o'clock meeting, he hated any further delay. He headed south, back to town. From the road, he called Wendy.

"What's she like?" Wendy asked.

"She's detached," he said. "I think she's still in shock. She rambles when she talks about what happened. It's the strangest thing in the world. Wendy, she's as frail as a kitten, but ferocious."

"Why doesn't she go home? Why is she hiding?"

"She's scared. And she's been sick. I think she doesn't want to put her family through such a shock. It's almost understandable in a way."

Wendy made him promise he would be careful. "I don't like any of this," she said. "It all sounds so strange. Too strange, Charlie."

"I'm fine. This will be over soon. I'll be back in the office. Strictly nine-to-five after this. We'll get our lives back to normal." He told his wife he loved her and couldn't wait to be home. "But, Wend, one thing. Please don't say a word about this. Not to anyone."

Writing up an accident investigation report could take two years. The final report would sprawl to hundreds of pages, chock full of highly vetted technical data, reports, interviews, summaries, analyses, and conclusions. He used to dread the very idea of it, all that office work, the minutiae, endless meetings and tedious arguments over syntax and style. But now he saw it differently. He'd pack a lunch in the morning and kiss his wife when he got home every night. For so long he'd dreamed about working a major. Now that had happened, and soon, he'd be back to the routines. He was surprised at how much he missed his ordinary life, missed the predictability of the daily grind. Having been away more than two weeks, he was ready to be home.

"I love you, Wendy," he said again.

"I love you too," she said. "Charlie, I just want you home. We have to make some decisions, and I can't do it alone."

During the rest of the ride into town, he thought about his legacy, about the path he would leave behind. He thought about Dickie Gray, and all the work the man had done now only to be ignored. He thought about his father too, about the walls the man had built. But after all that work, only the stones remained, with no trace of the craftsman. So much disappeared. So much vanished into thin air. He wondered if he was too naïve, too idealistic to work in a town as cynical as Washington.

It was still early when he reached the outskirts of town, and he didn't want to make Erin nervous. Ahead, a sign for a roadside bar beckoned, so Radford stopped. One drink, he told himself, just to take the edge off. He looked around the bar. A few ornery patrons claimed barstools inside. Drinking in the early afternoon was a time and space reserved for the desperate and the detached, he told himself. So where did that put him?

"Get you a beer?" the bartender asked.

Radford checked his watch and nodded. He read through his questions once more, wondering if she'd laugh at them. When he returned to Kansas, with the completed interview and the pieces of this puzzle finally put together, he'd be sure to staple a copy to Shep Ellsworth's door. Whatever else came of this, Radford had a sense of who his friends were at the agency. He wanted to let Lucy

Masterson know what he'd found, what he'd learned. He wanted to celebrate this news with someone.

He looked again at the form. What did any of these questions have to do with what happened to Erin Geraghty? What would her answers reveal about the fall? He fought an urge to throw the form into the trash can behind the bar.

When the bartender returned with his beer, Radford glanced up at the television. A bright red breaking news banner flashed on-screen as the local news came on. The credits rolled, the dramatic music, a shot of the mountains in autumn, a helicopter in flight, a reporter in front of a burning building.

"News Five, your leader in breaking news for the Shenandoah Valley. Let's go to our ABC affiliate in Washington, and to Pamela King, who's on the ground in Augusta County with some stunning news."

Radford set his drink on the bar. On the screen, the scene cut to a reporter standing in front of Sandy's restaurant. This time, he recognized the woman immediately—she was the one in the hotel lobby who'd wished him a safe trip. At least a half dozen news vans, satellite poles extended, framed the back of the shot.

"I'm outside a popular local establishment here in Augusta County, Virginia, where I've learned that the mysterious Falling Woman, the lone survivor from the crash of Pointer Airlines flight 795, may be working right here at this roadside restaurant."

Radford grabbed some cash out of his wallet and threw it on the bar. He didn't even look at the bills.

In the car, racing south, he tried to figure how long this reporter had been trailing him. Could she have been the woman

who talked to Wendy too? And who had tipped her off? Someone
had leaked his name a long time ago. Ulrich? Lucy Masterson?
Shep Ellsworth? What the hell sense did that make?

Then it hit. A cold wave of panic flashed through him. It
couldn't be true, but what else explained it? The only person who
knew what was happening, the only person he'd even hinted to
about a destination, the only person with an axe to grind against
the agency, was Dickie Gray. Gray had read his notes. Gray had
seen the words, the address in his notepad. No one else knew.

"Fuck me," Radford said.

Was it possible? What would possess his mentor, his hero, to
betray him like this? No reason made sense, but no other explanation presented itself.

He called the main line at the headquarters and asked to be
put through to Gray's extension. Holding the phone in one hand,
the wheel with the other, he drove close to eighty miles an hour. If
the state police spotted him, he had no intention of pulling over.

"Aviation Division," a woman's voice said.

"This is Charlie Radford. I need to talk to Gray immediately."

"I'm sorry," the woman said. "But Mr. Gray is in the field today."

"What field?" Radford almost shouted. "What's he working on?"

Before the woman could answer, Radford slammed down the
phone and pressed the gas. The restaurant was still several minutes
away.

What would she do now? The first thing she'd do was blame
him. All his work—not just the past couple of weeks on this woman
but his entire career, his entire life's journey, from the time he was
ten years old—began to crumble. She'd never trust him now. He

might as well have punched her in the mouth. Ahead, Radford spotted a helicopter hovering over the trees.

He had to think. If Erin Geraghty was still at the diner, if he could somehow get to her before the press did, then maybe they could slip away. The key was to get her out of there. He'd keep her from being exposed. If she still trusted him, which seemed almost impossible now, he could sneak her out. After that, he didn't know what he'd do, but it was a start.

What could they really know? Gray knew only the location, so if he had tipped them, it meant someone in town had to fill in the rest. Unless Erin Geraghty decided to talk, the press still knew nothing. Since this story began, everything about it rested on half-truths, speculation, and scant evidence. He just needed to get inside the restaurant and convince her he hadn't called the press. There was still time.

He spotted the building ahead. More than a dozen news vans jockeyed for position in the parking lot. Crews from local channels, D.C. stations, and two national networks were setting up. A crowd of locals stood nearby. The shades were drawn in the restaurant's windows, and the Closed sign was lit, even in broad daylight.

There was no way to get inside through the front, but he remembered the side door, behind the dumpster. He parked the car down an adjacent alley and donned a baseball cap. If the bartender and the owner didn't shoot him on sight, he'd try to slip inside the restaurant and plead his case. Two helicopters now circled overhead. The one thing she'd wanted to avoid, the one thing he'd promised her wouldn't happen, was unfolding.

He slipped behind the dumpster, startling a squirrel. He tried the side door but found it locked. He knocked twice, but no one answered. Circling around back, past the smelly dumpster, he stopped by a small window that was partially open. He thought about trying to climb through, but the opening looked too small. A low stone wall ran along the back of the building, separating the restaurant from an adjacent car wash. Could he climb from the wall to the roof, maybe find a door up there? Instead, he picked up a large stone and made his way back to the side door. With as much power as he could muster, he smashed the stone against the wooden door. Paint splintered off, then chips of wood. He must have hit the door a dozen times before he heard footsteps inside.

"Go away," a woman's voice said. "We're closed. We ain't talkin' to no reporters."

"I'm not a reporter," he said. "Tell her it's Charlie. Tell Erin I didn't do this. Tell her I didn't call the press."

A long pause followed while Radford tried to think of another way in.

"You got a lot of nerve," a different woman's voice said. Was it Erin? He couldn't tell over the roar of the helicopters flying overhead.

"I didn't call the press," he said, almost shouting straight into the hinges. "There's no way in the world I want them here."

"Go away," the voice said. He still wasn't sure if it was her. But who else could it be?

"Erin, listen to me. I can get you out of this. But you need to trust me."

He waited, but there was no reply. The rock was still in his left hand. He didn't know what he'd do if she refused to open the door. What the hell had Dickie Gray done? And why? Not only had the entire investigation been strange from the start, but now the very people who should know better appeared to be running down personal agendas rather than doing their jobs. Revenge. That was the only thing that made sense. Gray must've wanted to exact revenge on the agency for leaving him behind. A senior, venerated investigator had been jilted. No other reason he'd do something as stupid as call the goddamn press.

Radford smashed the rock into the door again. He wouldn't leave. No matter what, he'd see this through to the end. Erin Geraghty deserved that much at least.

After a few seconds, the lock jiggled and the door creaked open. He grabbed the door with his hands and pulled it open wide, stepped inside, and quickly shut it behind him. Inside the kitchen, the angry bartender pointed a double-barrel shotgun at Radford's knees. In the corner, Erin Geraghty sat on a metal stool amidst shelves of sugar and jars of canned fruit.

"I didn't call the press," he said again.

"I don't believe you," she said. She turned and waved at the armed bartender. "Hazard, it's okay."

The bartender lowered his shotgun and locked the door.

"It's the last goddamn thing I need at this point," Radford said. "But I am responsible for this now. And I'm the only one who can get you out of here."

In the bar, Hazard poured Erin a glass of whiskey. The restaurant appeared from different angles, in three panels, on the flat-screen above the bar. There were even more people outside now, with the parking lot full and the highway traffic slowing to a standstill. Waiters and busboys huddled around a television, trying to understand how their backwoods hamlet had suddenly become the center of the universe.

Radford knelt beside Erin. The idea forming in his head seemed absurd, the worst possible plan given the situation unfolding outside, but nothing else suggested a way out.

"I need you to trust me," he said. "I know that goes against every instinct you have, but at this point, I may be the only person who can help you."

"I don't care anymore," she said. "I'm ready to walk out there and let them ask their questions."

"That's an option," he said. "It is. In some ways, that may even be the simplest option. But then they own your story and control your future. I know you don't want that. I think I have another way out of this."

He was lying about that. He barely had a plan to get her out of town and to safety. But about her future, about what came next, he had no earthly idea. At best, he could buy her time, time to figure out her next move, and maybe, he hoped, time to still answer some of the questions he had. For the next few hours, if she trusted him, he could hold the wolves at bay. After that, he figured, she could decide how to come forward on her own terms.

"You need to listen to me," he said. "I know this is hard to believe. But I am on your side."

"You caused this," she said. "Maybe you didn't call the press, but you caused this. You put this in motion."

"I did," Radford said. "That's true. But remember, I was just doing my job. You put this in motion before I set foot in Kansas. You knew this was going to happen." He pointed toward the front door. "This was only a matter of time."

"Why should I trust you?" she asked.

"Because right now, you don't have a better option."

Radford went up to Sandy and Hazard, who stood in front of the television watching the ongoing coverage.

"I'm going to take her out of here," he said. "Give us thirty seconds, and then one of you needs to walk out there and tell them she's not inside."

"Frankly, mister," Sandy said, "I'm inclined to tell you to go to hell. I don't know what is going on out there. I just know that this woman is scared, and right now, she seems to blame you."

"It will all be clear soon," he said. "But if I don't get her out of here, one of us has to walk her out the front door. So, it's a matter of who you trust more—me or them?"

"I don't trust anyone," Hazard said.

"Look, they're not going to go away," Radford said. "She can't hide in a town this small for very long."

"And you have a better option?" Sandy said.

"I do," he said.

Ten minutes later, they were ready to leave, but as Radford took Erin by the arm, she stopped and turned to Sandy and Hazard and the rest of the staff. They were all standing stock-still, watching her.

"Sandy, all of you," she said, "you've been so good to me. I'm sorry to have turned your lives upside down like this. But I need to ask you one more favor. What you've never quite understood, what I've never wanted to tell you, is that I am dying. I've been on my way to death for many months now, and I came here to live out my final days in quiet, undetected by the curious world that would make something else of me. But now they're all outside, waiting for me to surrender, and I just can't do that. The favor I need from you is to ask that you please, please keep my secret. Don't talk to these people, don't point them toward me. They'll ask you questions about me—don't answer them. They'll show you pictures—turn away, please. Let me go. Let me be free."

There was a pause, and then Sandy spoke: "Babe, I don't know what you're talking about. I don't know who you are or that you ever existed. We sell beer and meatloaf. None of what is going on outside there has anything to do with us, right, guys?"

There was a low murmur of assent. Erin grabbed Sandy and embraced her, then she and Radford slipped out the side door. Erin wore Radford's NTSB windbreaker, turned inside out, and Hazard's baseball cap. They scaled down the stone wall behind the restaurant. Radford's car was away from the street, but they still had to stay low to avoid being seen. Rain started to fall, which made the ground slippery. A news helicopter circled overhead, trying to stay beneath the lowering clouds. They were like fugitives, evading detection, though no one had committed a crime. When they reached his car, they were both drenched. He hoped the storm might force the reporters inside, but floodlights lit the vans as he looked back down the road.

"We'll stop by your cabin," he said as they reached the highway. "You can get your things. But we have to be quick."

"What difference does it make," she asked. "You're only delaying the inevitable."

"No, I'm not giving up," he said.

At the cabin, he looked around for a towel. While she packed, he stepped outside to call Ulrich. With less than forty-eight hours until the public hearing, he owed it to his boss to at least warn him. But when Ulrich answered, it was clear that he already had seen the news.

"What the fuck is going on in Virginia?" he said. "And why am I finding out on the news?"

"That's where I am," Radford said. "Right now."

"You called the press?" Ulrich said.

"Of course not. I think Dickie Gray tipped them off. He was the only one who knew where I was going."

"I don't care," Ulrich said. "Tell me you have something I can use at the hearing on Friday. Jesus, Charlie. Tell me you found her."

"I'm coming back tonight," he said. "I need you to authorize me to purchase two plane tickets."

"So, it's true?" Ulrich asked. "What's her name, Charlie?"

"Just authorize the purchase. There's enough wild bullshit floating around now that I need boots."

When Radford had finished on the phone, he went inside the cabin. But Erin hadn't finished packing. She hadn't even dried herself off. Mud from her shoes splattered the bedcover, where she lay, her head on the pillow. A small bag in the corner remained almost empty. He picked up the bag and tossed it to her.

"Pack," he said. "We need to go. I've booked us a flight out of Pittsburgh. No one will be looking there."

She sat up on the bed and began to laugh. Radford didn't know why, but she laughed harder, her head falling to her knees, her laughter filling the cabin. He thought maybe she'd cracked, that maybe the pressure was too much.

"What the hell is so funny?" he said.

"You think I'm getting on an airplane?" she said between gasps. "*Really*?"

38

THEY SPENT WEDNESDAY night in a motel off I-64. She didn't know where they were, only that they had crossed into West Virginia. Erin said nothing when Radford gave her the key and said good night. She thought about running, about disappearing, but where would she have gone? That night, she slept poorly if at all. When she did sleep, she had awful dreams, dreams of fire and falling, dreams that shook her awake. In the morning, Radford knocked on her door early, handed her a coffee, and said they had to get going. She went indifferently with him, like a prisoner.

They drove through the day on Thursday. A steady rain started to fall. Roads, towns, hours went by. She barely spoke. What she felt was numb, and confused, and entirely drained.

Radford drove in his stocking feet. He told Erin that they

would have to drive well into the night to make it back in time for the hearing on Friday. Erin replied that she didn't care.

"I'm sorry," he said. "I know this can't be easy."

"This is the way Adam came, but in reverse, when he brought me to the cabin," she said. "That feels like a century ago."

"I need to ask you something," he said. "How much do you trust him? Adam."

"I trusted him a lot," she said. "But then he went behind my back to you, so who knows?"

"But now," he said, "will you reach out to him?"

"For what?" she said. "What difference does it make?"

"Would he call the press?"

Erin shook her head. "Technically, he can't," she said. "He's also my lawyer."

They had stopped for dinner in Terre Haute, Indiana. They still had nine hours to go. As they finished dinner, Erin spotted the first news van. The white van zoomed past the restaurant. Radford saw it too.

"We'll have to get off the main roads," he said.

"Maybe it's not for us," she said.

"I can't take the chance," he said. "They could be tracking us somehow."

"What difference does it make?" she said. "Why not just hold a press conference right now?"

Driving away from the restaurant, she thought for the first time about the families still holding out hope for their loved ones on the plane. What could they be thinking? She thought about Claire and Tory. Were they paying attention to the media frenzy?

It had turned into a circus now. So much of what she'd done, so many of her decisions to disappear were meant to protect them from more suffering. It all seemed to have backfired.

"We've got to get off the main drag," he said again. "It will add time to the trip."

"You're going to have to sleep, Mr. Radford," she said. "Let's just stop. We're not going to drive all night."

"We are," he said. "I have no choice. The hearing is tomorrow afternoon. I have to be back."

"Why should I care about your hearing?" she said.

"Do you know what the easiest thing for me to do is?" he said. "To get on a plane, fly to my meeting, and just tell them who you are. I could end this all that easily."

"Then, why don't you?" she said.

The rain was steady and darkness had begun to fall. The hills in the distance released steam out of the treetops. She was exhausted, in need of solid rest, real sleep.

"I don't understand what you're doing," he said. "Maybe I don't need to. You have your reasons. Had the press not shown up at that restaurant, we could've handled it without all this bullshit. I'd already be in Kansas by now. I don't like what's happened to you. It's not how this should've gone down."

"I know what you're thinking," she said. "How could I disappear from my family? How could I choose to stay away?"

"In fact, yes," he said. "That's not my primary concern right now, but yes. Why?"

She stared out the window. The world raced by in a blur.

"It's an impossible question to answer unless you understand what it's like to say goodbye," she said. "I sent my daughters off to college in the fall with the expectation that I would be dead before spring. We were all prepared for that. We'd said our goodbyes. Claire and Tory helped write my advance directive. We cried, we laughed, we told stories."

"That doesn't explain your decision though," he said. "I'm sorry, but it doesn't."

"I don't have much time left. Why is that so hard to understand? Doug, Tory, and Claire, they'd already let me go. They deserved that crash to be the end. The goddamn chemo wasn't supposed to buy me so much time. And yet, after nearly dying, I suddenly felt so alive."

"What happened to you," he said, "what you went through—it's beyond an explanation."

"It would've been easier if I'd just died," she said.

"Yes," he said. "It would have."

She smiled. She appreciated his honesty. For some reason, the fact that he'd taken his shoes off while he drove made her trust him more. Finally, the tension in the car seemed to ease. Inexplicably, she realized she felt comfortable around this man, despite everything that had happened. She trusted him in a way she hadn't trusted anyone in a long time. As they drove, she closed her eyes and tried to sleep. The sound of the wheels and the steady thrum of the road beneath them was peaceful, but sleep eluded her.

"Don't I have a right to privacy?" she asked after a very long silence. They were outside Indianapolis by then, the lights of the city glowing on the dark horizon. At this hour, the roads were all but clear.

"Of course, you do," he said. "None of this is fair."

"And yet, here we are, dodging the press, rushing back to a hearing where you will expose me to the world, everyone will learn that I've been hiding."

"What are you so afraid of? What do you think is going to happen?"

She couldn't answer because she had no answer that would make sense.

RADFORD COULDN'T FIGURE out if the car was being tracked, but he was determined they were not going to be hunted down and forced to perform before TV cameras. If he was going to do this, if he was going to tell the world that he'd found this woman, then he was going to do it in the public hearing, like a professional.

Erin sprawled out in the back seat while he fiddled with the navigation app on his phone. The app kept trying to keep him on the interstate. He would plug in an alternate route, but the female voice kept coming on the phone's speaker: "Make a U-turn."

The flatlands of Indiana sprawled ahead as the pitch-dark night enveloped the car. Porch lights from distant farmhouses glowed like signal fires. He envied the simplicity of the lives inside those houses, envied their steadiness, their sleep, their faith in the land, and their predictable routines. Of course, what did he know of the people who lived inside those inviting-looking homes? Maybe their lives were just as confused and uncertain as his.

Erin stirred in the back seat.

"You need to sleep," she said.

"I'm fine," he said, lying to hide his exhaustion.

"You're stubborn," she said. "But dying on the road isn't going to bring me back any faster."

She was right. He'd already looked ahead to find a place to stop and rest. He didn't want to give up those precious hours, but endangering their lives made no sense.

"There's a motel just over the border in Illinois," he said. "We can stop there, shower, and sleep. But we need to get back on the road early. It's going to be tight."

"What are you going to do with me?" she asked.

"I don't know," he said. "But when the time comes, I'll be honest. I won't lie to you."

"I could just run," she said. "I used to run marathons before I got sick. I could just start running and disappear again."

"I don't think you will," he said. "I don't think you want to run anymore. You just want this to be over."

"Maybe you're right." She paused, then said, "The weird thing is, I sense that you're running too. Am I wrong?"

"My wife wants to have a baby," he said.

"Charlie, that's wonderful!"

Hearing her use his first name startled him a bit.

"I don't want kids," he said. "I never did. I'm breaking her heart every time we talk about it."

"Why don't you want kids?"

"I need to succeed at something. This job is important to me. I need to make something of myself." The words sounded hollow when he said them out loud. "Besides, I never saw myself as a father. Never thought it was something I could do well."

"No one does it well," she said. "When our friends started

having kids, when we did, everyone ran around reading books and putting their children in enrichment programs, hiring private coaches, choosing expensive private schools. It felt insane. No one knows how to be a parent, Charlie. Children find their own way. In spite of our best intentions, they're really on their own."

"Maybe I don't want all that chaos in my life," he said. "Maybe I want some control."

"Do you love your wife?" she asked.

"She's wonderful," he said. "I've never wanted anyone else. Never even really thought about other women."

"The idea of being a father frightens you that much?"

"It overwhelms me."

It felt good to talk to someone this openly. Many of the things he was telling her were things he had never said out loud before. He'd hinted at them with Wendy, danced around the truth.

"I miss sex," Erin said. "My husband and I . . . Let's just say that we didn't have a lot of passion left. When I woke up in the barn, I was filled with this intense desire to be awake again. I'd never experienced anything like it."

He turned on the high beams. She talked about other things she missed: Bacon. The smell of a lawn mower in June. The feel of a sweaty shirt on her back after a long run. A day with nothing in it but books.

"I was so tired of being sick," she said. "Death didn't frighten me. The treatment did. All those drugs, that radiation, the constant visits to the doctor. Treatment took away everything worth living for."

"Is there no hope?" he asked.

She smiled. "There's always hope, Charlie."

For a few moments, their lives felt easy, relaxed. He hated to acknowledge how much he simply liked her. Under normal circumstances, they could've been friends. Maybe even more, despite their age difference, or maybe because of it. He always played the part well. Always acted like he was immune to everyday temptations and missteps. But he was tempted by something with Erin, and it surprised him. He had judged her when he first heard about her affair with Adam. He categorized people in those black-and-white ways. Good and bad. Faithful people and cheaters. But was that fair? He wouldn't act on this feeling; he felt sure of that. But he had to admit that the constant good-guy act was growing thin. He was learning that life was a hell of a lot more complex than he once thought it was.

For a few minutes, they were just two people being honest with each other. How long since he'd been this vulnerable with someone? The reality was, he enjoyed this woman's company. He realized he didn't want their trip to end.

"How did you do it?" he asked. "How did you walk away from your life?"

She pondered his question a moment.

"I didn't. My life walked away from me. I finally just accepted that reality," she said. "How long have you been married, Charlie?"

"Just over five years," he said. "We've been together longer."

"You said you love her."

"I do," he said. "She pulled me out of a dark place. I suppose I pulled her out of a hole too."

"There will be other dark places. Life is a process. You change," she said. "You don't mean to. You don't decide to start behaving differently. It just happens slowly, bit by bit. A year passes, then a decade. And then you wake up one day next to a stranger."

Radford spotted the motel sign ahead. He didn't want to stop, but they couldn't go much farther without rest.

"The guy Wendy dated before me," he said, "he used to beat the shit out of her. When I found out, I wanted to kill him. For years after, I thought I might actually hurt the son of a bitch if I ever saw him."

"My father died when I was just a kid," Erin said. "I went to get a carton of milk, and by time I got home, he was gone. My sense of the world completely shattered."

"Life turns on a dime, doesn't it?" he said. "It looks so stable, so predictable, but none of it really is."

"Yet it can get so stale," she said. "Routines harden into habits. Habits turn into meaningless rituals. My husband is a good man. Doug took wonderful care of me when I became sick. But for years before that, I was invisible to him. Before, I was a piece of old furniture that shared the same address with him. I had walked away from the relationship long before I fell out of the airplane."

"But won't your new life end up that way too? In five years, in ten? Doesn't it always devolve into patterns?"

"Not mine, maybe yours," she said. "Maybe we need a way to reset. Every decade or so. We get to check out of our lives and experiment with a new one."

Radford slowed the car. He glanced in the mirrors to make sure no one was trailing them before he turned into the motel parking lot. They still had more than six hours of driving ahead. He'd started this trip sure of what he was doing, but he realized now that he wouldn't finish it that way. Erin's questions, their conversation, felt real and honest. He hadn't talked to anyone so openly in a long time. He couldn't simply dismiss her anymore as a piece of evidence, as a data point, a story he wanted to tell in order to advance his career. But what was the other choice?

She'd slipped into a deep silence. He kept trying to picture her body crashing through those trees, the barn roof, the hayloft, the earth. How was it possible? How could she have made it through? She was just sitting there, in the seat next to him, staring out the window, like it was just a normal day.

He parked the car behind the motel.

39

THEY WERE ALL over the news. In his motel room, Radford flipped from one cable news channel to the next, and even at this late hour, the reports still played. Footage of Wednesday's debacle at the restaurant in Virginia, the crowd in front, the satellite poles on the road. But they didn't have a name for her, and so far, no one had tracked them to this motel. The news reports only speculated. No one at the restaurant had talked, and as far as he could tell, they had managed to slip away from the news vans that were tracking them.

When had he first seen the reporter? The bar in Kansas. He'd thought she was flirting with him then. But had he seen her before? Had she been trailing him all along? It didn't matter now. If Gray had put that woman on his trail, then Gray would have to answer for it. Radford turned off the television. A few minutes later, there was a knock on his door.

Erin stood in the hallway with a bottle of wine and a corkscrew in her hand.

"Where the hell did you find that?" he asked.

"Where there's a will, there's a way," she said. "What's the agency policy on drinking with the subject of the investigation?"

He pulled the cork and retrieved two plastic cups from the bathroom.

"You've seen the news?" he asked.

"My fifteen minutes," she said. "Can I ask you a question?"

They toasted each other with the plastic cups. Radford sat on the edge of the bed. Erin sat on the floor, her back against the door.

"Why do you really not want kids?" she said. "I don't buy the career bullshit. I had a career. I managed both. You can too."

He took a long sip of wine, listening for the sound of news vans outside.

"My father wasn't the best role model," he said. "I don't know. Maybe I am making excuses. I suppose I wanted to figure myself out first."

"I used to dread the sound of Doug's feet in the morning," she said. She put the cup down and curled her arms around her legs. "The trickle of water from the sink, the clink of his razor on porcelain, the self-satisfied sigh as he splashed water on his face. I dreaded the light coming on in his closet, would close my eyes and pretend to be asleep. I could be hard and cruel. And yet I loved the man. I saw the singular decency of him in this world. He never complained, never resisted what life threw in his path. He was, by all measures and accounts, a good man."

"Meaning what?" he said.

"Maybe we never figure ourselves out," she said. "In the barn, in those long, dark, quiet hours after, I wondered what it was all for. What was I leaving behind? My life, Charlie. What has my life meant?"

"One might argue that such moral reflection is normal after trauma," he said. "Your life flashes before you. You take stock when the bottom falls out."

"But I saw something else too," she said. "I saw my life as a long straight line. What I once valued, the choices I once made, my lapses in judgment, my failings and shortfalls—it all ran in the same direction."

"Consistency," he said. "That's good."

"No, Charlie, that's not good. That's death. I'd done the best I could, mostly for the girls, but the longer I contemplated my life, the longer I tried to make sense of what it meant, the more I saw a new path. I didn't have to keep walking that line. The fall severed more than just my connection to the tangible world. Quite profoundly, it severed my connection to myself, or at least to the self I had been."

He refilled their cups.

"Why do you do this work?" she asked. "What inspired you to become an investigator?"

"I wanted to be a pilot," he said. "It was all I dreamed about growing up."

"And?"

"I was on my way. I was flying and really moving ahead, but then I had a medical problem. A heart valve issue. It prevented me from flying."

"How old were you?" she said.

"I was twenty-two," he said. "I was lost, devastated really. My heart was broken, literally and metaphorically."

"But why this work?" she asked. "Why did you end up investigating airplane crashes?"

The question made him uneasy, as if she was judging him, or if not judging him, then holding a mirror up so he could judge himself.

"I needed to prove myself," he said.

"To whom?"

"I don't know," he said, finishing his wine.

She smiled. "So why no kids?"

He'd almost forgotten she was a lawyer and could turn an argument back against him.

"That really is a strange question coming from a woman who's hiding from her family."

"I don't expect you to understand," she said.

"Try me."

He stood and crossed to the window. He glanced outside, but the dark parking lot remained unchanged.

"I love my daughters more than life itself," she said. "But even Lazarus only had to die twice."

Radford split the last of the wine between them.

"That's what I tell myself anyway," she said. "But there's hardly an hour that goes by when I don't question my decision. I miss them terribly. Their voices. Their laughs. The way they smell. But I won't impose my death on them again."

She finished her wine and then stood up.

"I guess I don't have a choice now," she said.

It was late, and they needed to be up early. He thanked her for the wine and checked the parking lot again. There was something more he wanted to say, some piece of himself he wanted to give her, but he wasn't sure what it was. Maybe he just appreciated the company, or the chance to be himself, his whole, authentic self in front of someone and not feel judged.

He walked her back to her room and told her that they needed to be on the road early, and then he waited outside her room until he could see, through the crack beneath her door, that her lights went off.

He was coming back to the investigation with an answer, but he wasn't sure what the question was anymore. If the Falling Woman had something to say, if her presence or absence might change the course of the investigation into Pointer 795, Charlie Radford was no longer sure it mattered.

Before they found the cancer, I was simply a wife, a mother, a lawyer, a lover. I was an avid gardener, a fiscally responsible Democrat, and a marathon runner. Before the chemo and the radiation scoured my organs and transformed my body, before the endless trips to the hospital, before the track marks in my arms, the blood in my stool, the radiation burns on my belly, before my life veered off in unimaginable directions, I was a suburban working mom who drove a Volvo to weekend soccer matches. Life was normal, privileged, safe, almost idyllic.

I once heard the poet David Whyte speak at a conference. This was a few months before I became sick. Whyte appeared onstage. Tall, rugged, with a square face and bangs that fell over his eye, he spoke with a British accent, each word formed with care and precision. As reverential as a parson, as confident as an actor, Whyte said, "Hiding is a way of holding ourselves until we are ready to come into the light."

I wanted to ask, "But what if I prefer to stay in the dark?"

Straw fell like snow. Flakes of straw, splinters of wood, sawdust, like golden icicles from the dark, all of it falling from the rafters and gathering, until the straw and sawdust covered me. Scratchy silage, one part blanket, one part torture. Hours and hours of it. Silence and straw. In the barn, after my fall, I lay there in the mud while the straw continued to fall.

I couldn't move, or if I could, I didn't, like a willed paralysis. The straw kept coming down, in the penetrating silence. Each stalk landed softly, the way snow sounds against the roof in a storm.

Time had stopped. Thick darkness encircled me. Lightning flashed in a gaping hole in the roof, illuminating the falling straw.

From outside came the lowing of cows. I tasted manure, blood, rusty pennies. Rain dripped from the roof. I had fallen out of the sky, and somehow, by some trick of fate or some quirk of physics, I had survived.

40

STORMS THREATENED AS they approached Wichita, the city's sky-line breaking the otherwise perfect flatness of the Great Plains. Compared with yesterday, their trip today had been quiet, sullen. They spoke very little for most of the morning. Erin stared out the window while Radford drove.

He had no idea what he would do when they arrived at the Holiday Inn. The hearing was scheduled to start at 3:00 p.m., and it was half past one now.

He'd bought her some time. He'd given her a chance to organize her thoughts. They'd driven practically halfway across the country, talked plenty, talked the damn thing nearly to death. He understood her story now, understood a bit more about why she'd disappeared. He didn't want to exploit her publicly; he'd keep her name out of it entirely if that were a possibility. But given the past two days, given the onslaught of media, her narrow escape, the pressure of the public hearing, her name would emerge, whether he wanted it to or not. Hell, for all he knew, the media had already reported it anyway.

"I'll take you to my room," he said. "You can shower, take a nap. You don't have to be at the hearing."

"It's not fair," she said. "The way this is going down."

"Fair has little to do with any of this," he said.

They were two minutes from the hotel, in light traffic. The clouds on the horizon had turned gray. Lightning flashed in the distance.

"When my father died," she said, "I never thought I'd get over it. But I did. I still missed him. I grieved for a long time, but after a while, I was okay. I laughed. I played. I couldn't help myself."

Radford turned off the highway. Erin seemed nervous, more agitated than he'd yet seen her. He was nervous too, energized in part by the end of the long journey. But he couldn't deny his own excitement about the timing of this whole thing. His colleagues had all but shunned him. No one took his work seriously, but they'd have to now. He thought of Shep Ellsworth. This would be as close to a knockout punch as it came.

"I've said my goodbyes. My daughters, my husband, they don't deserve this."

"What happened to you, it's . . . ," he said. "It's an incredible thing. Almost unheard of. But you'll get to the other side. Six months from now, you'll be happy you did this."

Erin laughed.

"Six months from now, I'll be dead."

"You don't know that," he said. "You certainly have beaten the odds so far."

He smiled, but she seemed unamused. Lightning flashed again, closer this time. Tornado warnings blanketed the state. Radford loved weather like this. He loved the anticipation, the moments before a storm hit. It made him feel like a child again.

There was no time to explain. Not now. They turned into the hotel parking garage.

"Look," he said, "I can't tell you how this will go down. Call your husband. Your girls. Maybe just let them hear your voice."

He worried that she'd try to run, but given the nature of what was happening, given all the attention, where could she go? No, he told himself, she was fighting, but inside, she must have known that the road had ended.

"Let's get you up to my room," he said.

They took the elevator from the parking garage. He hoped that no one spotted them on the way up. They were both exhausted from the road. He needed a shower too, a change of clothes, but he had to get down to the conference room. He stood in front of the door fiddling with the key card when he remembered the awful condition of his room. Papers everywhere, trash, mildewed towels, his clothes on the floor. She'd think he was crazy, which maybe he was. He opened the door.

Inside, someone had neatly stacked his files and papers, made the bed, scrubbed his bathroom. Even his clothes were folded. She followed him in and he closed the door. There'd be no time to explain.

He turned to her. She looked wounded, broken, defeated. He hated seeing her that way. But there was nothing he could do. He knew that downstairs the cameras were being set up. He turned on the television. A local news channel broadcast an image from the large conference room. No doubt Ulrich, Lucy, and Shep Ellsworth were there already, gathering near the front of the room.

"Take a shower," he said. "Make whatever phone calls you need to."

"Don't do this," she said. Her voice sounded desperate, like she was on the edge. He knew he shouldn't leave her alone, but he had to go.

"You'll be okay," he said. "You just need to rest."

"I won't go back," she said. Then she grabbed his arm. "I'm not going."

"What are you afraid of?" he said.

"I'm not afraid, Charlie. I just want to be left alone. Don't you see that? All this does is hurt people. Nothing good comes of me going home. It will only hurt the people who love me. It will only exploit their pain."

Something in her voice had changed. She wasn't negotiating anymore. His phone vibrated in his pocket.

"I'll be up after," he said. "I'll help you figure this out. Stay in this room. Just let yourself rest."

THE LAST PERSON Radford wanted to see on his way to the conference room was Dickie Gray, but there he stood in the hall, wearing cowboy boots, jeans, a flannel shirt, chomping on a toothpick. Radford bit down on an urge for physical violence.

Gray smiled, but Radford kept walking, refusing to even acknowledge the man who'd betrayed him.

"Hey, hotshot," Gray said. "I don't rate a hello?"

Radford turned. He was exhausted, confused, angrier than he'd been in years. The only thing that kept him from throwing a punch was Gray's age.

"You've got a lot of balls," Radford said. "I trusted you. I goddamn admired you."

"What are you talking about?" Gray asked.

"Forget it. You needed to get the last laugh, and you clearly got it."

Gray pulled the toothpick from his mouth and stepped toward him. He grabbed Radford's arm and pulled him out of the hallway toward an open door. Radford twisted and tried to rip away, but the old man's grip held firm. They stumbled together into the hotel's small business center, and Gray slammed the door.

"You got something to say to me, junior?" Gray said. His mouth was inches from Radford's face.

"You were the only one who knew where I was going," Radford said. "I trusted you."

"And?"

"Why the hell did you call the press?" Radford said.

Then Gray released his arm and laughed. The moment seemed surreal. Radford had been ready for a fight with a man old enough to be his father—actually old enough to be his grandfather—and the man had just doubled over with laughter.

When he stopped laughing, Gray stepped back and wiped a bit of spittle from the corner of his lips.

"You may be the dumbest son of a bitch to shit between two shoes," Gray said. "But you're earnest. I'll give you that."

"What are you saying?" Radford asked.

"I didn't call the press," Gray said. "Son, I've been doing this job for as long as you could walk. I've never called a reporter. I certainly don't intend to start now."

"Who then?" Radford asked. He was still mad, angrier now because of his confusion. "I didn't tell anyone else."

"You can't afford to be this naïve, son. You got caught up in a political battle."

Radford's thoughts swirled. Had he really been a pawn all along? Had the agency been using him? Had his work, his ambition, all been to serve someone else's agenda? Had they just been using him so that someone else could get the scoop?

"What questions do you need to ask?" Gray said.

"Why do this?" he said.

"No. That's the wrong question. You already know the answer to that. Who is this woman? Why is she hiding?"

"She's sick," Radford said. "She doesn't want to go home and die."

"You understand what's happening here?" Gray said.

"Not entirely," Radford said. "And I'm certainly not sure what to do about it."

Gray put the toothpick back in his mouth.

"It's pure theater," Gray said. "Always has been. The people on the ninth floor have different agendas. The spotlight has to shine on them, at all times."

"Aren't we all after the same thing?" Radford asked.

"Don't be obtuse," Gray said. "You want to solve the case. They want to advance their political careers. It's apples and ailerons, and you, my young friend, are about to learn your first valuable lesson in the art of politics. Finding this woman gets Carol Wilson and her cronies on the evening news. The evening news gets watched by a lot of people. Are you following me?"

Radford was stunned. He didn't care about the publicity. He wanted to do his job well. He wanted his work to count. Wasn't that what mattered? Or was this all a game?

Gray opened the door and stepped back into the hall. Radford followed, trying to unravel the pieces. Inside the conference room, the TV lights had just come on. Radford didn't understand the political angles. It made no sense. None of it did, least of all the fact that he was being asked to betray a woman he didn't want to betray. He'd only wanted to do his job.

They stood outside, still in the hall.

"There's the stage," Dickie Gray said. "And you're expected to play your part. So am I, in some way. If you aren't comfortable with doing what's expected of you, then get out of this city."

Ulrich spotted them and motioned for Radford to get inside. It was impossible to think. He held his notes in his left hand. She was upstairs in his room right now; she'd begged him not to go through with the hearing, not to reveal that he'd found her.

"Why do you do it?" Radford asked Gray. "Why do you play along?"

"I never did this work for them," Gray said. "I was here for answers. I was here to stop the next plane from crashing. That's all I could do. The work we do, that's about getting to the bottom of things, about figuring out what happened. Pure and simple. If you can't make that commitment, then no one will. What the politicians do, how they spin it, that's not our concern." He glanced inside the room. "It took me thirty years to figure that out."

There simply wasn't time to think. Gray's claims of moral ambivalence made sense but hardly offered a satisfying solution. Radford shook his mentor's hand and then stepped into the large conference room. Ulrich glared at him as he took a seat at the elevated conference table. Carol Wilson sat on the left, with two of her executive assistants. Shep Ellsworth had put on a shirt and tie. A few seconds later, Lucy Masterson came in and sat to his right.

The room was packed. Every seat was filled, and the doors were open in the back, with people spilling out into the lobby. There were dozens of cameras in the front row. Radford could smell his own stale musk on his shirt, and wished the hell he had shaved. He must have looked deranged compared with everyone else at the table.

Lucy flipped through her notes.

"Jesus, Charlie," she said. "You like dramatic entrances?"

He held his arms close to his sides to stifle his odor.

"It wasn't Gray," he said. "It wasn't Dickie Gray who called the press."

He knew Lucy understood what Gray meant to him, but she had no way of knowing everything that had gone down in the past few days. She went back to her notes. Radford pulled out his notes too. He had to get his head together, had to figure this out.

For a few minutes, no one spoke. Ulrich seemed to be waiting for a signal from Wilson, who talked into her phone. Murmurs from the audience grew louder.

"Why aren't we starting?" he asked.

"You haven't heard?" Lucy asked.

Radford shook his head.

"FBI found bomb residue in a section of the cargo hold," she said. "Ulrich is waiting for an explosives report. I think it's Shep's head that might explode!"

"Now? After three weeks?"

"It's a shit show," Lucy said. "No one buys the bomb angle. But the FBI wanted to be onstage too. I sure hope you have something solid."

Radford thought of the woman up in his room. Erin. The Falling Woman. He wondered if she was watching the hearing. What must she be feeling now? Strange thoughts mixed in his head. Could she be suicidal? Would he walk back to his room and find her hanging from the shower? Would she run? Or would she recognize the futility of her situation and embrace her reentry into the world? Next to a vision of her hanging from his shower stood another, one in which her twin daughters embraced their mother suddenly back from the dead. He pictured shaking hands with the woman's husband.

From the left, a team of three suited FBI agents entered and crossed up to the front. One of the agents leaned in and whispered to Ulrich. Before long, Shep Ellsworth stood and interrupted the conversation, which clearly grew tenser by the second. When Ellsworth slammed his fist into the table, Wilson put down her phone and broke up the huddle. Lost in the middle of the fight,

Ulrich seemed to shrink from the pressure of stronger forces surrounding him.

A moment later, Wilson straightened her suit coat and approached the microphone.

"Ladies and gentlemen, thank you for being here," she said. "We'd like to remind you that the purpose of this hearing is to update the public about the investigation into the crash of Pointer 795. This is a preliminary report. The analysis remains in the earliest phases. And while a public hearing is a significant milestone, it is not—I repeat, *not*—the final chapter. And with that, I'm going to turn this over to Gordon Ulrich, the Investigator-in-Charge."

Ulrich stood and straightened his tie. Radford didn't envy him. Whatever the FBI agents had just whispered in his ear caused him to blanch. For several minutes, Ulrich talked about the early phases of the work, especially about the extensive recovery efforts. He reiterated that numerous probes remained opened, and any of the inquiries could affect the outcome. "We've taken great care to collect the victims of this accident, to make a positive identification for each. It has been difficult, and that work remains ongoing."

Radford expected him to mention the Falling Woman, but Ulrich sidestepped the topic, talking now about the reconstruction team, about the hundreds of engineers, scientists, and experts who'd come together to figure out what had happened that spring night over Kansas.

"We've come to the end of the recovery phase," Ulrich said with a beam of pride in his voice. "The long, slow process ahead will provide the answers we all want and need."

Whatever the FBI had found clearly rattled Ellsworth too. He flipped through his notes and typed into his laptop while Ulrich went over a detailed time line, starting with the flight path Pointer 795 took and concluding with the Go Team's arrival in Kansas. Ulrich spoke for more than ten minutes, and continued to avoid any mention of the Falling Woman or Radford's work. The more he avoided the topic, the more the pressure built around it.

"I'm going to turn the floor over to our working group leaders," Ulrich said. "Each will issue a brief statement, and then we will open the floor to questions."

Lucy would go first. She took a deep breath, collected her files, stood, and crossed to the microphone. She began talking about the ID procedure for the bodies, stepping through the complicated logistical process that Radford had started three weeks ago. She thanked the state coroner, Cheney High School's administrators, the local cops, and the Red Cross volunteers. Then she nodded at Radford and thanked him for his work at the beginning of the investigation. After that, she provided a general analysis of the types of injures involved. With great delicacy and tact, she assured the families that the victims were being handled with the utmost care and urgency.

"We won't stop until we have accounted for every single passenger," she said.

Like Ulrich, she dodged the topic of the Falling Woman. Radford grew more anxious. Very clearly, everyone onstage still wanted to distance themselves from any association with the woman currently waiting in Charlie Radford's hotel room. Why had he left her alone, without any support? In a few minutes, he'd stand up in front of the cameras and all the people watching, and he still had no idea what exactly he was going to say, how he was going to present his findings. Four more working group leaders followed Lucy. Each spoke briefly while Ellsworth continued to type into his computer. Ulrich crossed behind the table and leaned down to Radford.

"You're going after Shep," he said while a structural engineer droned on about metal warping and burn patterns. "The shit just hit the fan with his theory. Goddamn FBI meddling where they shouldn't. Please tell me you have something conclusive. I need one thing to go right today."

Ellsworth had loosened his tie by the time he stood up to talk. His face glistened with sweat. For a man who normally bristled with confidence, he now looked like he might throw up. Radford took no small measure of joy in Ellsworth's distress.

"We are investigating every phase of the accident," he said, glancing down at his notes. "There are several factors that indicate the explosive decompression was triggered by ignition in the center fuel tank, possibly caused by a lightning strike."

He paused and glanced at the FBI agents, who stared straight ahead, not making eye contact.

"However," he said, with a tone of open disgust, "an explosives team with the Federal Bureau of Investigation has just reported that they found trace elements of explosives in the baggage compartment." The mood in the room grew agitated. Reporters typed into their phones. "I emphasize the word *trace*," Ellsworth said. He was hot, ready to blow. "We have no concrete reason to think that there was an explosive device aboard this plane."

The mood verged on bedlam now. People shuffled in their

seats. Someone cried out, "We need answers!" A woman on the left side of the room, more than likely a relative of a victim, covered her mouth. Carol Wilson stepped to the microphone. She smiled, tried to regain control of the room.

"I want to tell all of you how important transparency is to this investigative process, and to me personally as the director," she said. She assured the audience that every step was being taken to complete the most thorough investigation possible. She repeated that they were being transparent, open, forthcoming. Radford wondered where that transparency stopped. Apparently, some-where short of his investigation.

"Let's open the floor to questions now," the director said.

Radford glanced at Lucy and then at Ulrich. Had he just been skipped? Had the director really just passed over his briefing? Lucy shrugged. Down the long table, Ulrich stared straight ahead. Wilson chose a reporter from the side.

"We'd like an update on the Falling Woman," the reporter said. "We've all heard reports that she was found in Virginia."

"We'd like to stick to the technical questions first," Wilson said. She pointed at another reporter, who also asked about the Falling Woman. Radford scanned the crowd, hoping at least to spot Dickie Gray out among the many faces staring back. It was all happening too fast. When the third reporter in a row asked a similar question, Wilson yielded the microphone to Ulrich.

Ulrich looked exhausted. If the fallout from this meeting was going to land anywhere, it was going to land on Ulrich's head. That was why Dickie Gray had been brought in. That was why Carol

Wilson had just taken over the hearing. Though technically still in charge, Ulrich now faced his own insignificance, a feeling Radford understood well.

"Ten days ago," Ulrich said, "we opened a special investigation into reports about a possible survivor. I'm going to let the lead investigator brief you on the progress."

Radford again thought about Erin up in his room. Was she watching the hearing? What could she be feeling? He glanced out at the room and pictured each of those seven families, some of them in the audience now. Dickie Gray was right. He was a pawn in this game, easily sacrificed, hardly valued, never missed.

He stood, crossed to the dais, cleared his throat, and took a sip of water.

"The most difficult part of this investigation," he said, "is knowing that there are families out there in need of closure. There have been so many rumors, so many stories about what has happened. I hope to clarify some of this now."

He took a deep breath. He didn't know what he'd say next until the words actually came out.

"There is no credible evidence that anyone survived the explosion of Pointer 795," he said. His voice didn't even catch. "I have no evidence to support any claims about a woman falling out of the plane and surviving." The words echoed off the back of the room. Then came a pause, a moment of complete silence, before reporters began to shout questions.

Ulrich stood and pressed into Radford, almost shoving him away from the microphone.

"What the fuck are you doing?" he said.

"I don't have her," Radford said. "Don't make this worse. Let me take their questions."

Both men's careers teetered on the edge of a cliff, and Radford was hanging by the slimmest of threads. Ulrich stepped aside from the dais, and Radford came forward again. He'd never run a press conference before, and had no way to get control. But finally, one reporter stood. It was the woman from the bar, the woman in the hotel lobby, the woman he'd seen on television. She looked angry, betrayed, ready to throw something at Radford's head.

"What about the report of the woman in Virginia?" she asked. "Several credible sources revealed that your agency had located and identified a passenger from the flight."

"As you may know," Radford said, "I've just returned from western Virginia. I have interviewed several people, including a woman who had recently moved there. I could find no conclusive link between this woman and any passengers on the flight. The woman has made no such claims and is requesting privacy."

The lies came so fast and so easily that Radford marveled at his own efficacy. It felt incredible.

"What about these reports?" the reporter demanded over the clamor in the room.

"Pure speculation," Radford said. Ulrich looked queasy. Lucy Masterson refused to lift her eyes from her notes. He needed to reel himself back, to remain, at least, professional, or they'd simply think he'd gone off the rails. At the microphone for almost twenty minutes, he answered every question that was asked, never once revealing that Erin Geraghty was just a few floors above all of them. When it was over, when the last question was answered and everyone settled back down, he wondered what he'd just done. The only person who seemed pleased was Shep Ellsworth.

Ulrich came to the dais and the meeting continued for a few minutes, with a smattering of questions about the investigation and where it would go from here. Radford didn't wait for the end. As soon as the focus was off him, he slid out the side door and raced back to his room.

He had lied. He had lied at an official investigation. As he left the room, he saw Dickie Gray looking at him with a knowing smile. Would he keep this secret? Radford could only hope.

41

Erin hadn't intended to fall asleep. But the shower was hot and the bed comfortable, and she knew there was nothing more she could she do at that point. When the door opened and Radford stepped inside, Erin awoke.

It wasn't as if she'd expected clarity or resolution, but what she felt on waking was a profound and gentle warmth. The afternoon light fell across her body. The thick blanket wrapped around her shoulders. There was no reason to climb out of that bed.

She kept her eyes closed. Radford seemed to be gathering his files. He was audibly mumbling to himself. What was the next step? Where could she hide to keep the press away from her? And what of Doug and the girls? It would be terrible for them. All the attention—just what she'd wanted to avoid.

"The files," he said, talking to himself, "all the technical data, photographs, research, every printed document in this room belongs to the NTSB."

"What's wrong?" she asked

"If I have any chance at keeping my job, or getting a paycheck next month, I need to make sure that every document is in perfect order."

He seemed panicky, rushing around the small room, throwing papers and files into boxes.

"I need the receipts," he said, rifling through a pile of papers on the nightstand. "I'll need to log the hours, to make a perfect accounting of my time."

She sat up in bed. Her hair was still wet from the shower.

"I fell asleep," she said. "Is the hearing over?"

He kneeled beside the bed. "We need to get you out of here."

"How bad is it?"

"It's bad," he said. "But not for you. You need to get your things. I don't have much time."

He told her that they'd come looking for him. He said he was surprised they hadn't banged on his door already. At most he had a few hours to get her somewhere safe so he could get back to the hotel and take care of things. She stared at him—he was making no sense.

"Charlie, slow down. What happened? What did you do?"

"I'm going to meet you up the street," he said. "Gather your things and walk out of here like you haven't a care in the world. But don't linger."

"I just want to sleep," she said.

"We don't have time," he said. "There's a gas station about a block from here, to the left when you leave the hotel. I'll pick you up there."

"I'm tired of running," she said.

"You can decide all that later," he said. "But right now, I need to get you out of this hotel."

SHE MUST'VE HAD questions. She must've wondered what had happened, but she didn't appear to care. He'd burst in the room and prattled on like a madman, but she hadn't even climbed out of bed. Radford almost admired her ability to react without anxiety, to press ahead with only partial information and no plan. It was a type of grace, that willingness to go with the flow. Did you have to face down death to get there? he wondered. Or was there a simpler way? The past few hours of his life indicated that maybe he'd found a bit of that within himself. Right up until the minute he stood at the microphone and unleashed his lies, he'd lacked such an ability.

Five minutes later, while idling in the car a block away from the hotel, he spotted her making her way up the street, a bag looped over her left shoulder. For the first time it hit him—what the fuck had he done? And why? But if regrets or doubts threatened his decision, they passed quickly. You did something right, he thought, something that didn't fit with what everyone expected you to do.

His whole life, he'd behaved exactly as expected. Hadn't he come back to his father at the air show? Hadn't he followed the doctor's orders and taken his heart medicine? For ten years, hadn't he accepted his fate? Ulrich, Wilson, his father, his goddamn high school football coach. He'd been following orders his whole life. He'd finally done something authentic, finally done something without seeking someone else's approval first. It might cost him everything, but he didn't care. When Erin climbed into his car, he wanted to kiss her. He finally understood her decision not to do the expected things. Many would call her decision selfish, but he finally understood how brave she was.

"I saw the news," she said. "Jesus, Charlie. Why? Why did you lie?"

"I had no choice," he said. "The way you are being tossed around in all this. The government doesn't care about you. They just want to exploit you, and then they want you to go away. So, why not let you go away on your own terms?"

"This has been so sudden. I don't know what I'm doing anymore," she said.

"I have a plan," he said. "I don't know if it will make any sense, but it buys you some time. Maybe we both just need some time."

"I'm hungry," she said. "Does your plan include dinner?"

He thought about what he'd do when he returned to the hotel to face his boss, the team. Would there be an explanation that made sense? Would he still have a job? Did it matter anymore? And he had to call Wendy; she must be completely confused. He drove west, without explaining where they were heading. Erin stared out the window while he drove.

"It's beautiful here," she said.

The storm had passed north of the city, but the lightning was still vivid in the dark clouds in the distance. The plains held light and dark in equal measure. Balance. Everything felt balanced here.

He'd read somewhere that humans respond on some innate level to ideal landscapes, ones that include water, trees, rocks for shelter, grazing animals, and open space. Radford didn't know if that was true, but driving out of the city, he felt a deep connection with this place, the ancient prairie that had mostly been plowed over now. Only a faint echo of that long-ago time remained, in the way light cast long shadows over the roads, or in the ability to see far off toward the distant horizon. Kansas was a good place, he thought, despite everything that had happened, despite all the darkness he'd seen. They would figure out what brought down that airliner. The questions would be answered, even the most pressing ones. Nothing he'd done today hurt the investigation. He believed that standing up for this woman, refusing to bend, would eventually make sense too. A streak of lightning flashed over the city skyline now.

"I'm going to miss you, Charlie," Erin said. "Surprisingly, I've really enjoyed spending time with you."

He didn't know what to say. He'd felt the same way, felt like they'd become true friends, even though they were forced together by circumstance. He didn't like the idea of their time together coming to an end.

"You asked me how I ended up doing this work," he said. "Why I do this and not something else."

"I didn't think you liked that question," she said.

"I was afraid all the time as a kid. I was nervous. Sickly. My mother nurtured me, but she was overprotective, clingy. I used to throw up and cry whenever anything frightened me. When I was ten years old, my father took me to an air show. We drove together down this beautiful road. It's the only time I remember being alone with my father. It was one of those moments, one of those magical little windows into what life could be like."

She twisted around in the passenger seat so she was facing him.

"It was like falling in love," he said. "When I saw planes flying overhead. I didn't have anything in my life that was as pure, as magical. I loved them. I wanted to be with them, to be one of those people who could fly. It was all I wanted to do."

"You found something that you connected with deeply," she said. "Something that was purely yours."

"I thought if I could do what those pilots did, then I could make my fear go away."

"Did it work?"

He smiled and shook his head.

"I used to pray when I was little," he said. "I used to pray for courage. I just wanted to be brave, like my father, like my brother."

"You are brave," she said. "But this work? Isn't this a corruption of what you wanted? Shouldn't you find another way to fly? Maybe I'm out of line to say that."

He exited the highway and slowed. He'd come to Kansas filled with ambition, eager, even excited to get to work on a major accident. He'd experienced things that he couldn't have imagined a month ago. The woman sitting next to him seemed utterly normal, just a good person to talk with, to spend time with. The fact she'd somehow been blown out of an exploding jetliner and fallen from almost six miles up, and then crashed through a barn roof, and by some incredible quirk had survived—this story felt secondary. The miracle of it was beside the point. The world was full of awe-inspiring things. All you had to do was notice.

He turned left at the stop sign. Darkness had begun to fall in the east, but a purple-umber sky glowed in front of them, with bands of pink-orange cloud stretching out as far as they could see. He switched on the headlights as they drove, the darkness slowly circling the car, the road, the prairie around them. Ahead, faintly glowing in the distance, lights from a farmhouse guided the way.

"Here?" she said. "You're taking me here?"

She leaned across the seat and kissed him on his cheek. "You are a sweet man, Charlie Radford, and brave too. You have given me back my life, and I will always be grateful to you for that. And you know what? You will make a wonderful father."

42

"Almost a year has passed since the public hearing in Kansas, Mr. Radford. And now you've come forward to tell us that you lied at the hearing. Do you have any regrets about the lies you told?"

"It wasn't my job to expose that woman," he says. "My job was to ask the right questions. She had a right to her privacy, a right to decide what to do with her own story."

"And now, a year later, all the bodies have been identified, all except one. And now you come forward to tell us that you knew all along. And you want us to accept your explanation?"

"You can believe what you want. I'm here to answer your questions."

"Then please answer the question that was asked. Do you regret what you did at the public hearing?"

"I do not," he says. "I believe I did the right thing."

"Where did you take her after the public hearing?"

"To the farm in Goddard. Yes. The same one where she was found after the plane exploded. There seemed a certain symmetry to that. I had a feeling about those people, about Millie and Norbert Werner. I knew they'd take care of her. Help her figure out what to do next."

"And you told no one until now?"

"Yes. She lived as she wanted. Quietly, comfortably. The world eventually forgot the story, went back to its own concerns."

"And yet so many families held on to false hope. Doesn't that bother you?"

"It does and that's why I'm coming forward now."

"And her family, Mr. Radford. You are now telling them that their mother, their daughter, their wife was alive for months without their knowledge. How do you think they'll take that news?"

"I hope they will understand what she did. I hope they will see that her decision was intended to spare them more pain."

"How is that possible to believe? Wasn't she just being selfish?"

"You can think that if you want. I did for a while. But there's another explanation."

He took a long sip of water and cleared his throat.

"Please understand the great irony here. Mrs. Geraghty was sick. She was dying. When she got on that airplane, she was traveling to California to a retreat for cancer victims. She knew that her cancer would eventually come back. Her family had been mourning her for several months, and the retreat was for her an opportunity to consider how she wanted to deal with the remaining time she had. That she, of all the people on that Pointer flight, should have survived in such a miraculous manner was ironic in a way that feels almost cruel. Her family had mourned the inevitability of her death from cancer, and then, suddenly, they had to mourn her death in the plane crash. To go home, back to all the attention and notoriety around her fall, would have made her life crazy, and I think she wanted to spare her family that. Falling out of that plane changed her. How could it not? It reshaped the way she understood the world. She knew she didn't have much time. I don't think we have a right to judge her."

"You were reassigned after the public hearing?"

"Yes, to the highway division. I didn't object to the reassignment. It seemed a fair outcome, considering what I'd put the agency through."

"We still don't have a cause for the crash. We still don't know what caused the explosion. Does that concern you?"

"Nothing I did during the investigation, and nothing about that woman's story, would have helped solve the mystery of Pointer 795. They will find answers. I have faith in that. In six months, or a year, or longer, we will all understand what happened to that plane. Or maybe we won't. Maybe some things can't be fully understood."

"Why now? Why come forward with this now?"

Radford stares up at the Great Seal on the wall. He remembers seeing the number flash across his phone's screen. He remembers the wave of panic when he recognized the Kansas area code. "She's gone," he said. "The Werners took care of her until they couldn't, and then called in a hospice nurse. Erin . . . Mrs. Geraghty did not want more treatment for her cancer when it came back. Before she died, she sent me her responses to my questionnaire. That was her way of saying that it was time to tell her story. At least that's what I believe."

Radford glances around the room. He's not certain that his testimony will change anything. He's not certain he will be taken seriously or that his words will somehow sanctify or even clarify the choices Erin made. The prevailing wisdom will be that Radford is now trying to sell a book, to exploit this story for his own gain. But he knows nothing could be further from the truth. He simply felt an obligation to tell the story. What happens now, what people choose to believe, that is no longer his concern.

"She had a choice," he says. "And I believe she made the right one. She took the long road home."

"And this is your official statement? This is how you want it entered on the record?"

"It is. Erin Geraghty survived the explosion of Pointer 795. She fell out of the sky and survived. That is the conclusion I've reached. I know nothing more."

RADFORD TAXIES THE Cessna to the holding area and runs through his checklist again. Flaps ten degrees. Altimeter set to field elevation. Fuel mixture, rich. Carb heat, on. A crisp spring afternoon covers the valley. High clouds keep the temperature cool and stabilize the air so that the orange windsock at the runway's end luffs lazily against the pole.

He glances skyward and then down the runway, all the while holding the brakes with his feet. When he pushes in the throttle, the nosewheel digs into the earth. Then he releases the brakes. Surging forward, the plane swings around onto the center of the runway.

Wendy waves from behind the chain-link fence. She is pregnant, with a little girl they plan to name Amelia.

Though this isn't Radford's first solo—that took place almost fifteen years earlier—the moment feels every bit as exciting, perhaps even more so now since he understands what it means to lose the thing he once loved the most.

After two months of flying lessons, a waiver from the heart doctor, and a fair amount of negotiating with his wife, the flight school, the FAA, and the insurance company, Radford is set to fly again. He holds the plane steady on the runway and checks the windsock again. The perfect day for it. Then he clicks the mike button.

"Manassas Tower, Cessna 714 *Charlie Pop*, ready to depart runway thirty-four-right."

"Cessna 714 *Charlie Pop*, you are cleared for takeoff. Wind calm."

He presses the throttle and engine noise fills the cockpit. The plane lunges forward, pulling to the left as the propeller accelerates. He counters the plane's natural yaw with right rudder, holding the nose straight and true. The wings shake as the rough pavement jostles the wheels. The smell of gasoline fills the cockpit, along with the drone of the engine. Glancing down, he verifies that all his gauges are good.

He'll never be like Chuck Yeager. He'll never fly a jumbo jet over the ocean. He'll never be a Blue Angel. He'll never live the dream as fully as he once hoped he would, but maybe that's okay. Maybe he just needs to be back in the air. As gently as he can, he pulls back on the wheel and waits. A second later, the nose lifts and the ground falls away. The plane climbs, gray clouds coming closer, the wings responding like an extension of his body. He turns south, away from the airfield. Below him, the bright umber and green leaves of the Virginia countryside look surreal, almost like they've been painted by an artist.

This is what he's missed. Not the rigid need to prove something about his manhood. Not the certifications, the ratings, and the accomplishments. Not power or speed or danger. All along, he's simply missed the view. He thinks about Erin falling through the sky and wonders, if she were still alive, whether she might have enjoyed this view. More than anything, he wishes he could have taken her flying, to show her how everything looks clearer up in the sky. But then he thinks that perhaps she already saw enough of this view.

He banks the starboard wing toward the Occoquan Reservoir. Water silvers in the lowering sun, the reservoir shimmering like a mirror.

Thirty minutes later, he touches down. Wendy hugs him when he climbs out of the cockpit, and he feels her growing stomach press against him. He is still adjusting to the idea of being a father, but each day he grows more confident. He knows it will be the most important thing he will ever do.

NTSB: WITNESS DOCUMENT 1.18.4.5

I've come to the last question, the one you were gracious enough not to ask: What does it all mean?

The more times I've thought about that fateful night, the more hours I've had to contemplate what occurred, the more I think that any explanation only detracts. If I talk about how it affected me, if I try to contextualize it, I slide further from the truth.

The most extraordinary thing did happen to me, but it wasn't falling from an airplane. The extraordinary thing was walking through this life. Against all odds, I emerged from nothing, from a darkness and a void at least as silent the one that will follow. We spend so much time worrying about death, but so little trying to understand the silence before we entered the world. My life, your life, all of our lives, are miracles far greater than what happened the night I fell from the sky.

I took chances. I loved, laughed, lost, cried, screamed, became bored, impatient. I was stubborn and ignorant and full of passion and wisdom too. There never was enough time. I didn't do any of it well. But I lived.

Falling out of an airplane was but one small part of my time here. Those two minutes didn't define my life. I've made peace with my choices, as hard as they've been. My only regret, my only lingering doubt, is that I may have kept hope alive for some families longer than I should have. If there is some way, please apologize to them on my behalf.

These answers must stand in for my story. If they don't suffice, if they merely lapse into a contrived statement, then just burn them. But if you do one day choose to share them, if you decide there is some merit in telling this story, then please tell the whole thing. Don't make me out to be someone I wasn't. And please be sure my daughters see these answers, whatever else happens. I know it will take time for them to understand what I did. I don't expect them to forgive me right away. But in time, I hope that my choices will make sense to them.

In the end, I have been well loved. I have been nurtured and cared for my whole life. If I've failed to see that, if I've failed to notice the abundance of goodness and light around me, I can only hope that some of my lapses can be understood, and if not understood, then at least forgiven.

I'm tired. Lately, more and more, I'm run down by the simplest tasks. I could sleep for a thousand years and still not be rested enough. One gift of the fall, perhaps, is that I'm not afraid of what comes next. I feared pain before, some return to those sharpest minutes of suffering. But after the fall, even that fear passed. I am ready, as they used to say in the old songs, when people still sang about death.

You should know that my reluctance, my deep need for privacy, was nearly ruined. You preserved that for me. Somehow, you understood and protected me. I am grateful for that, beyond what I'll be able to express on this questionnaire. You've done a very brave thing. A selfless thing. You stood to gain nothing. In fact, you lost a great deal because of your actions, which makes them all the more staggering.

You are a good man, Charlie Radford. A bit stiff around the edges, overly concerned with what everyone else thinks. You're still young in that sense. You're just beginning to move out into the world. But you will do well, I think. You possess good instincts.

Most nights, after dinner, I go out and sit alone near the barn. I like to watch the sun go down, to feel the coolness of evening's approach. I mark the end of another day. Somehow, that feels more important now.

Everything glows here in the evenings. Dusk paints the barn, the sky, the corn stalks, a miasma of purple, orange, and gold. As I wait for that color to hit, my body lightens. My soul expands, and spreads into the air around me, as if the countryside, the sky, the world, is inside me and outside me at the same time. And then the barn swallows return.

There is no way to describe my joy, my utter elation when the swallows begin circling. The sound of air off their wings as they bank. Their gleeful, manic, keening song. They circle, descend toward the barn rafters, and then, at the last second, zoom back into the sky. They remind me of children playing outside, refusing to come in, refusing to yield to the demands of the world. They want to fly longer, to dance in the sky a few more seconds, and I am filled with the most abundant sense of wholeness when I watch them. Holiness, perhaps as well. Somehow, I catch their joy in flight and am able to let go, and, like the barn swallows, I too surrender. I twirl my arm in front of me in a ballerina move, a port de bras in the air, my gesture to join them. I am not flying exactly, but borrowing their movement and sound and grace. I allow them to pull my spirit into the sky. Gravity releases me as the sunlight glows and fades. We were meant to fly. The sole purpose of our lives is to rediscover our wings. The swallows circle above my head, zoom left, climb, hundreds of birds engaged in this incredible, intricate, ancient dance, their wingtips so close that no light comes through, before they all lift over the barn roof and disappear, only to flash once more above and around me. The sky darkens, the colors fade, but the birds keep flying. They circle back, soar again, every bird reaching higher, resisting the urge to land, and the evening fills with their song. As they soar, I imagine myself among them, and I imagine the thrill, the ecstatic freedom that comes with flight. My own invisible wings flutter in my soul. It is almost dark now, the Kansas sky leached of color and light. The first stars appear on the horizon. The birds soar off, far away from the barn, extending their reach, perhaps never to return. But then, just before their songs fade to silence, just before their wings flutter overhead one last time, I remember. I remember the grace of flight. Finally, in a desperate flash, the birds surrender, yield to darkness, dive toward me and disappear into the barn. And so, I will go that way too.